RENDEZVOUS

RENDEZVOUS

RENDEZVOUS
A WESTERN DOUBLE

LEVI JOHNSON MOUNTAIN MAN SCOUT
BOOK SIX

ASH LINGAM

WOLFPACK
PUBLISHING
— EST 2013 —

CONTENTS

RENDEZVOUS

MAYHEM ON THE OREGON TRAIL

Rendezvous

Rendezvous

Levi Johnson Mountain Man
Scout 11

I dedicate this book to my work dog, Lola. Congratulations for arriving to certified police- trained defense dog. Three years of training and still moving forward, and she never steps backward regardless of the threat. She's a bonified maligator.

"Everybody wants to reach the next peak, but there is no growth on the top of a mountain. It is in the valley that we slog through, the lush grass and rich soil, learning and becoming what enables us to summit life's next peak."

Andy Andrews

PREFACE

Mountain men from all over the Rocky Mountains descended on a spot cut out of the wilderness in the valley to have their yearly Rendezvous. The American Fur Trading Company, the Rocky Mountain Fur Trading Company, and the Canadian Fur Trading Company organized the trade fair. Each firm negotiated for the best position to acquire the highly prized, cold-water beaver pelts. These made top hats for the East Coast American markets and even Europe, i.e., England, France, and Germany. This saved the trappers the trip to St. Louis when they could sell their pelts right there in the Rocky Mountains for a reasonable price.

The earliest meet recorded was held at the junction of the North Platte and Laramie Rivers in Wyoming, and it took place in 1815. Salespeople, gamblers, con artists, harlots, card sharps, and thieves traveled great distances to spend two weeks in a place so remote and wild there was no law other than that of the men who inhabited the mountains and their counterparts, the American Indians. Marksmanship contests were held along with axe-throwing, archery, wrestling, and log-cutting competitions, among tests of other skills practiced in the wilderness. The excess of free whiskey guaranteed the entertainment sought out by men who lived fifty weeks a year in isolated stretches of mountains.

Fur companies organized endless teamster-driven mule trains, which carried whiskey, tobacco, coffee, steel tools, and rifles, among other items unavailable to the frontiersmen and the Indian tribes alike. A predetermined place was announced each spring to set up their trading fair. When the meet was over, the British company buyers packed up their purchases and returned to Fort Vancouver in the Pacific Northwest. The American fur companies headed for St. Louis and farther east.

The Rendezvous was known to be a lively and fun place where everything was on the table, and nothing was illegal. Some people came from as far away as England to visit the meet. It was a time and place where White men and Indians alike could frolic with all sorts of extravagances. A temporary truce was called between the Whites and the local tribes. The Blackfeet Indians broke this truce at more than one Rendezvous.

Past Rendezvous were held in La Ramee, Wyoming; McKinnon, Wyoming; Cache Valley, Utah; Bear Lake, Utah; Lander, Wyoming; Riverton, Wyoming; Pierre's Hole, Idaho; Upper Green River, Wyoming; and Granger and Daniel, Wyoming. Some were the sites of several Rendezvous. The last held was at Daniel, Wyoming, in 1840. It was attended by Catholic missionaries who traveled west with Father Jean De Smet.

A conversation was recorded between Newell and one Joe Meek, mountain man. Joe was considered the wittiest, saltiest, most shameless wag and jester to ever wear moccasins in the Rockies. Upon leaving the last Rendezvous, Newell said to Meek, *Come. We're done with this life in the mountains—done with wading in beaver dams and freezing or starving alternately. Done with Indian trading and Indian fighting. The fur trade is dead in the Rocky Mountains, and it is no place for us now if it ever was. We are young yet and have life before us. We cannot waste it here; we cannot or will not return to the States. Let us go down the Wallamet (Willamette Valley, Oregon) and take farms. What do you say, Meek? Shall we turn American settlers?*

BLACKFEET

DUST CORKSCREWED BEHIND TWO RIDERS AS A STRING OF mules followed. Flies hovered over the bloody skins, buzzing in the air. After a week's trek down the mountains, they finally had the end of the trail below in sight. The mules protested as the path became steeper before it opened onto the green valley floor. Hooves plodded silently on the lush grass. The animals of burden were loaded down with buffalo hides. The wind blew the long grass, making it roll like ocean waves. The buffalo hadn't gotten to this valley yet, or it would be razed to the nub. Wherever the millions of bison traveled, they left the land void of grass.

Vultures made lazy circles in the sky, lured to the smell of the bloody cargo. A raccoon walked to the trail's edge, stood on its hind legs, and sniffed the air. It saw the humans, turned around, and scampered away. Hooves pushed dust clouds across the ground as the sun bore down, creating heat waves in the distance. The smell of pines filled the air as mosquitos searched for mammal blood. Sweat glistened on the riders' faces.

"I don't know if we're going from the skillet to the frying pan, or it's just my mind playing tricks on me," Captain Forrester said as he pulled up spur-to-spur with Virgil. He stood in his stirrups and had a better look ahead. "We'll be out of Crow territory half a day from now, but then we'll be trespassing on Blackfoot land, and Chief Hachta's promise can't protect us anymore. We'll have to watch both our point and drag from here on out."

"I've been watching my drag all my life." Virgil chuckled. "That's something I learned as a little boy and something you're just learning, even if it's for a different reason. You have no idea, young man. There's more than one world out there. Some are worlds that a lot of folks choose not to see."

"It's a miracle you saved me back in the mountains, Virgil," Captain Will Forrester said. "I have no idea what worlds I've seen or lived, but I know I'm forever in your debt. I suppose I've already told you that a dozen times, but I'm not reluctant to tell you again."

"Why, I was gonna say the same thing to you, Will." Lovejoy laughed. The captain didn't notice, but it was the first time Virgil had used his actual name—he had just learned it back at the mountain men's compound and had felt reluctant until now. He stared hard for a reaction but saw none—it was like the captain hadn't noticed. "And I'd suggest that you use caution about going around sayin' you'll be forever in someone's dept. Forever's a long time, pilgrim. It even transcends the grave. Surely ya don't wanna have that kind of responsibility, do ya? Somebody might just take ya up on it." He cackled like a rooster, and the amusement reached his eyes.

"Anyway, don't change the subject. Your friends that you don't remember got us out of these mountains. Otherwise, I reckon we'd have been eaten by the wolves just like Bud and Clinch, God rest their souls. And you say you felt nothing when you were with those nice folks? Not even a little?"

"Not a thing, Virgil," the captain replied. "The way I see it, I was lookin' at strangers. It's hard to try to feel somethin' that's not there. I don't know that I like wearing my feelings on my sleeve anyway. It's just a notion I've got."

"Well, they sure as shootin' knew you and knew you well," Virgil grinned as he looked at his friend. "Like I said, iffin it weren't for them, that fierce chief would have killed us both. I thought we were a goner when he showed up at the mountaineers' cabins. I almost wet my pants."

"Fool me once, shame on you—fool me twice, shame on me," Forrester hissed like a viper. "If he shows up again, he won't catch me by surprise." Suddenly, his eyes were full of anger and violence.

"Why, it's a miracle we're even alive," Virgil continued, ignoring the captain's reply. "Like I said, iffin it wasn't for your friends, we'd have been long gone and dead with that Hachta after us. I've never seen a man who looked so dangerous."

"Like I keep telling you, I only have little flashes of past memories as slim as a razor, which don't add up to squat," Forrester replied. "It's almost like shadows pass through my mind, but I can't quite make them out. Strangely enough, the only thing I remember are smells, but I don't have people or places to put them together with. What was physically drilled into me and learned in school still seems to be there. It's just people, faces, and places that all elude my grasp—me included. The other day, I looked at my reflection in the water and found myself looking at a stranger. It was the oddest thing, not even remembering what I look like." He shook his head in near desperation. As soon as the captain realized he was showing weakness, he jutted his chin out, narrowed his eyes, and spat a brown stream of juice into the dirt.

"Why don't ya tell me what cha see even if it is foggy?" Virgil asked. "Or whatcha smell and hear? When you heard Rusty Steel's voice, you said you seemed to recognize it at first. Maybe if you talk about it, something may sneak past that black veil you seem to have in your mind. I don't know about that fancy name you put on it, but it seems like a dark curtain to me, and all ya gotta do is figure out how to draw it back."

"Amnesia? That's just a name for no memory. How can I tell you what I *don't* know, Virgil?" The captain's eyes looked tired.

"Well, don't just stand there like one o'clock half-struck. Start by tellin' me what cha *do* know." Virgil smiled. "That's the more important issue."

Will looked at his only friend. Lovejoy was the only one left alive that he remembered. Even though he and Virgil had met minutes after he lost his memory, he felt like he had known him all his life. Perhaps it was because of the circumstance of their encounter. Sure, he had met the people back at the compound, and it was apparent they knew him, or at least they thought they did. At this point, he didn't even know himself. Still, there was too much pressure to do what they wanted when he didn't even know what he wanted yet. This fact blocked out his willingness to cave and accept what they said. But how could you explain a love you didn't feel? It would be impossible.

"I know I could see the pain in Johnson's eyes when he said we were best friends, and I told him I didn't remember a thing about him. It was the truth. Had I seen him in the street in some town, I'd never give him a second glance."

Now, they weren't deep in the mountains, so they knew daylight would last longer. In the Rockies, as soon as the sun dipped behind one of the highest peaks, everything fell into shadows, and the temperature dropped. Now, it was warmer, and the going suddenly became easy for the mules, but still, the day had been long. The beasts of burden bore heavy loads, and the last stretch of the mountain was some of the most treacherous.

"Why don't we stop by that spring over there a way?" Virgil pointed. "We can camp in that stand of trees. These mules deserve a well-earned rest."

The two riders wheeled their mounts toward the spring. They closed in on the refreshment. Nine mules and four horses stepped up their pace when they smelled the water. They waded in up to their knees and slurped. Animal tracks were scattered around the watering hole. Forrester instantly knew predators came to this spot to kill their prey as they sought relief from thirst. It was almost as dangerous as when they tended to their personal needs. These were moments of vulnerability.

It took nearly two hours to unload the mules,

unsaddle the horses, and start a fire. They worked as quickly as they could to beat the vanishing daylight. All four mounts were hobbled and left to fill their thirst with crystal clear water and graze on the green grass. Once the mules were free of their burdens, they rushed to the spring and waded in up to their bellies, allowing the cold liquid to cool them down.

"I don't know if we should risk a fire or not," the captain said. "Though I have no doubt that every Indian within five miles already knows we're here. Nine mules are kind of hard to hide. Especially with all those smelly hides. I'll be glad when we're rid of them."

"You and me both, brother." Virgil snickered. "It's gonna take a month for the smell to wear off. I reckon them flies will continue to follow us around for a spell after we sell our buff hides." The captain didn't even hear the word *we*.

"You've earned yourself a small fortune, Virgil. You'll be a wealthy man when we get this to the Rendezvous. It's going to fetch a pretty penny." The captain smiled.

Virgil looked at the captain and raised an eyebrow. "Why, I reckon them buffalo skins are just as much yours now as mine. You fought for 'em and risked your scalp just like Bud and Clinch." He shook his head. "It's a shame about the boys, but it is what it is. A man gets used to death and dangerous surprises once he gets along a little in life."

"Why, you're not old, Virgil. You've got your whole life ahead of you. You don't have a gray hair on your head."

"No, I ain't old, but I sure ain't young like you. I ain't sayin' it's a bad thing either. With a little age comes a wagonload of knowledge. You just wait and see, young man. All ya gotta do is keep a keen ear out and always be open to learnin' somethin' new. If you keep your eyes on the target you won't miss. I guarantee you that."

In the end, they made a fire. They knew deep inside nothing went on in the mountains that the various Indian tribes didn't know about. At least they could make a warm meal even if they didn't need the fire to ward off the cold. In the valley, the nights were cool but not cold, and warmer weather was on its way.

They had a meal and a few coffees. When they were done, they poured the rest of the pot onto the fire. The orange cinders hissed as they turned gray and cold, and steam rose until it disappeared a few feet above the cooling coals.

That night, they took turns keeping watch in three-hour shifts. Virgil took the first shift, and Forrester took the second. On the third shift, they kept watch together. They knew this was the Indians' favorite time to attack. The night dragged on, minute by minute and hour by hour. Millions of stars twinkled overhead as they peered into the darkness. When the wedge of moon rose, it cast hazy silver shadows on everything around them, making their surroundings seem to come alive as their eyes played tricks on them.

Coyotes and wolves howled in the early morning. They had spent the night hunting and would be returning to their dens. Owls hooted out to one another. They, too, had feasted on field mice and small animals during the hours most mammals were slumbering. Their large eyes blinked in the dark as their curious heads turned at impossible angles.

Morning came and went, and nothing happened. Both men were still jittery. They had been convinced they would be hit before dawn, but there hadn't been a sign of human life, and in the morning, they saw no footprints nor smelled anything out of place. Virgil prepared coffee and biscuits so quickly that the food seemed to appear like magic.

"Those are some fine-tasting biscuits, partner," Forrester said. He stabbed another piece of bacon hanging on a steel rod over the fire. Hot grease dripped into the coals and sizzled as they cast an orange glow into the eyes of the two men.

"I use my mother's recipe, which was passed down from my great-grandmother," Virgil said. "Yes, sir, my folks were famous for their vittles. At least we were known for something positive. Too many folks are known for all the wrong reasons and few right ones. Most famous men this far west are largely fabrication. The yarn stretching is done by the newspapers, who take a molehill and turn it into a mountain."

"I'd say you're making quite a reputation for yourself when it comes to hunting buffalo," the captain said. "I believe every Indian in this part of the Rockies heard about Crow Chief Hachta chasing us. Probably most people that aren't Indians too. I heard Rusty Steel say that Indian gossip travels as fast as the wind."

They started the process all over again. Each day, they were closer to their destination and freedom from the horrid smell. They loaded the mules, saddled two horses, and were on the trail heading west a couple of hours after first light. Reaching this year's site for the Rendezvous would take another week. Luckily for them, this season's gathering was relatively close.

The captain heard the whirling sound as the steel hatchet whizzed past his ear. Sunlight flashed off the blade, blinding the blue-eyed captain for a heartbeat. It embedded deep in the head of Virgil's horse with a thud, dropping the horse and throwing Virgil to the ground. The captain was right behind him as he dove for cover, pulling his rifle as he leaped. His mustang screamed and ran off, spooked by the sudden smell of blood. Virgil took cover behind the carcass of his dead animal. The disinterested mules continued down the trail, but the other horses groaned and screamed. It seemed like it took them forever to return fire, but it must have only been a few seconds. Soon, pistol barrels flashed as chunks of lead hammered into trees and bushes where the warriors hid.

Just as quickly as it began, it ended. The only sound was flies buzzing around the smelly buffalo skins. It was far too quiet, but it appeared the braves had gone. Or was this what they wanted the trespassers to believe? Perhaps they were waiting to ambush them. It was impossible to imagine what a Blackfoot warrior thought, at least for anyone who wasn't an Indian.

"You wait here and cover me with the rifles," the captain said as he exposed himself despite the danger. "I figure they've just come to test our resolve. Now they know what we're made of, so it'll be more serious next time. If anybody's still there, I'll draw them out, and you shoot."

"Ain't ya takin' too big a risk, Captain?" Virgil asked. "Maybe we should just mosey on down the trail, and perchance they'll leave us alone now they see we ain't a piece of cake to kill."

But Captain Forrester had already vanished. It was a

habit that Lovejoy was having difficulty getting used to. Especially as, usually, the deaths of several men followed. The captain's skills hadn't escaped Virgil. He was very aware his new friend was a killing machine when threatened. Then again, that was what was expected of a US Calvary officer. Lovejoy knew he had been an Indian fighter, knew from Levi Johnson that he and the captain had been in many battles with Indians. They had even fought the most dreaded tribe of them all, the Comanche. Just the thought made chills run up their spines.

Lovejoy still didn't know if that killing machine mentality was a trait that he liked or not, but it had saved their lives already, and it would probably save them again. He saw the captain's image flash between the trees and disappear again. He knew better than to shoot, so he held his breath and forced himself to wait, and he was usually a patient man. Knowing Will Forrester was out there on his own gave Virgil pause. He didn't know if he was the bravest man he'd ever seen or was simply crazy. He didn't appear to have a frightened bone in his body.

After a couple of weeks with the captain, Virgil, too, forgot he was missing an arm. The captain gave its absence no regard whatsoever, so people with him eventually forgot too. It certainly didn't hinder his abilities. If anything, it had made him a more focused man. Any more focus and he could become dangerous, even for his friend. This was something that Virgil knew but he was also aware that these same skills made it possible to trespass on Indian land with nine mules loaded with poached buffalo hides.

If the Blackfeet came in force, Lovejoy knew they

didn't have the wherewithal to protect themselves. This fact had shaken him up and thrown him off his game. Still, he held fast and doubled his resolve as he stared down the barrel to the gunsight. He traced it across the trees. He knew if he shot, he had to make sure who he was firing at, and he wouldn't have the luxury of a miss, with the captain roaming somewhere behind whoever it was trying to kill them. Somehow, Virgil seemed to sense what the captain was up to. He felt he had no choice but to follow.

It wasn't that Forrester acted like a captain or even a leader other than during instances of defensive violence. Then, he got a little bossy, but he obviously knew better what to do than anybody his Black friend had ever met. At least, that was all that Virgil Lovejoy had witnessed until then. He usually was like most men, although he did have an inherent suspicion of the enemy. Then again, that had kept them alive so far. Every man he killed was trying to kill them, and he clearly showed no mercy and took no prisoners. Virgil wondered how a man with one arm could still be so deadly to his enemies. He thanked the heavens he was on his side, or he wouldn't be long for this world.

As the captain raced through the forest, he suddenly stopped, frozen in place like a syringe full of ice was injected into his veins. He silently dropped to the ground and pulled all four pistols, carefully pulling back the hammers before laying them on the ground before him. His eyes narrowed as his sharp hearing detected movement to his front, so he patiently waited. Now, they were the prey, and he was the predator. A wicked smile crossed the officer's face.

The captain had already turned the tables. They

probably never imagined the captain and the buffalo hunter would attack them, but here he was, waiting for his moment. He knew he would recognize it when it came. He knew this deep inside, even though he couldn't remember how he knew so much for such a young officer about fighting Indians. Still, he was somehow aware he had done this before and even felt an angry fire burn deep inside, although he didn't know why. Beaver Johnson had told him of the battles; still, it all sounded foreign and impossible to him because he remembered nothing. So, the stories went in one ear and out the other, and he retained little of what was said.

He shook his head to clear his mind. The hole in his head still throbbed, but the wound was healing nicely, with Virgil keeping a close eye on it for infection. As far as his memory went, he still remembered nothing. Everything before Virgil found him on the cliff had a dark curtain hiding all the details, but they were impossible to see for the captain. Since he couldn't see or remember it, he had difficulty accepting it as fact. Time would tell if he ever regained his memory. At this point, he didn't seem to care if he did or not. As long as the captain had a purpose and some sort of plan, he was focused and pondered little on anything other than what he was doing right then.

His breathing slowed, and his heart barely murmured as he waited. His pulse calmed like a receding tide. The clever hunter knew to sit tight and place himself in the victim's path. They would never expect the tables to have turned so quickly, but here he was, waiting to ambush the men trailing them.

Captain Forrester peeked out from under his hat,

and the bright sunlight flashed in his eyes. He heard a light rustling of grass, but the dead giveaway was what he sensed when he drew in a breath. He sniffed the air and smelled Indians. He didn't know how he knew they were Blackfeet, but he did just the same.

Forgotten

Levi gasped when the last mule disappeared into the trees and down the winding trail. He felt sure he had lost his best friend. An inkling of regret dug into his conscious like a thorn. Of course, he was in love with his new wife, but he and the captain had been best friends, and Johnson believed they still had many adventures ahead of them. Especially the time they spent together fighting for their lives against their enemies, the Comanche. Was all that about to change now? Johnson couldn't fathom how a man could forget such an event. Beaver had never been as scared as those days.

Sharing times of battle and risking their lives for each other created a bond that eclipsed any other, and now Forrester didn't even remember it. Levi was having difficulty absorbing such a thing happening to a close friend. What if he, too, had had a wife? Would he have forgotten her too? Beaver had heard about amnesia but didn't really understand it, nor had he met anybody who had experienced a similar affliction, so he was clueless as to how to proceed. All he could do was wait for the Rendezvous and see what happened. Maybe a miracle would occur, and Will would get all those cherished memories back. It was almost as though the old Will Forrester had died, and Levi had difficulty facing the fact. Also, the valued memories were only Johnson's now that Will had no memory at all.

Had he really died like they had come close to doing several times, Beaver wouldn't have such a hard time accepting their fate. But with the captain alive and well, he just hurt worse and felt all the more confused.

When pondering what the captain had suffered, he couldn't help but wonder how such a thing would affect him were it to happen to him. He realized he could never grasp the depth of the affliction. His friend was nearly like the brother he never had, so Levi tried to put himself in his shoes. He wondered if it happened suddenly, or did it come on him slowly like a lazy sleep? Virgil Lovejoy said it was from a nasty fall, so Blaze was definitely dead. The captain was lucky he didn't go over the side too.

No horse, not even the captain's white stallion, could withstand such an impact from a three-hundred-foot drop. He wondered why and how Will didn't go over with his mount. It showed them all how fragile their existences were. They were held in an indubitably delicate balance, and any exterior influence could affect their future for good or for bad.

Johnson counted his blessings and regrets and suddenly realized he had many of both in the last year. The question was, which outweighed the other? Of course, he would see Will at the Rendezvous, but would it be the same? He knew his new friend Virgil would have to sell his buffalo hides, and Johnson had both their beaver cold-water pelts and those of Crow Chief Hachta's people to trade. Could they repeat the friendship they once had after so much change? Or would there be nothing left of a brotherhood in tatters? It took two to make an alliance.

"Next week, we'll be startin' down the mountain with all the beaver pelts." Rusty smiled. "That'll give us a couple of extra days before the Rendezvous starts. I wanna see if Levi here can beat me this year—or maybe not, and he ain't up to the task." He wiggled his eyebrows.

"Beat ya at what?" Johnson asked, his mind elsewhere. He looked at his mentor with questioning eyes.

"Everything." Rusty smiled. "I figure you've gotten too big for your britches and need to be taken down a notch or three. Last year, there were a dozen contests to enter, and all of 'em had handsome prizes—not to mention the bragging rights for a whole year. All you tried was the shootin' contest. That's 'cause we came from such a dangerous trip across Kansas. This time, I intend to spend the whole two weeks at the Rendezvous and sign up for anything that provides a good challenge. I'm feelin' my oats, youngster. You know as well as anybody I'm hell on wheels when I get my dander up. Plus, there's free food and whiskey all week. They even supply our firewood, so we don't miss any time drinkin'."

"Levi is gonna be busier than a snake in a cage full of birds." Angus laughed. "Especially with that wildcat that you call your wife." Angus cackled. It echoed off the mountains. "You don't know what cha got yourself into, Beaver. I know, 'cause Pine Needle is my third

Crow wife. It's the first one or two that takes gettin' used to. After the second, the third one comes easy."

"She'll be just fine at the Rendezvous, but she's already planning to enter every event I do," Levi said, puzzled. "Why does she feel she has to do everything better than me when I'm her husband?"

"'Cause she be a mix of Crow war chief and mountain lion, I reckon." Rusty laughed. "Indian women folk ain't like the ones you find back east. Why, Angus and I even made a wager to see iffin she beats you or not."

Shock showed on Johnson's face. "And who are you betting on, Rusty?" Levi asked, a little offended. "You better be bettin' on me."

"Of course, I'm bettin' on ya, pilgrim, but some of the boys ain't of the same opinion as me. You know how Angus is." Rusty spat a yard of brown juice off the side of the porch. "Whatever I say, he'll answer the opposite. Ain't that right, you old fool?"

"I'll always bet on a Crow warrior, no matter if it be a he or a her," Angus replied. "Everybody knows a warrior brave can outfight any man that ain't Indian. Just because she be a woman don't make a breath of difference. Why, my Pine Needle gets ornery once in a while and all, and before ya know it, I find myself on my behind and seein' stars. Even I don't dare mess with her. I've seen her get ahold of a few lonely widows who were eyeing me, and she liked to take 'em apart."

"But I'm three times Dahteste's size and weight." Levi snickered. "She ain't much bigger than a corn nugget. How is a little Indian woman gonna go up against men as big as me?"

"Some mighty mean critters come in small packages." Angus chuckled. "Take a honey badger. It's half the size of Rusty's dog, but it'll take on a lion and chase it all the way home. That's what I reckon you married, Beaver. I can see it in her eyes how she challenges everything you do." Laughter echoed in the canyons. "I sure am glad you two came down to visit 'cause it was gettin' mighty borin' around here with both you and Forrester gone. Sam, Pete, and Bob hardly talk anyway, and Angus don't do nothin' but complain and be contrary. The only reasonable conversation I have is with Mountain Dennis, and even that's limited to his dim wit."

"I'm standin' right here behind ya, Rusty," Dennis grumbled. "Ya can't talk down on a friend when he's listenin'. It ain't polite."

"Well, excuse me, Reverend." Rusty smiled. "Had I known you were there, I'd have called ya intellectually deficient."

"That's more like it," Dennis replied puzzledly. He never knew if he outsmarted Rusty or not. His mind wasn't up to the challenge.

When she showed up for dinner, Dahteste had a look of helplessness on her face, yet behind that, she held something far more profound. She was playing and wasn't scared at all, but it was her first day, and she would test them all. First, they would have their resolve analyzed. Then she would evaluate their emotions. Levi watched, amazed, but he had seen her do it before.

She tried to do it to him, but he was too clever. He doubted that Rusty or Angus would be fooled, either, but maybe the other men would be won over and would fall under her spell. Johnson had seen it back in the Crow camp. Half the young men in the stronghold walked around with lovestruck faces and their mouths hanging open like lost pups. These same braves gave him dirty looks when they passed. He had stolen the prize of many a warrior. To add insult to injury for her warriors, Levi was White.

When they were back in the Indian village, Levi was amazed how Dahteste ordered the warriors in her charge about. Nobody questioned her authority. Johnson had mistakenly nearly laughed the first time he saw her growl at one of her braves, but a sharp look from her big brown eyes cut his words short.

Seven men and one woman sat at the table as Angus fiddled about making a fuss over supper. He complained constantly he had to cook for everybody when the truth was, he wouldn't let anybody cook for him anymore. Everything they made he found fault in, so he begrudgingly cooked most dinners. He also made breakfast for those in his cabin, although with Levi and Dahteste living in the tipi and Forrester gone, the cabin seemed a little empty.

Before, Angus grumbled the house was too crowded, and now he complained it was too boring. Each year, he seemed to get more cantankerous, but Rusty paid him little mind, which upset old McFarlin even more. Sometimes it took an earthquake to rile Rusty Steel up, but the consequences were brutal and unforgiving once he was angered.

"Whatcha cookin' up tonight?" Levi asked with his knife and fork in hand. "I'm so hungry I could eat a polecat."

"Do you smell polecat?" Angus retorted. "I imagine iffin I was cookin' skunk, you might get a whiff of it. And you call yourself a full-blooded mountain man, and ya can't even smell what's for dinner."

Soon, steaks the size of hams were forked onto tin

plates as the hungry people of the compound patiently waited. Blood pooled under the meat as steam rose, and the smell of grilled steak made their mouths water.

Levi breathed in deeply and smiled. "I knew it was meat, but I didn't know what kind. You can make pretty good tastin' steaks from most game animals or even a horse, Angus, but none are as good as elk. I ain't ever tasted any as good as you grill up, either."

"I've tasted delicious horse meat," Dahteste said. "You have to know what kind of horse is best. But Indians, we eat anything when we're hungry. I have heard from the elders, in the old days, some Indians ate White men. They say the meat tastes sweet." She grinned as she blinked her long, curly lashes. Mischief danced in her big brown eyes.

"You and most folks, I reckon" Rusty grinned. "I've eaten a rat or two when I was nearly starvin' in a cave back when I first came to the mountains and lived with the Plains Indians. At first, they didn't take too kindly to me, but once I showed 'em I could handle the wilderness, they slowly took a shinin' to me despite the color of my skin."

"I don't eat any animal I give a name," Sam said, "and I name all my horses. Why, it would be like you eatin' your dog, Rusty."

"I reckon if we come to starvin', it'll be Dog eatin' me before I'll be eatin' him." Rusty chuckled. "I wouldn't be surprised iffin he couldn't take down a bear. Ain't that right, boy?"

Dog lay under the table with his head on Rusty's feet. Every time his name, Dog, was mentioned, his canine's tail hammered the wood-plank floor. His long red tongue hung out the side of his mouth as he sniffed at the bone Rusty had just given him. Soon, his massive jaws were crushing the T-bone into pieces like it was bacon.

"Now you're talkin' nonsense," Angus retorted. "A bear would swat 'im away like a tiny fly. I've seen cats that scared me more."

The banter stopped for several minutes as knives and forks scraped clean the tin plates. Two loaves of freshly baked bread were used to wipe them clean. The smell of coffee and baked dough filled the air. Finally, Angus pushed himself from the table and patted his belly.

"Go be a good friend and bring us the coffee kettle, Levi," Angus said. "I can hardly move after that chunk of meat." He stifled a burp with his fist due to the lady's presence.

Even the wildest mountain men respected women and demanded a code of honor be followed, or it was considered poor manners, usually followed by a severe beating, especially in their compound, where sass was answered with a sound thump from a heavy pistol barrel. There were so few women west of the Missouri River they were held on a pedestal and cherished. Some said White men were a hundred to every White woman, although most of them weren't your marrying type of girls. At least not for folks that don't come from the wilderness. For them, almost any woman would do.

"How about I get the coffee, and Dahteste here opens a few cans of peaches?" Levi grinned. "Maybe if we stay busy, we can stay out of trouble with you two." He grinned at both Angus and Rusty as he gave them an amused look.

After the meal, the men and even the Crow warrior

pulled out corncob and ceramic pipes and stuffed them with tobacco. Matches sparked the cured, sweet leaf to life, leaving the smell of sulfur in the air. They all puffed thoughtfully as the evening breeze pushed the smoke off the porch and into the swaying pines. The sun neared the peak over the compound and suddenly disappeared. The sky behind the snow caps turned a fiery orange, then they were plunged into semidarkness.

Lightning bugs flashed here and then somewhere else a few seconds later as the night predators scurried through the dense vegetation surrounding the three cabins and one buffalo hide tipi.

THE AMBUSH

THREE BLACKFOOT WARRIORS LAY IN THE LONG GRASS that rolled like waves in the wind. They whispered into each other's ears to avoid making any sounds. Their quivers were full of arrows, and their bows were in their hands. Their faces were painted black with red stripes shooting out from their eyes. Long white incisors were drawn on their bottom lips. In the shadows, it made them appear to be dangerous wild animals. They looked frightening beyond imagination.

Black scalps were sewn into their rust-dyed buckskin shirts, and colorful ribbons and multicolored beads were woven into their hair. They hardly made a sound, but their accumulated body odor was what gave them away to the sharp awareness of the soldier. Few men would notice skilled warriors who moved with such care. Still, the captain knew they were there. Even though he didn't know how he knew, he just did. He supposed it was the Indian fighter in him.

Locusts chattered, then stopped only to resume their noisy choir. Woodpeckers hammered on trees as vultures made lazy circles high above, waiting for their next meal to appear. Unseen animals moved through the underbrush as bushes rustled with life. Not even the insects and small animals noticed the cautious warriors. It was like they blended into the very ground they lay on, and beyond them was the hidden soldier. He lay frozen and almost breathless. He blended in even better than the talented Blackfeet.

"We must crawl to where the cowards hide," the largest warrior whispered to the leader of the three-person war party. "We will catch them by surprise and attack them when they least expect it. Now, we know they know how to shoot, but we will kill them silently with our poison arrows. They won't have time to use their guns."

When the war party left to follow the trespassers, they only intended to badger the buffalo hunters and maybe steal a few of their buffalo hides if not all. Every Indian in the mountains knew they were on their way down. They had all heard the drums and seen the smoke signals. Of course, they were only three, so attacking two armed men could always be dangerous. But one of these trespassers only had one arm, so they asked themselves, how much of a challenge could he be? Indeed, he would be less than half a man with such a deficit. Three against one and a half men might work in their favor.

The braves began to dream of glory and fame by being the first of their tribe to slaughter a White and a Black man in the same battle. Victory swam around in their heads, making them slightly giddy, and the battle had yet to begin. They were already drunk on the blood they planned to spill and the gushing respect they would receive from the tribe and their peers when they returned victorious. Each one already imagined the reception they would receive both from the elders of the tribe and the most desired women.

"They will be easy to kill if they don't run away first like the cowards we know them to be," the leader smiled. It looked like shadowy tombstones wavered in his eyes. "I want the yellow scalp. Nobody kills the army man—he's all mine. I want to feel his warm blood on my hands and see his shiny scalp on my buckskins. Maybe I will cut his heart out and eat it to capture the soldier chief's power. I wonder what his hair feels like. I heard yellow hair is soft like rabbit fur. We will be in the elders' songs soon." He smiled, making his painted fangs grow, and his face became more fierce-looking than before. "Come and follow me, and don't make a sound. Be patient now. I don't intend to hurry into a trap. They will be ours in a short time. It is best to savor the moment and enjoy the victory."

The Blackfoot leader smiled and turned to crawl closer to where they thought the enemy was. One smaller and one larger warrior brave followed. They couldn't see more than three feet in front of them as they moved forward inch by inch. The shiny blades of their knives flashed between their teeth. The attack was imminent. They silently closed in as slow as slugs. Their eyes never wavered, nor did their intent. They knew they could easily take the trespassers' lives. All they had to do was get close enough. It would be as easy as killing a couple of dogs. Maybe even easier.

Dogs had some value in guarding the camp, but the intruders on Blackfoot land had no worth at all. Only the officer's yellow hair was of value, and that would be quite a trophy. They were two worthless men who stole their game and, when convenient, killed innocent Indians. Today, the earth's people would kill them and take their hair so they would wander aimlessly through the spirit world for eternity.

Today, these two would die. Images of blond hair flashed in the leader's mind. He was hypnotized from the moment he laid eyes on the soldier. He believed him to be some sort of army chief. He saw the long sword he wore on his belt. The warrior planned to keep that too. He also noticed the missing arm. He wondered how he lost it. He looked too young to have much experience, unlike these three veteran warriors. Little did they know they had just met their match.

———

THE CAPTAIN LAY in the tall grass so close to the Blackfeet warriors he could smell their breath. Somehow, he was so still he had gone unnoticed even though he was nearly at their feet. Tufts of grass covered his pistols as he carefully inched his hand nearer his sword. Forrester even used his eyelids to hood his sky-blue eyes so the Indians wouldn't notice the icy cold color. His heart was a faint whisper as he focused, slowing his breathing even more. One by one, four fingers and a thumb wrapped around the grip until they slipped through the bell guard of his saber.

He lay on his back, hearing trained on his surroundings as he focused with closed eyes. He used only his senses of sound and smell to guide him to his target. He could feel them getting nearer. When he finally spread his eyes wide, he saw cotton-like clouds cross the sky between the heavens and earth. The tips of giant pine trees swayed in the wind. He began to silently count backward from ten as he held his breath.

A branch broke, and everybody froze. It wasn't the captain because he had yet to move, so it had to be the Blackfeet warriors. Now, they would assume they were discovered and would change their plan, but the captain knew he had to catch them before they reorganized. Hopefully, they didn't have a plan B ready and waiting. The captain had lost much of his element of surprise with their mistake.

You just never knew how things could go wrong, but they always seemed to go wrong at the most dangerous moment, just before the attack. An expert fighter would know the time to take advantage of the situation and do the last thing they expected. He could feel how close they hid in the tall grass just a few feet from him. His senses of smell and sound guided him directly to them.

As they carefully crawled on their bellies, the few agonizing seconds it took seemed to stretch into minutes for the warrior braves. Eventually, it seemed like an eternity.

The cavalry captain squeezed his fist around the grip of his sword. He could feel the claret come to a stop in his veins. Bloody fingernails dug into his palm. Now the captain had that one-in-a-million shot. His blood suddenly sped into overdrive, and he lurched forward, making his silent attack. He knew where there were three Blackfeet Indians; more would be nearby, so he had to make as little noise as possible. If he killed them silently, they might be able to escape unseen or unheard if there were others close by.

The first and last thing the three Blackfeet

warriors saw was the flash of steel. As the war party leader turned his head to look back, it toppled off his shoulders and rolled off onto the ground in one smooth movement. When the head came to a stop, its sightless eyes stared directly into the sun. The captain's sword followed through and lobbed off the second head in the same graceful motion as the first. The largest warrior jumped up to run when twin thrusts pierced him in the back, rupturing each lung. The last man to be mortally wounded opened and closed his mouth like a dying fish as he unsuccessfully tried to gobble enough air to stop the burning in his chest.

"You stabbed me in the back!" the Blackfoot brave said in broken Spanish. It shocked the captain that he understood what he said. He must speak Spanish too, which must come from his education—maybe from New York.

"If you wanted to get stabbed in the front, you should have been running toward me and not away from me," the captain spat, wiping his mouth with the back of his hand, the saber still in his bloody fist. Viscus red liquid dripped from the tip.

The largest Indian let out a long chattering breath, and his eyes crawled back into his head, leaving only the whites visible. Three dead warriors lay in the dirt as blood pooled under their lifeless bodies. The two detached heads lay several feet away. The wind rolled around, and the waves of grass flowed in a new direction.

"I've said this before, but you're either the bravest man I've ever seen or the craziest," Virgil whispered, amazed, after he stood and walked to the captain. "If the

United States Army saw what you did, you'd be given a brace of medals, no doubt."

"I can't see myself in a uniform festooned with medals, and I don't take to trophies," the captain replied.

"I reckon they was plannin' to get themselves a fine trophy and all," Virgil guessed. "I thought it would be touch and go with you against three, but those poor souls never had a chance in Hades. I do believe the first two were dead before they knew you were there."

"And what trophy might that be, Virgil?" Forrester asked.

"Why, that shiny yellow hair of yours, Captain." Virgil chuckled nervously. "These boys like to collect scalps. Just look at their buckskins. That black hair be Indian or Mexican scalps they're wearin' like medals of their own. I reckon the leader there fancied a yellow one to go with the rest. It does stand out like a crow in a flock of doves, the yellow hair, I mean."

Virgil stood over the dead men with his open Bible in his hands and said, "Everything starts dyin' the minute it's born. Some lives are shorter than others." Then he mumbled a passage from his Good Book and closed his eyes in prayer. "Good men must die, but death cannot kill their names. As long as we live, they too will live, as they are now part of us, as we remember them. Only love gives us a taste of eternity. The only truly dead are those who have been forgotten."

The captain got an uneasy feeling every time his friend read from his Bible, and he did so every night if the situation permitted. He also spoke a few words over the dead, whether they were Christian like him or not— even their enemies, like now. Forrester couldn't remember if he had been a religious man or not. For all he knew, he may have been at one time, but for the life of him, he couldn't remember, and it wasn't one of those things he still had notions of, like his studies. Even his education escaped him if he thought about precisely what subjects were his majors, but bits and pieces came to him in the course of a normal day.

Military strategy seemed to come to him all on its own, so he assumed he was well-educated and versed in such activities. He knew his sword was an extension of his arm, and he didn't miss when using his rifle because he never shot before, he was sure he would kill his target. He supposed his religious beliefs would appear sometime soon, like most of what he retained in his memory from lifelong practices.

Virgil had mentioned one day that he had a New York accent, whatever that was supposed to be. Still, he recognized Lovejoy's deep southern accent and didn't know how or why. Each of the mountain men had slightly different ways of speech and vernacular particular to from whence they hailed. This was a puzzle that the captain was still trying to work out.

LEAVING THE PAST

DESPITE THE HEAVILY LOADED MULES, VIRGIL LOVEJOY and Captain William Forrester knew they had to move as quickly as possible. If they didn't leave for lower lands now, they would be caught by any other Blackfeet warriors that were nearby. When the three warrior braves didn't turn up, they would surely be missed, and somebody would be sent out to see what happened. It was just a matter of time before their bodies were found.

Hopefully, some of them would turn back to take the dead home, but they knew others would follow, seeking restitution for what the captain had done. They both doubted severed heads would make much way in the Indian's spirit world. Virgil had never heard of something like that happening, so he didn't know what response to expect, but he imagined, even knowing the Indian ways as little as he did, they wouldn't be happy. Death was the way of a warrior, but losing their heads made a much bigger statement.

Virgil knew the captain didn't intend to offend every Blackfoot Indian within fifty miles, but he had probably done just that. All the Indian Nations were finicky about warriors passing into the spirit world intact. That was the reason they removed their enemy's scalps. That, and to obtain the power from the brave they beat in a life-and-death battle. Some went even further, like the Shoshone, who removed their enemy's hearts and ate them to attain the power of the dead.

With the growing moon, they traveled during the day and late into the night whenever the trail permitted. As they got near the bottom, rather than getting better, the switchback trail became even more treacherous. They stopped making fires, be it day or night, because they knew they weren't alone, although it appeared they had not been pinpointed yet. They hoped that if they kept moving, their pursuers would have to keep moving too. It was a race to see who was run to death first.

Lucky for them, Virgil had been aware of the need for excellent animals while preparing his team of shooters to hunt buffalo in the hundreds. They couldn't risk the whole hunt for incapable animals, so he'd only bought the best. Now, it was paying off and had been money well spent. The mules were focused and held up against the strenuous climb down the mountains. Often, the animals had a more difficult time riding down a hill than up, just like horses.

They were riding down the steep trail at night despite the captain's words of caution. Virgil believed it was more dangerous staying in the mountains and being captured by hostile Indians than falling any day. They rode around a deep bend in the path and could finally see the valley below them stretching out for miles. It was bathed in silver moonlight. Virgil looked relieved as he let out a breath he felt like he'd been holding for days. As Lovejoy turned his horse for the edge of the trail, grinning, he winked his approval, and the captain smiled back.

"It looks like we made it despite having the whole Blackfoot Nation after us," Virgil said. Again, there was that moment of nervous laughter.

"All we saw were a few warrior braves." The captain chuckled. "And where do you come up with the whole Blackfoot Nation? Most of what we've seen have been tracks and footprints. If we had a whole Indian camp after us, we'd have never made it out of the mountains."

"Just the same, I thank my lucky stars." Virgil smiled. "It ain't but a hoot and holler to that valley down there."

"It's farther than it looks," the captain said, but he didn't really know why. He just knew. "Distances are deceiving at night—especially from up here on the hills."

Virgil was getting so accustomed to following the captain's instincts that he didn't give an ounce of protest. Even though most of Forrester's actions created more dangerous situations, he still trusted his skills more than he did his own, especially at fighting Indians. Even though Virgil Lovejoy had more reason than most to wreak the wrath on many men he encountered, he was a happy-go-lucky type of guy and usually avoided confrontation like the plague. Maybe that was some of the way he grew up sticking with him. After all, he was raised as a slave.

Even though Virgil was dead tired, a new strength seemed to arise from somewhere deep inside him, like steam from the earth's core. Just the sight of the valley gave him a new source of energy. Even the mules and horses seemed to feel it because they, too, picked up their pace despite the heavy loads. Suddenly, they were riding across flat ground, and the shadows of the mountains stood tall behind them but now at a distance. The highest peaks above them all summer now seemed far away in the distance behind hazy silver clouds.

As daybreak came, rays of sun slanted through the trees like rain, warming their faces after the cool night. The pungent smell of subalpine fir and Engelmann spruce filled their senses. Like the captain said, it took much longer to reach the valley floor than it appeared. They rode all through the day, only occasionally seeing the valley, but it seemed just as far as it did at first glance. Still, they plodded on, knowing it had to be close. The day passed as evening neared, and they knew they couldn't ride through another night, even if it was slowly.

They couldn't risk losing any animals because they had no spare mules to replace one if it came up lame. If the truth be known, Virgil had never imagined having such a successful hunting trip, although it cost him both his shooters. Clinch West had been an old friend, and Bud Gunns had been a lazy good-for-nothing, but just the same, he had been too young to die like that. Lovejoy knew in the wilderness it was best not to make too many close friends, but if you had to, pick somebody able, like Virgil did. The captain was a handful for any outlaw or Indian and made the ideal traveling partner for such dangerous country.

They followed a narrow creek that spilled into a pond and stopped to refresh the horses. Dragonflies bounced on puffs of air just above the water's surface. When they neared, dozens of bullfrogs protested, leaped, and swam to safety.

The first thing the captain did was to inspect the waterhole for visible enemy tracks, but he found none. That wasn't the case with wildlife, which was obviously abundant because there were tracks of both small and large game all around the small pond. Carp made lazy circles in the center of the waterhole.

"Soon, we'll be at the Rendezvous," Virgil observed as they unsaddled the horses. "I reckon them nice folks from the cabins in the mountains will be there too. You remember who I mean, don't cha? That fella that went by the name of Levi Johnson."

The captain's heart started to pound. He wondered if Virgil could hear the bass drum hammering in his chest. He bunched his lips and shrugged, then sniffed and shook his head. For some reason, it reminded him of things he didn't want to hear or discuss. Things he had put away somewhere deep in his veiled memory, and he no longer possessed the key to open the door. Maybe it was better to have an unknown past. It allowed a man to start over again.

Virgil eyed the captain carefully as he curled an amused smile. Forrester locked looks with him, his eyes drawing wide. They were full of questions.

"Take no offense, friend, but I'm afraid you appear to have a host of hate in ya," Virgil offered. "Don't get me wrong, 'cause I care for ya like a brother, but when you're dishing out justice, it leaves me in awe. I've never seen such violent eyes."

"Everybody has to pay like those past paid before us," the captain blurted out without thinking. "What do you mean by a host of hate?"

"The evil has to be drawn out of ya," Virgil whispered. "By an agent of the Devil like a snake. Lucifer makes for a dangerous bed partner."

"What in the world are you talking about?" the captain asked as he shot a glance sideways at his friend.

"'They may build, but I will tear asunder,'" Virgil quoted from the Bible. "'They may repent, but judgment is still mine.'"

"Sometimes I wonder who you are, Virgil," Forrester replied. "What is it you're talking about now? And you say I'm strange? Compared to you, I'm as solid as a rock."

He didn't answer but instead busied himself unloading the buffalo hides from the mules. Hopefully, this would be the last time they had to unload and load them again.

It suddenly dawned on the captain that they had just about made it safely to their destination despite his actions with the Blackfeet. He wondered if they had found the headless bodies yet.

The following morning, they risked a fire so they could finally have a hot meal. Both men worked on the grub as one made cast-iron skillet biscuits and the other fried eggs sunny side up. Slabs of bacon roasted over the hot coals. Steam hissed as the grease struck the orange cinders below.

After the last strip of bacon was devoured, they sat and drank the last two cups of coffee. Virgil wondered how much the buffalo hides were worth, and the captain wondered who he was before the fall.

"Considering my situation, what advice would you give to a man in my position?" Forrester asked. He turned his head and locked eyes with Virgil. "You're obviously a wiser man than I."

"My advice?" Virgil asked, surprised. "I've never had anybody ask me for advice. But I reckon my answer is to be decisive. Right or wrong, make a decision. The trail is full of flat squirrels that couldn't make up their mind."

"It looks like we have a conundrum," Forrester replied in realization. "This is what I would call a dilemma."

"And what's that?" Virgil asked. "I know what dilemma means. So, what conundrum are ya talkin' about?"

His mind was ultimately at rest when it hit him like the hot kiss at the end of an iron fist. It came with such sudden clarity it threw his brain into turmoil.

"Now that we're nearly to the Rendezvous, I feel nervous," the captain said. "I don't know if I *want* to find out who I was or not. Maybe I won't like the man I was. I know once I get to the meet, I'll be challenged by everyone to show me who I am. As it is, I feel I could walk away and never know. I'm tempted to do just that."

"Come on, now, you're worryin' about nothin'," Virgil said. "Why, if I were you, I'd be jumpin' at the chance of findin' out who I am."

"Yeah, but I'm not," the captain replied. "I feel like I've got to make too big a decision."

That night, the captain took the first watch. He was supposed to wake Virgil halfway through the night, but he didn't feel like sleeping, so he let him rest as he stared at the moon. It was so bright it was like an early morning.

They finally made it to the valley the next day, and the meet was in sight. First, they saw the dust cloud that hung above the small tent city that had been constructed from one day to the next, but they could hear them long before they could see them. It sounded like a big party, and it was still the day before it all started. The streets were already thick with humanity. A man came running up to their mules and jotted down a number.

He looked up from his notepad and said, "I can offer ya top dollar right now. How about I take that big, smelly load of hides off your hands?"

"That's what we came here for." Virgil smiled. "Whatcha say, Captain? I say it's about time we stop luggin' all these smelly skins and turn 'em into money."

The captain's mouth was no more than a gash. Virgil could see his tortured eyes. He was so clueless as to who he was now, he appeared afraid to find out, and fear wasn't something that Forrester pondered much. Lovejoy turned back to the businessman and smiled.

"Well, be my guest and lead the way," Virgil said.

The gaunt man led them to a large tent, pulling aside the flap. Inside were piles of furs already bought and paid for. Some traders came early, so they caught the first trappers before the others did. The prices would change depending on how many furs the mountain men provided. If they were too numerous, of course, the price would go down; too few, and they would go up. But Virgil had more hides than he'd ever counted on, so he wasn't bothered if he got a few pennies less. He believed it was best to get rid of the buffalo skins before somebody else tried to steal them.

The tent was so crowded with hairy men that it felt

like a thousand people were present. A cloud of smoke hovered a foot below the canvas ceiling. Tobacco stains streaked the sawdust-covered dirt floor. An overpowering smell of sweat filled the trader's tent; combined with that of dead hides, it was nearly unbearable. Some of the mountain men smelled worse than the hides.

THE RENDEZVOUS

SINCE 1820, THE VARIOUS RENDEZVOUS, OR FUR TRADING meets, were held in different locations at the foothills of the Rocky Mountains. This year, almost twenty years later, it was to be held on the same tract of land as the first. The last time Rusty and the boys had attended was twelve months before, back when Levi Johnson and Captain Will Forrester had just arrived from the Kansas Plains. Johnson and the captain had come with the very mountain men who would lead them to a new and adventure-filled. The Rendezvous had even led Levi to marriage.

Johnson would have never thought in a million years he would have taken an Indian wife, but as soon as he met Dahteste, there was no question about their destiny. They both felt the same from the beginning and knew there were no others for either of them despite their significantly different cultures. Time would tell how they worked out their differences, which were many. At first, it appeared they were limited, but as the first strike of Cupid's arrow wore off, the apparent divergences stood out loud and bold.

Both husband and wife were strong-headed, too, so they each wanted the other to bend and shift their ways toward their own, and they weren't even aware of what they were doing. It came naturally to them both. Who would have thought that their cultures were so deeply embedded? Their marriage would be a test of their love and their different upbringings. Lucky for Levi, he had been raised in the wilderness of Southern Indiana on the Ohio River. This made the leap from the ways of White men to Indian life easier, but still, their upbringings had been very different, and his existence less primitive.

Tents littered the cleared ground. It looked like they had been preparing the place for days ahead of the event. Large white wooden signs announced the various American and Canadian fur trading companies. Many said FREE WHISKEY in bold red letters. It was still twenty-four hours to the official opening, but it was already thick with traffic. The noise level rose with each passing minute as more and more rugged men and women streamed down from the most remote parts of the Rockies.

Most of the people who lived in the mountains only had this one time a year to speak to more than a dozen people and get updated on the current events from back east. They might even find some tidbit in the tent, hardware, or gun shops that were scattered among other traders, some cherished objects they could take back to the mountains when they returned. But as the years passed and cold-water beaver pelts became more and more valuable, the event grew from a few dozen trappers to five hundred strong, plus all those providing the services. It was like a small town had magically appeared from one moment to the next.

Long, thin, red banners snapped with gusts of wind, drawing the new arrivals' eyes to the saloons. The large traders had organized free drinks to grease the gears of the rugged mountain men and the Indians so they might talk them out of their pelts for a pittance. Free whiskey flowed in excess, and a drink was never denied. A few drunken men with long hair and beards lay in the shade along the provisional road sleeping off what they'd imbibed the night before.

"Why, it looks like a party's already started without us. And here I thought we were arrivin' early." Rusty grinned as they walked the horses into the temporary compound. Hooves pushed small dust clouds as they rode for the livery.

Makeshift stables were made of wire and wooden posts and were already teeming with animals. A cloud of dust hovered a few yards above the nervous animals. A separate corral held beef to feed the hungry trappers for two weeks. Barrels of whiskey were stacked high in each of the fur trading company's saloons. Roughhewn planks lay across empty barrels to make makeshift bars and dining tables. Empty buckboard wagons and prairie schooners littered the edges of the Rendezvous. A pine post protruded from the ground, and a gate was attached to allow livestock to enter and leave the corral without losing any animals.

Dozens of tents populated every square inch of cleared land. Some were so large they held over fifty people; others were so small they passed the liquor out the flap, and you drank in the street. Several little tents with red lamps hanging out front dotted the temporary town as women plied humanity's oldest trade.

The mountain men stood in a long line to have their knives sharpened by an expert. Bright sparks showering off the shiny blade were like a hymn in church to the men. The blacksmith wiped a mixture of sweat and dirt off his face and neck with a wet rag. The smell of burning hair floated on puffs of air. His foot worked the pedal that turned the pulley attached to the stone wheel with a leather belt.

Two dozen men exchanged tales and lies about their experiences with the large knives the mountain men carried. The sun flashed off blades and bore down, baking the dirt into a dry powder.

A cloud of flies followed the mules with bundles of cured beaver furs. They also had bear, raccoon, fox, and wolf skins, among others. They had brought every mule they had, plus a string from Crow Chief Hachta's stable to carry his part of the hides.

Levi couldn't help but crane his neck, looking for some sign of his friend, Will Forrester. Maybe they had already sold the buffalo hides and left. It looked like business was already brisk. The fur trading companies didn't let pelt one escape them. They would mark them up five times the price they paid when sold back east and double that in Europe. As they rode down the newly leveled street, it looked like preparations were being made for a circus more than a fur trading meet.

Makeshift dwellings held everything from remedies to cure-all ailments to Gypsies telling fortunes. With each hour, more men filed down from the mountains and neighboring trails. It was like a flood of creeks flowing into a pond of people. Others came from the closest civilization to take advantage of the isolated trappers. All sorts of humanity were lured like magnets to the Rendezvous.

An ample open space was made for the visitors to camp. Forty campfires circled by stones were already prepared. Each one bore the provider's name. Stacks of firewood waited for nightfall. Everything the mountaineers needed was provided in the hope they would sell their mountains of beaver skins to the company that treated them the best.

Soon, the alcohol would take hold, and with men of such a wild nature, like every year, chaos and bedlam would follow. Men who were used to fighting grizzly bears wouldn't hesitate to fight any man who challenged them. Some came to the event with the intended purpose of creating havoc. All sorts of men lived in the Rocky Mountains. Some were outlaws escaping crimes, and others were just as wild as the animals that populated the mountains.

They rode past a tent as the flap door opened on the front. A pale-looking man pushed it aside and stepped out. His face was gaunt and drawn. His brown hair was stringy and was held in place with a leather string like an Indian. His eyes were a soft hazel and mistrusting like a deer's. They noticed the pallor of his face. A hat hung from his hand at his side.

"They have the habit of dying off like deer flies at the end of summer," the man said as two men followed. "You gents be careful with all that money. Not everybody here are mountain men like us. Some be thieves and bandits."

"Is that a fact, Mr. Line?" Virgil replied.

Drag Line was an aging California buckaroo turned

fur trader. He slipped on his cowboy hat and walked down the main drag with bowed legs. He had four pistols shoved into a wide belt.

Levi hoisted himself into his saddle and stood in the stirrups as he had a peek. Will Forrester and his new friend Virgil Lovejoy followed the ill-looking man. The black man held a leather pouch full of something. With the missing buffalo hides, it must be the gold coins he got in exchange. When the captain looked right past him, Levi's heart sank. He waved at them, catching the buffalo hunter's eye. Still, Forrester hadn't noticed them stopped in the middle of the wide trail. He was obviously busy looking for somebody with ill intentions for Virgil's gold.

Angus McFarlin wore that reproving-older-brother look. "Don't go gettin' your hopes up, Levi. A man without expectations is a man free of disappointments."

Rusty Steel watched as he scratched his bushy beard, squinting his intelligent eyes. He nodded affirmation, tight-lipped.

Finally, he said, "Don't you worry, Beaver. Everything will work out just like it's supposed to. We don't have so much say-so when you stand back and look at the big picture anyway. Only then can you see just how complex everybody's lives are. Most people bounce from one train wreck to another simply tryin' to get to the end of the trail in one piece."

Levi swallowed appreciatively, yet there was a heaviness in his eyes. He had already seen and experienced enough to know he had little to no control over the future. They forfeited that as soon as they decided to live in the Rocky Mountains. But although he knew Rusty was right, it still hurt. He could see from where he sat astride his horse—he hadn't even entered Will's mind since they last saw each other. He knew deep down inside he was staring at a stranger. Finally, the captain felt eyes on him, and he turned his eyes to lock with Beaver's.

He expressionlessly nodded. Virgil waved and grinned. They had already done what they came here for. Levi wondered if they would stay or if they would wander off. Then he would know the truth. He knew his old friend could never intentionally hide anything from him. He just didn't know who he was anymore.

TENT CITY

When Dahteste walked up to the man signing fighters up and taking bets on the wrestling contest, he had to take a second glance. He shook his head and wondered what the Crow woman wanted. The shock on Levi's face was apparent, but Rusty, Angus, and Dennis all had a good laugh. This didn't come as a surprise to them at all. Angus had told them all about Crow women warriors—especially Beaver's wife, who was known by all the tribe. This just pushed the bets higher.

"What can I do for ya, ma'am?" Bobby the Baptist asked. "Do you wanna place a bet?"

The man tending the event was as wide as a door. He got the name by dragging his victims to the river and drowning them back in the East End of London, England, where he was born and raised. He ran his hand over his smooth head as he towered over Dahteste. He was nearly as tall as Levi Johnson. He tugged on his beard as he awaited her answer.

"No, I want to enter the competition," Dahteste said

with her hands on her hips and her chin jutted out, daring him to challenge her.

"But don't you think you're a tad on the small side?" Bobby chuckled like it was a joke. "You're no bigger than a mamma bear cub."

"Where do I sign?" Dahteste replied as she pushed the admission fee toward the man leaning on two wide pine planks laid across a pair of wooden barrels.

His dishwater eyes spread as his chin dropped to his chest, and he asked, "Are you serious, ma'am? You're so little it looks like you got caught in the rain and shrunk up. Have you had a look at the size of the fellas already signin' up for this string of matches?"

"My husband is one of them," Dahteste replied as she nodded at Levi. The six-foot-seven frontiersman nodded, but his eyes were full of confusion. He wanted to say something but didn't know where to start.

Angus cackled again and said, "I'll double that bet right now, pilgrim."

"And I'll double it again, fool," Rusty growled.

Angus McFarlin crossed his arms and rested his chin in his hand as he had a close look at the men in line behind Dahteste. He nodded and replied, "All right then. Double it is."

"Come on, Levi," Dahteste said. "I want you to sign up too. Put your mark on the paper just like me."

"But I ain't gonna fight my own wife," Levi argued, more confused by the minute. "I just ain't gonna do it."

"Don't worry, Beaver." Rusty chuckled. "By the time you get around to the last winners, she'll have long lost. Just look at the faces on those fellas waitin' in line." He laughed until he was red in the face. "You just remember, I've got a lot of money ridin' on ya."

"I've seen meaner-lookin' men taken down by Crow braves," Angus said. "Just because they're big and dirty don't mean they be ornery or even dangerous."

The men in line were all as scraggly as wharf cats. Two of them were Sioux Indians wearing the remnants of US Army clothing. They had Indian scouts painted all over their faces. Not a man in the bunch looked like a daisy. This made Levi frown even more despite what Rusty's assurances. He just shook his head and allowed himself to be led to the slaughter—or that of his wife.

"Do you know what nemesis means?" Bobby asked. "It means a righteous infliction of retribution manifested by an appropriate agent. In this case, personified by a bunch of mean hombres. That would be the men there standin' in line, ma'am." Bobby the Baptist grinned, showing a mouth full of yellow teeth.

"They're nothin' but a house of cards ready to fall with the first breath of wind." Dahteste smiled with eyes full of confidence. She looked at her husband and couldn't help but snicker at the uncomfortable look on his face.

Angus stood before Rusty, spat in his hand, and then held it out. Steel did likewise, and they shook on the bet.

"You hold the money, Dennis," Angus said. "I wanna make sure I get paid this year."

They each pulled out four two-bit coins and dropped them in Dennis's hand.

"You mean to tell me you're only bettin' a dollar on me?" Levi said. "I thought you said double, then double that."

"That's right," Rusty replied. "Four times two bits is a dollar. I know how to count."

Dahteste was grinning, and her eyes danced with

delight. She knew that Levi disapproved of her entering a wrestling contest, but back in the Crow stronghold, she had participated in many events of all sorts and usually won too. She didn't see why it should be any different with White men. Especially as she now lived with one.

In the end, forty men signed up for twenty fights. The ones that lost would be eliminated; then the twenty remaining contestants would pair off until only one wrestler stood.

"When are ya gonna get this show on the road?" Rusty Steel asked. "I'm bitin' at the bit to whip me a few young whippersnappers."

"At first light tomorrow morning," Bobby the Baptist said. "Why, the Rendezvous don't even officially start until tomorrow. You sure are itchin' to get a whippin', ain't cha, old man?"

The blow came so suddenly and unexpectedly that Bobby didn't even have time to grab his victim by the scruff of the neck and drag him off to the nearest stream to drown. By the time he saw the heavy pistol barrel, it was too late even to flinch. It hit him square on the temple. A rivulet of blood dripped from his brow and soaked into the fluffy dust. He lay on the ground staring up at the sky, sightless. He was out cold.

"How dare you call me an old man, fool!" Rusty retorted as he stood over the unconscious body. A drop of blood fell from the barrel of his pistol before he slipped it back into his belt. He spat a stream of brown juice on his forehead. "You'll know better next time."

Angus's eyes stretched wide as he grumbled, "Oh, my God. There ya go again. Makin' friends like there's no tomorrow."

"You know I don't take kindly to smart-alecky sorts," Rusty replied. "He called me an old man. I don't kin to strappy talk from any man, no matter how big they be. Bobby the Baptist. He's lucky I don't drag him down to the creek and do to him what he's said to have done to others."

"I thought we came here to have a good time," Levi said.

"And that's exactly what I'm havin'." Rusty grinned. "A good time. There ain't nothing that gets my blood flowin' better than a little scrap. Especially with a lump of lard like Bobby. This ain't the first time I run into him. He best mind his manners next time he sees me. He knew better anyway."

"Now you've gone and done it!" Angus cried when Bobby didn't move. "You've done murdered 'im. What do I always say? Pay your bills, and don't kill nobody, and it'll be all right. Well, now you've done it."

"No, I ain't killed 'im," Rusty replied. "Any fool knows dead men don't keep breathin'. I like 'im better laid out on the ground anyway. You know I don't tolerate bad manners or sassy talk."

"Well, leave 'im be, or we ain't gonna have our fight tomorrow iffin you do kill 'im," Dennis said. "I reckon this one ain't gonna make it to the end of the Rendezvous. He's got too big a mouth."

Bobby groaned, and his eyelids fluttered open and closed like he was trying to come back to consciousness but was having a hard time. Finally, his eyelids flipped open, but his dull gray eyes were vacant and still rolled back into his head.

By the time they got the mules unloaded and the horses brushed down and fed, it was pitch dark outside the Rendezvous. Inside, it was lit up like daytime. Fires roared every few yards. Insects crackled as they flew into the flames. A banjo and fiddle played *Old Zipp Coon* somewhere inside the growing mass of humanity.

ROUND ONE

BEHIND THE IMPROVISED COUNTER WHERE THEY HAD signed up for the wrestling match was a thick fencepost ring. It was twice the size of a standard boxing ring. All around it roared a crowd a dozen deep of rowdy men of all colors and origins, and they all wanted to see the event of the day. Flags from the American Fur Trading Company hung from flagpoles at each corner as they whipped in the wind. This marked the beginning of the two-week Rendezvous. The event was officially on.

Along both sides of the ring, long planks lay on tall sawhorses, where the company promoting the fight gave out free drinks. They were also giving chips for free visits to the fortune teller, the bathhouse, or one of the other services offered along the temporary main drag. Jugs of liquor were placed every three feet, and the mountain men gladly helped themselves. The alcohol just fueled the growing frenzy of the wrestling competition, and soon, everybody was yelling and shouting.

Bobby the Baptist was standing behind the counter. He had a white bandage around his head, blood-stained red over his temple, but he appeared to have recovered from the blow. They had paid and signed up the day before, so all they had to do now was wait until their names were picked out of a hat. Once the fighting partners were drawn, the first fight would begin. Men and a few women pushed and shoved to get a closer look. The news of the Crow Indian woman ran through the crowd like smallpox. A woman in a wrestling match among frontiersmen was unheard of, and everybody wanted to watch.

Of course, everyone knew Rusty Steel and was aware that, despite his beginning to age, he was still a danger to reckon with. Not to mention his new mentee, whom he had brought the previous summer. Levi had proved his skills at shooting then, so the spectators were expecting a similar show of wrestling now. The public was as excited as the fighters, as bets were made, and money exchanged hands. Everybody was getting in on the action as gambling fever raced through the crowd like the measles.

Rusty Steel walked right up to the man he'd pistol-whipped the day before like nothing had happened. He grinned and wiggled his eyebrows.

"Howdy, Bob," Rusty said. "It sure is a fine day for a scrap, ain't it?"

This time, Mr. Baptist minded his manners and didn't shoot off his big mouth. He hardly made eye contact with the old mountain man and simply nodded in reply. The doctor that had tended to him had heard of Rusty Steel, and he assured the Londoner he was lucky to be alive. Steel was said to have killed countless enemy Indian warriors.

"Here we are, pilgrim." Rusty smiled as he rocked

back and forth on the balls of his feet, full of energy. "Now we're all gonna see just what you're made of."

Bobby opened his mouth like he was going to give him some sass, but he slapped it shut, deciding better. He nodded, his mouth a hard line, but not a peep escaped him.

As the names were pulled out of the hat, Bobby called out who was to fight whom. Levi was paired off with a trapper called Cheese Flagstaff. His dull gray eyes were like a deer's, full of distrust and suspicion. Even Dahteste was paired off with a mountain man. His name was Gorgeous George, a Scotsman from Glasgow. His red hair and beard stood out in the crowd, making him easy to spot, and Levi didn't like what he saw.

Cheese was five feet nine with a barrel chest and a mop of hair pushed back on his head. He liked to fight for sport unless they were Indians; then, it wasn't a sport anymore. He felt it was more a religious task, and he was God's punisher because he considered everyone but Christians heathens. He believed himself quite the card and more intelligent than most, if not all.

When Gorgeous George was paired with the woman Crow war chief, he laughed. His friends slapped him on the back as if he had already won the fight just from the draw. Of course, some men would be harder to defeat than others. The whole competition was about pairing dangerous men against each other and making bets to see who would win. Nothing could be more exciting after twelve months of near solitude in the farthest stretches of the Rocky Mountains. They had gone from hardly a sound—beyond Mother Nature—to near bedlam and total chaos.

"No weapons allowed in this fight! Only hands, fists,

and feet!" Bobby shouted over the roar of the mob. "The fight's over when one man is down and out. That's the only rule there is. On the bell, gentlemen." Then he looked at Dahteste and nodded, adding, "Ma'am."

BANG, BANG, BANG rang the triangular dinner bell, and the fight was on. Roaring cheers rose from the crowd of rugged men. They were all there to see a few suitable matches. There would probably be a friendly fight or two in the crowd as well. It was anything-goes at the Rendezvous, where massive wild men walked the streets of the temporary tent town inebriated.

"You've gotta win this one, pig or pork, girl," Levi whispered into his wife's ear. "Don't wait around. End it before it starts, and you'll have the chance to take another shot. Maybe your next opponent will be smaller."

"Don't worry so much," Dahteste replied as she looked into Johnson's eyes. "It's only a wrestling match. The worst that can happen is I lose." She jumped from her corner into the ring, smiling and ready to go.

Gorgeous George grinned from ear to ear as he looked the little Crow warrior over from head to toe. Dribble seeped out of the edge of his mouth, and his eyes glazed over.

"Come on over here, girl, and give us a kiss," the Scotsman leered. "I know ya want it." He grotesquely rubbed his crouch.

Levi almost jumped the fence and went for George, but Angus, Rusty, and Dennis wrestled him down and held him back. It was like trying to manhandle a bull. Johnson's nose flared as the veins in his neck bulged. He growled like a wounded animal as his heart throbbed between his ears.

"Whatcha doin', fool?" Angus huffed. "You're gonna get us eliminated! It's just a wrestling match. You're gonna have to grow tougher skin than that iffin you wanna keep a Crow wife."

"Didn't you hear what he said?" Levi growled as he wrestled to get free. "I won't have any man talk to my wife like that. I'm gonna kill 'im!"

"Don't be such a dad-gummed fool," Rusty spat. "If you get us tossed out, I lose my bet."

"That's my wife in there," Levi growled. "I've got to stop this right now." He struggled some more, and Yosemite Bob, Portland Pete, and Syracuse Sam had to jump in to keep him from stopping the match and ripping Gorgeous George apart. His mentor, Steel, had never seen him so angry.

Rusty gave Johnson a stiff slap in the face and yelled, "Get a hold of yourself, pilgrim! Calm down now and stop actin' like a teenager. Don't you think Dahteste can take care of herself? Why, she'd be shamed if she saw you act like this. Remember, you're married to a war chief, not some river girl from back home. You can't treat her like she's helpless. You just watch. Somethin' tells me she knows exactly what she's doin'."

Levi snapped his head toward the ring and frowned. George was closing in with an evil grin, and his eyes were full of lust, and everybody saw it, but nobody did anything to stop what was about to happen. And nobody missed Dahteste's beauty. That was something she was counting on. The Crow woman batted her big brown eyes and looked puzzled at her opponent. He smiled, and that was all it took.

George hesitated for a second, giving Dahteste that instant she needed as she landed a well-placed kick to his groin. It didn't look like she had it in her, but the blow lifted her opponent's feet off the ground. His knees crossed, and he doubled over as his eyes popped wide, and a painful groan came from deep inside. He struggled to stay standing but finally dropped to his knees as he covered his privates and fell onto his side. The fight was over before it started. At first, nobody said a thing. It was so quiet they could hear a rat fart.

Then suddenly, the crowd went wild over the little Crow woman kicking Gorgeous George's butt within seconds after the bell. She casually slapped the dirt off her hands and turned for her corner with a grin. Her eyes caught Johnson's, and they were full of wonder. Dahteste loved how she affected men.

"Attaway!" Angus laughed as he slapped his knee.

Rusty, Levi, Angus, and their friends all patted Dahteste on the back and laughed. She was their new hero. Despite the rugged looks of the men challenging them, it was clear they wouldn't come in last despite one of the team being a woman—a Crow woman at that.

"If this is how things are gonna go for us, I reckon we'll do all right." Levi grinned.

Dahteste let Levi wrap his long arms around her. He was so proud he beamed. She looked up, pulled him down, and kissed him on the cheek. Her smile reached her eyes.

"Thank you for waiting," she whispered in his ear. "I'm glad you didn't jump in and stop the fight. Now, you see that I can take care of myself. But thank you for wanting to defend me. I would do the same for you."

That wasn't exactly what Levi wanted to hear, but he knew he had much to learn about his new wife, and she probably had a bit to learn about him too. He had misjudged her on the first opportunity and was now embarrassed about how he'd acted. His eyes met those of his mountain men friends, but theirs all danced with laughter. The first match had just ended with an upset that would set the pace for the next two days of wrestling matches.

At the side of the ring stood a man in a black suit with a satchel in his hand. He waited patiently as the fights began. He was the only doctor they could convince to come from Old Fort Boise. But even though he was really a horse doctor, he would suffice in these harsh wilderness conditions. He was up to the task if anybody needed a bone set or even a lead slug removed. Most mountain men have done such operations on themselves as there were no doctors in the Rockies, only medicine men from the various tribes.

Doc Black would stay for the duration of the Rendezvous. The Canadian trading company paid him to help lure more of the trappers to a better deal. Sure, many trappers were of the opinion that only Americans could be trusted, when the truth was, nobody could be trusted in the wilderness and surrounding area. The men from north of the border had English and European tools and goods at lower prices as a member of the Commonwealth. The American trading companies had to pay import tax to purchase the pricy goods.

"How did you know?" Levi asked.

"I just knew, even before the ugly man with red hair was vulgar," Dahteste grinned. "I don't cotton to sass, either. Just like Rusty Steel."

"Where'd you learn to talk like that?" Levi asked with raised brows.

"Rusty's been teaching me proper English," Dahteste replied, her eyes twinkling with mischief.

"Why, Rusty can hardly speak English himself." Levi laughed. "He uses more slang and misplaced words than most. I wouldn't consider him havin' a teacher's skill level."

"Wipe that drool off your face," Rusty laughed. "You're next in the ring, pilgrim."

Levi's opponent, Cheese Flagstaff, stepped through the fence posts that formed the ring. There was nothing soft about it. If you were slammed into the bark-covered logs, it could do considerable damage, especially to a man's head. The opponent sat in the corner as two buckskin-clad men coached him. Levi's opponent's eyes flashed back and forth like he was looking for a way out. But he saw none, so he gritted his teeth and stood up to the young giant.

He was drunk when he signed up and now regretted his bold actions. Everybody knew only the toughest mountain men were interested in such a dangerous confrontation. His friends had encouraged Flagstaff, only for him to find out later that none of them had signed up. They had been making fun of him since. Now, he was facing a six-foot-seven giant, the husband of the woman who had just decimated Gorgeous George.

Rusty slapped Beaver on the back to encourage him, and Dahteste rubbed his arms and back with bear grease, making it harder for his opponent to hold on. When Johnson stood to step into the ring, he towered over Cheese. You could see Cheese's Adam's apple bobbing up and down as he swallowed with a dry mouth. It looked like Flagstaff had caught an unlucky break in the draw. He was obviously slightly drunk, as his body weaved back and forth. He'd needed whiskey to give him the courage to take on Levi Johnson.

The clanking of the starting bell came fast and unexpectedly. There was only one round, and it lasted as long as it took for one contestant to beat the other into submission. There was no maximum time, and short of a knockout, there was no end. Cheese knew he had signed his death sentence, especially knowing the young mountain man lived with Rusty Steel. There were few people in the Rocky Mountains who hadn't heard of the trapper, hunter, and Indian fighter. Most Indians feared him, and he was a blood brother of a Crow chief.

Cheese circled. Levi crouched and growled like a dog. He was looking for the same opportunity Dahteste had seen, but Levi never took an opponent for granted and treated them all as dangerous. He kept him just out of reach until he could see his plan. They slowly circled each other crouched, cross-stepping as they moved around the ring. Both men remained in perfect balance. It appeared the drink had suddenly worn off Flagstaff. The roar of the crowd had disappeared for the two opponents. All their focus was on each other.

The sun bore down as the morning crept by, and both contestants' faces shined with sweat. The crowd began to jeer because they weren't making contact. They wanted to see blood. Levi smelled something fishy, so he held back until he couldn't hold it anymore without being called a coward. He lunged for Cheese. Halfway to his opponent, sunlight flashed off a shiny steel blade immediately after Johnson felt warm blood run down his side. Lucky for Beaver, his reflexes were primed, and he managed to turn his torso, evading the blade puncturing his kidney.

Levi jumped back with his heart in a frenzy. Right then, his stomach fell off a cliff. Cheese had been hiding a knife. It was hidden in his hand, so the referee didn't see it, but he had seen the flash of light off the shiny blade. He backed away with his eyes fixed on the wild man. He touched his side and saw the blood on his hand. Then he turned his eyes to Flagstaff. His head was reeling from the narrow escape. Levi shifted closer as his eyes grew more focused. If he tried to tell the referee, Cheese would take advantage of the lapse and stab him. He would have to finish this now and by himself.

There was only one way to end this, and Beaver intended to end it now. His legs felt like rubber, then they folded like a card table under him. *It's just a flesh wound,* he thought. *Shake it off or lose your life.*

Cheese had broken the rules. Blood dripped from the knife in his hand as he stood before Levi. He had cheated. He waved his frontiersman's knife in front of Levi's face. When the gunshot rang out, nobody knew where it came from or where it went. It was customary for drunken mountain men to shoot their guns to celebrate their arrival. But this time, the crowd went silent again. They looked at the fight organizer and saw he held a long gun with a smoking barrel.

They all turned in unison toward Cheese. A large but neat hole appeared in his chest right over his heart. Blood began to pump out in spurts spraying six feet. He bled out so fast he was ghost white in seconds.

"I done told 'im the rules," Bobby the Baptist called out. "There were to be no weapons. If you break the rules and try to take a man's life, then you forfeit your life. It's as simple as that. So iffin one of you scruffy fellas think you're gonna cheat in my fight, ya got another think comin'. Now, Fred, you drag that body out of the ring, and let's get our next two contestants up here and ready to go. I declare Levi Johnson the winner, and we go on to the next challenge."

Then the pain hit Levi, and he buckled. The cut was worse than he thought. His shirt, britches, and moccasins were stained red, wet, and sticky. Doc Black slipped through the wood posts and into the ring. As he tended to Johnson's wounds, two men dragged Cheese's body out and to the back, where they kept the pigs.

Rusty and his gang of mountain men had spent the entire day at the fight and hadn't taken time out to see the sights.

"Come on, y'all." Rusty laughed. "That's enough of all this fightin' for a spell. Why don't we go get somethin' to eat? Remember, everything's free if we go to the fur trading saloons. That means both food and drink."

"Let's go try some Canadian food," Dahteste said. "I've never had food from another country."

"Why, you can hardly tell where the Canadian border is, so it's pretty much the same on this side as the other," Angus said. "That is, until you get to the part the Frenchies settled. The boys speak Chinook Wawa. That's a mix of the English and French jargon."

"Well, come on then, I am starvin'," Angus said.

CHAOS

AS THE SEVEN MOUNTAIN MEN AND ONE CROW WOMAN walked down the street, things seemed to be reaching bedlam. Where there were no tents, furs were stacked high where traders worked in the blazing sun. A half dozen tipis were scattered here and there. Indians from several tribes had come to trade pelts for steel tools, hatchets, and the odd rifle.

Dozens of trails of smoke rose into the sky from the camp and cookfires. A wagon train of supplies fifty wagons strong was just pulling into the already over-flowing meet. Mules and horses rode in teams with barrels of supplies and hard liquor. This train of bull-whackers was the Rocky Mountain Fur Trading Company. They had arrived just in time to be in line for the best pelts. Cold-water beaver furs were what brought the highest price and the most bidders.

Indians from several tribes used the meet to call a truce for two weeks, so they all could get their much-desired coffee and tobacco. These were the items most traded with the locals. The aroma of complimentary, freshly perked coffee filled the air. Every person in sight seemed to have a cup of java or whiskey, or both, in one hand and a pipe in the other.

Armed men kept watch over the plot reserved for the local trading companies. The thirty men standing guard looked determined, and nobody questioned their claim. Fisticuffs and bribes would attain any other prime spots. Some clever businessmen had claimed special plots only to pass them on to the highest bidder. The closer to the fur trading companies, the more traffic, thus the more money they stood to make.

Rusty spotted the odd Crow Indian from Hachta's tribe but acted like he didn't see them. He knew the chief would disapprove of their presence, but who was he to judge? He came here to let off some steam after a lonely, cold winter. Now, they were in lush green valleys full of wild game. It was a rest from the daily battle to survive not only the dangers of the wilderness but also the various hostile Indian tribes that also called those mountains home.

Saloons that held as many as fifty people were bursting at the brims. The flow of human beings into the Rendezvous seemed constant, and it felt like humanity would soon overflow. The noise of more than five hundred men, hundreds of mules and horses, and creaky wagon wheels made it all but impossible to hear what a person right next to you was saying. Yet, there were mostly smiling faces in the dense crowd. For a few days, the men would live the opposite of the lives they had survived the last twelve months.

Everybody seemed to know Rusty Steel. He was constantly stopped and proffered a hand by some old acquaintance. Angus liked the attention, but he preferred it secondhand. He liked for Rusty to bask in the warmth of knowing so many people, respected and even, in some cases, feared. He was glad he was his trapping partner, even if he was lazy as sin.

Levi and Dahteste walked hand in hand. She was in awe at all the confusion. She had never seen a sea of people who weren't Indians. He marveled at all the colors of hair and skin. Johnson walked proudly beside his new wife. She had beaten Gorgeous George in the wrestling match. Maybe he didn't have to look out for her so much after all. She seemed to be doing an excellent job of taking care of herself.

"Lookee at that sign over there," Angus said as he pointed. It said FREE FOOD. "The best food I've ever had was free. It must be the idea of it that appeals to me so much. You know, not havin' to pay and all."

"I wonder what else is free." Rusty cackled. "I heard drinks weren't the only thing on the house. I think I'm gonna have to dig deeper into this."

They took seats on long benches made of freshly split logs. Sawhorses stood under wide wooden planks, and food was stacked on top. Steam rose from several buckets of fried chicken. Fifty ears of boiled corn sat beside a vat of butter. Every cut of beef imaginable was skewering over the spits. Hot fat dripped onto the coals and hissed. Indian women sold strings of sweet bread for two bits.

A man with long hair and a beard brought a tin tray as he weaved his way through the mass of people. Three dozen baked apples covered in honey and cinnamon filled the air with fresh smells as honeybees buzzed over the sweet treat. Mouths watered as their senses were assaulted by the delicious smells.

At the other end of the tent saloon, three men played instruments. The man on the banjo tapped his feet to an unheard beat as another played a harmonica and the third a juice harp. But the music was lost in the high decibels of the roar of the crowd. Suddenly, all of them had raging appetites, and they ate everything in sight. When they were done, another eight people were waiting to take their places. More food was brought out like on a conveyor belt from some mysterious, endless supply behind cookfire smoke.

An Indian woman came running up to Rusty and said something in broken Crow. She grabbed his hand, dragged him to a very small tipi, and motioned inside. There was something familiar about the woman. Rusty's brow furrowed.

"You help," she said. "You know the young warrior. You get help, make him get well." She pulled him to the flap and entrance to the tipi, which was barely Levi's height. Usually, the center of the Indians' dwellings towered over his head.

This small tent smelled like stagnant water or burned meat on a spit. The bullet wound was puffed up and swollen. The skin around it was jagged and ugly, and the exit wound was just as nasty. He looked up as the light began to dim in his eyes, shaking his head while making a gurgling sound. Strangled whimpers struggled from his throat to his mouth. Spittle mixed with blood seeped from his mouth and down his chin. When they arrived, he was gasping and out of breath as he made a failed attempt to gobble air.

"That there's Chaska, that Sioux warrior boy," Rusty said as he dropped to his knees beside the young brave. "What happened to ya, son?"

He sucked in a bolstering breath, gobbling air as he made a monumental effort to talk. Dark thoughts began to worm into Rusty's brain.

"I'll go get that horse doctor," Dennis said as he peered in from outside. With Levi, Rusty, and Dahteste, they barely had room to stand in the tiny tipi.

The Sioux warrior looked into Rusty's eyes. He nodded. You could see on his face that he knew he was already dead. He was just saying goodbye, but why now, after nearly a year? How had he known Rusty was there? Maybe because every mountain man within a hundred miles was there. He shuddered, one last chattery breath escaped his lungs, and his heart stopped. His eyes crawled back into his head until only the whites showed.

"I wonder who shot 'im," Rusty said. "He was a scrappy young fella. It must have been somebody with skills."

"I wonder even more why he fetched us," Angus said.

"There's more to this story than meets the eye," Rusty said. "I reckon he was comin' with beaver pelts like everybody else, and he was bushwhacked. I doubt just anybody could kill Chaska, either. It would take somebody with determination, 'cause he weren't no easy mark. I'm thinking more than one did it. Maybe three men."

"It could be other Indians, too," Dahteste said. "We are all at war with each other all the time. Even when we make a short peace with one tribe, we will fight three more. Our people are warriors. Just because he was shot doesn't mean it was a White man. You and your people aren't the only ones with guns anymore."

"The French Canadians be sellin' guns over the border," Angus agreed. "They want instability."

Rusty reached into his britches pocket and brought out a gold coin. He dropped it into the Sioux woman's hand, and he pressed it closed in his.

"See that this body is taken back home and put to rest all proper-like," Rusty said to the Sioux woman in perfect Crow. "When I first met Chaska, we were enemies, so we didn't meet in the most favorable conditions, but he was a good man just the same. He proved that to us all in the end."

"We have pelt poachers in our presence," Levi said, frowning. "I know I wouldn't take kindly to someone stealing all the pelts we trapped during the long winter. I wouldn't mind teachin' some poachers a lesson or two."

"Come on, boys," Rusty said. "We can't do nothin' for 'im now, can we? We best mosey along and check out the rest of the activities before we've got to be back for my fight."

"We better spot Sam and Bob a spell so they can get somethin' to eat too," Levi said. "Dahteste and I will take a turn on guardin' the furs. With seein' Chaska shot like that, I figure the sooner we get 'em off our hands, the better."

"Yeah, but then we won't get the best prices," Rusty replied. "This is business, Beaver. The nervous and impatient man gets the worst deal, especially with the quality of our furs. Any of the companies will be hard-pressed to find better-cured beaver skins. We know we have only the very best pelts, so we can let 'em bid on what we've got. All we have to do is make sure nobody steals our furs first."

"With the way things are looking around here, that may be a tall order," Levi fretted. "I'd say we're borderin' chaos right about now. Just wait until tonight when everybody's tight and in their whiskey. Then the bedlam will start."

"Considerin' Chaska's fate tonight, we should all stay put with our furs," Angus said. "I reckon if they're gonna steal 'em it'll be at night. I'd expect a run of thefts this first day or two before the mountaineers settle down. Some of 'em will get drunk first thing, and as soon as they drop their guard, the thieves will get 'em. Then, iffin some of the trappers catch the thieves and string 'em up, there'll be a lull for a few days, but somebody else will arrive at the Rendezvous, or some still here will work up the courage and have another go."

The fur trading companies hired Indian scouts and ex-lawmen to guard their fortune in furs. More than two hundred wagons would leave the Rendezvous once it was all over. Every mule available would also be stacked high with furs. Nobody was taking any chances. High-quality beaver pelts were like money, so they treated them as such. Nobody ever successfully robbed the trading companies. Sometimes, the very traders them-selves were the thieves by stealing the hard-earned skins from drunken trappers. Only when the party was over would the trappers realize they were going home with nothing.

Gambling was also present in every form possible, from straight-up poker games to penny pitches. They also bet on every event and competition. Much of the money made trapping during the coldest months of the year was lost gambling. Every way that existed to extract money from the trappers was used and was often successful. Still, it was dodgy business messing with the mountain men. They were often quick to anger, and they attacked first and asked questions later, especially if they had a few drinks in them.

"We can keep a two-man watch, and each do shifts," Rusty said. "Like always, just before dawn is the most likely hour. Especially if the bushwhackers are from one of the tribes."

"There ain't nobody gonna steal our beaver pelts," Angus said as he patted his pistols. "We ain't your normal seasonal trappers. We be the real deal."

RUSTY STEEL

THE FIGHTS CONTINUED ALL DAY, AND IT LOOKED LIKE they would finish all twenty matches. But the second to last fight was a knock-down, drag-out between two long-time rivals, and today they had the opportunity to sort things out once and for all. Both brawlers were big and burly mountain men with long hair and beards; they had been sworn enemies for a decade.

It was said that every time they saw each other over the years, they immediately attacked, and often one or both ended up at the doctor. Still, neither one had managed to kill the other, so they made a date in the ring during the meet. They planned to end the feud once and for all. They both looked more like bears than men. They even sounded like grizzlies.

They began by trading blow for blow like mountain goat rams banging heads. It was a test of who could take the hardest beating—punch for punch, kick for kick. They even traded headbutts. By the end of the match, they were so bloody and battered it was hard to tell who had won and who had lost—if there was, in fact, a winner. They were so bruised and swollen it was hard to tell which one was which. They fought until they didn't have an ounce of strength left, and they both dropped, heaving, to the ground. They gasped for air like a couple of beached trout. Bobby asked Doc Black to see if he could determine who was the worse for wear, but a verdict was impossible.

Doc Black said the only way to find out who was more damaged was to wait a few days and see what turned up broken or if they began to pass or vomit blood, or even if one of them died. All were sure signs of deeper problems. They were both nearly blind from the swollen eyes and torn eyebrows. Split lips accompanied broken noses, and every few minutes, one of the two would fish around in his mouth with his tongue and spit out another tooth.

They were too tired even to argue, and both were prepared to let bygones be bygones. They staggered out of the ring in a daze as their friends helped them, one on either side dragging their feet. They were so beaten they didn't even remember what they were fighting about and could barely see who was in front of them. Their eyes were nearly swollen shut. Bobby the Baptist was at a loss for who had won and who had lost. In the end, they were both declared losers due to the fact nobody clearly beat the other. So, Bobby deemed them disqualified.

Finally came the twentieth fight and the end of the day. The sun lay low on the horizon, and after that long last match, many wondered if the light would hold until the fight was finished. If not, Bobby the Baptist promised it would be repeated the following day regardless of the state of the contestants when the sun set. It would resume with the break of dawn. There were no excuses or exceptions in Bobby's game. Despite his mouth, he knew how to do business and was a skilled organizer. That was why the fur trading companies hired him.

The bets were trading briskly as one pair of opponents after another made their way to the crude boxing ring. One was dispatched, and one survived to fight again. The dirt floor of the ring even had rocks buried with jagged pieces sticking out. They had to watch where they stepped, or they might trip, and their opponent would have a moment of advantage.

"Come on, Rusty, you're up, boss," Levi said, full of confidence. "Who ya fightin'?"

"A fella by the name of Harlan Crow," Angus replied as he looked at some notes on a piece of paper. "I've never heard of 'im. Has anybody seen 'im before?"

"It could be anybody," Levi replied. "I reckon you'll be seein' 'im real soon anyway. Come on, or we're gonna be late."

Rusty, Angus, and Levi rushed to their corner. Johnson brought a washrag and a half bucket of water. Dahteste came at the last moment with bear fat to rub Rusty down and make him slippery. Still, they waited for Harlan Crow. At first, Rusty thought he wasn't going to show. It was true that Mr. Steel had a reputation for being dangerous if crossed. Despite his graying hair and beard, he was still as perilous as a rattlesnake.

Eventually, a tall, lanky man stepped leisurely into the ring. It was apparent he wasn't in a hurry, and his feathers weren't ruffled. He pushed back his dirty-blond hair, and his black eyes pierced the distance to the other corner. It almost looked like he was of Asian descent, at least partially. He was calm and collected for a man his age. He wasn't much older than Levi and the captain but was dressed in buckskins from some other tribe than those of the Rockies. The style and design were strikingly different. Maybe he came from Canadian Indians far to the north. Despite his lanky body, he moved with an unusual grace. It was almost like the movements of a deer.

Rusty pulled his spyglass from his large buckskin pocket and removed his lion claw necklace. The bear canines clattered on a leather string as they hung from his wrist. He pulled his massive knife and gave it to Angus for safekeeping. After removing his shirt, he pulled back his long gray hair and tied it in a knot at the base of his neck. For a man his age, muscles still rippled across his chest, arms, and back. Living in the wilderness made men rugged and hard.

Steel was calm and relaxed as he observed the young man sitting on the box in the other corner. He had nobody to cheer him on, as he appeared to be alone. Still, Rusty saw a calm confidence in his eyes, especially for such a young man. It didn't seem to bother him that he was on his own without moral support. A hint of a smile touched his lips, but just for a second, then it was gone. Rusty felt it was only for him. It gave him a little glimpse of the man behind the emotionless face.

Bobby banged the iron rod inside the steel triangle, and the last round of the day began. Rusty was in one place one instant; the next, he was behind Harlan Crow, standing in his shadow, snickering. He had fought alongside Crow Chief Hachta and knew how to fight with the best of the Indians. The Indian medicine men had also taught him to shadow-walk. They used the shadows and difficult places to see to blend in with their surroundings, making them appear to be someplace they weren't.

"Hey, youngster." Rusty laughed. "I'm over here. You're lookin' the wrong way."

As soon as Mr. Crow looked, he was on yet another side. For an aging man, Rusty was quick, like snapping your fingers. He seemed to mingle in the shadows cast over the ring by the people who were now standing on the fence. One and all were drunk and wanted to see one more fight like the last one. Patches of blood could still be seen in the dirt.

Rusty had one heck of a reputation from the Rockies to the Montana Plains, then back to St. Louis. He had cornered and fought every kind of two-legged creature that ever walked the earth at one time or another. Nobody was agreeable at this point of intoxication, but he was sober as a judge and ready to use the consumed alcohol against his opponent.

"Come on, youngin'." Rusty smiled. "I ain't gonna wait on ya all day."

The lanky man dropped to the ground and used his long leg to sweep the ground and knock Rusty's feet out from under him, but the aging mountain man skipped over his move like he was jumping rope. He seemed as nimble as a nineteen-year-old. Now, the mountain man could see his new opponent was skilled, although, he felt, differently than him.

Steel nimbly shifted his weight to the balls of his feet and prepared to make a pass. So far, he had run rings around his opponent, and now he planned to go in for the kill. Rusty didn't even see where the blow came from. He heard somebody shout in alarm, but he didn't even have time to react. His jaw twisted like it was broken. He only saw the flash of a foot before it hit him. He felt like he'd been kicked by a horse. Rusty wiggled his chin with his hand, and it clicked and slipped back into place.

There was no hint in Harlan's body language. He was so calm it was like water on a mill pond. But he had struck with the speed of a viper.

Rusty opened his eyes foggily while his head spun. His heartbeat was loud, pounding like it was in an echo chamber. He bit back his fear and faced his opponent. He knew he was going to take it up a notch. He was going to have to reach down deep inside and pull out all the resolve he had to beat this young man. Harlan Crow snickered with a curling, sly grin. His breath was slow and even, and his eyes held an uncanny calm. The breeze bent the single eagle feather in his hair.

Steel creakily pulled himself back to consciousness and up and on his feet. His heart rate flew off the charts, and his agitation needle slammed into the red. Rusty's heart was in a sprint, and his mind was jumbled and confused.

With blood pounding between his ears, he jumped up and hit the ground at a full run. He realized that this time, he had melded with a serious fighter. He swallowed grudgingly. He corrected his stance and prepared for another attack. He'd never seen a man fight like this before. None of the mountain men had. He was going to have to fight dirty.

"So, you know who I am, huh?" Rusty asked. His voice croaked, and pain shot from the hinges of his jaw.

If Rusty's heart rate could be measured, it would

have been in the red. His eyes grew wide and angry. He had to stop for a moment to take a couple of breaths.

Despite the fact Harlan looked drawn and pale, his movements were as quick as lighting and as smooth as silk. Sweat glistened off his shaved head and face. He wore a strange rosary around his neck.

Rusty nodded as his brow furrowed in thought. His expression seemed to say, *There's no way I'm gonna lose.* But he now recognized his challenger for what he was. He had to assume he was just as dangerous as Steel.

"Well, whaddaya know?" Harlan smiled. "You aren't as dumb as most of your types."

Rusty shrugged mutely, evincing a slight smile.

"And exactly who is it that's my type?" Rusty growled. "I sure don't know anybody like me."

For a split second, their eyes locked. That was when Rusty's mind and blood went on a rampage. He dodged hand chops and kicks as he twirled like a Crow warrior going in for the kill. His war cry was so unnerving goose bumps sprouted on the arms of every man and woman there. He faked a punch and then slammed his elbow into Harlan's throat, nearly breaking his windpipe. His eyes popped wide as he struggled to gasp for air. All the scrappiness instantly vanished, and the calm was replaced with a panic to catch his breath as he fought for air.

The control of the situation had been wrenched from Harlan, leaving him off balance and lost for what to do next. His fingers clutched as his throat as he fought for his breath from his knees.

"I can't breathe." Harlon Crow's voice croaked and held a tone of desperation. He haltingly stood and made his way back to his corner.

Rusty Steel shrugged, looked back, and said, "He'll live." He raised an eyebrow warningly when he looked at Harlan again. He motioned with his chin to go back to the opponent's corner. "Mosey on along now. This fight's over, youngster. Be a good lad and give it up while ya can."

The dead spark in Harlan Crow's eye was unmistakable. His body held a host of hate. He had heard of Rusty Steel and had come to best one of the most famous; then, he would acquire his fame. But it wasn't meant to be. The man off the ship from mainland China vanished into the mass of humanity, shamed by one of the great old mountain men of the Rocky Mountains.

Levi was speechless when he saw that Will Forrester had signed up for the wrestling contest. He was so focused on Dahteste then Rusty that he didn't see him standing at the back of the crowd. When he did spot him, he was watching the fight and never turned Levi's way.

"Lookee over there," Levi whispered to Rusty. "It's the captain. I see a black eye and a busted lip. I'd say he's signed up for the contest too. Either that or he slept with a wildcat last night."

"He must have been in one of the rounds when we went to eat," Rusty said. "Now ain't the time to be shootin' the bull, boy. Let's get this show on the road."

The following morning, it was time for the first fight after the elimination rounds. Once again, the names went into the hat, and the remainder of the contestants were paired up for their individual fights. Eventually, there would be one man standing. Or woman, were that to be the case. Of course, the betting was off the charts as the odds got better and better for Dahteste. They'd seen how quick she was and how powerful her kick was, so they knew she couldn't be ignored or taken lightly.

The crowd had already taken their champion even if she didn't win in the end. She had shown she had a wagonload of grit, especially to stand up to Gorgeous George and put him down in seconds. The fight would go down in history as the shortest fight in all the years of Rendezvous.

Levi was still shocked that Will Forrester had signed up for the wrestling contest. He wondered who would be put against him next. Would it be Levi or maybe even Rusty Steel, or would it be one of the other contestants waiting to learn their fate? Names were written down on small pieces of paper and folded over twice. Then a hat was held overhead, and the names for the coming matches were called out.

THE CAPTAIN

BOBBY THE BAPTIST STOOD ON A SMALL BARREL, SO HIS head was above the waiting crowd. He cupped his hands around his mouth and yelled, "The next to fight are Captain Forrester and the Sioux Indian scout, Tatanka Ptecila, or Little Bull! From now on, each man who wins stays in the ring until he wins another round or gets beaten. This is the last pass, and then we'll see who's left standing. Good luck to y'all, and the Lord willin', nobody'll get killed."

A roar went up in the crowd. Of course, Dahteste was still their favorite, but some of the attention swayed to the man with the yellow hair. He stood in the corner with a black man as his second. Virgil Lovejoy covered the captain's torso in bear fat, making him hard to hold onto. The whole time the officer seemed strangely detached—like he didn't even know what he was doing there. Or maybe he wasn't quite sure exactly where he was.

He blinked his eyes in what appeared to be bewilderment, but no confusion was present as soon as the iron chow bell rang. He was bare-chested, and his stump showed. It was cut off right above the elbow, but the captain never gave his missing appendix the slightest notice. He acted like he was like every other man there. Ripples of muscle crossed his arm, shoulders, neck, and dorsal, making him broad and strong. His one good arm sported a massive bicep. It was clear that using one hand to do two hands' worth of work had bulged his remaining appendage with muscle.

The Indian approached the captain like he intended to chop him down like a big tree. The sooner he had the White officer on the ground, the less chance of defeat or even being seriously wounded. More than a couple of the contestants had cracked skulls, and one even had a punctured lung from a broken rib.

Many men who'd challenged each other over the last two days had broken their arms, hands, fingers, or ribs, or fractured their skulls. Luckily for most mountain men, their heads were as hard as rocks. Even the wounded were in the crowd, sipping whiskey to numb the pain. Still, they didn't mind. It was one of the year's events, and they wouldn't miss it for anything. Not even a broken arm or a few busted fingers.

Captain Forrester sidestepped the Sioux warrior's advance and hit him on the back of his neck so hard the crack was heard in the first rows despite the noisy crowd. The Sioux scout tumbled with the fall and was instantly back on his feet like he hadn't even been hit. Still, Will knew he was dazed, so he had to keep it up, or he would recuperate. He intended to keep the pressure on until he cracked.

Again, the Indian scout attacked savagely, and again Will sidestepped him at the very last fraction of a second. He was well-balanced and quick on his feet. The warrior's flailing hands and fists punched the air because the captain wasn't where he was an instant before. Again, he gave him another hard punch at the base of his neck. He knew it was his last move this time, so he put all his weight into it. He nearly broke his hand.

This time the people closest heard the Indian's neck crack. It happened so quickly that everybody was shocked. At least everybody except the captain, who knew exactly what he was doing. Yet he had gone too far, and a man with a broken neck lay in the dirt. He appeared paralyzed from the neck down, but Forrester didn't give him a second thought. His mind was already on the next match.

The crowd roared just the same as two men came running with a stretcher, rolled the brave's limp but living body on, lifted him up, and ran off with the motionless carcass. His eyes shot all over the place but not even his lips moved. Will Forrester didn't seem to notice what had happened. He had won the fight, and that was all that counted. Virgil had had the big idea of placing Bud Gunn's and Clinch West's part of the money from the buffalo skins on a sure thing. He was counting on the captain to win, and he came through with flying colors.

Virgil ran to the corner and poured a tin cup of water into Forrester's mouth. He washed it around before spitting it out and wiping his mouth with the back of his only hand.

"Who's next?" Captain Forrester asked.

Virgil cupped his hand behind his ear to better hear what Bobby said. He was back on the barrel and was now blaring from a metal megaphone. The name of a fur trading company was painted on the side in red letters.

"The next event is with Captain Forrester, who won the last match against Little Bull. Crow War Chief Dahteste will challenge him. Will the challenger take her corner, and we'll get on with the next fight."

Levi instantly turned to Dahteste. He was ready to protect her with his life. There was no way he intended to allow her to go into the ring with an Indian fighter, and especially not Will Forrester. He would have her for breakfast.

"I ain't gonna let Dahteste go in there with the captain," Levi Johnson said. "We're all friends, for Pete's sake. The captain don't remember who we are, but I know who he is, and he's as dangerous as any man I know this far west of the Missouri River."

"And who do you think you are to tell me what I can or can't do?" Dahteste asked, clearly angry.

"You're my wife, and I say you ain't gonna fight the captain," Levi said. "He may not remember it, but he's my best friend."

"And don't you think I have a say-so in this?" Dahteste asked. "Just because we're married don't mean that I have to do everything you say. I'll fight whoever is the next name drawn. The rules apply to everybody equally, Levi. Remember, I am a war chief and will fight whenever I decide it's necessary. Now, don't interfere again."

"Yeah, and why is it necessary today?" Levi asked. Anger flashed in his eyes, but it was brought on by fear of something happening to his new wife.

"Because I am here on behalf of Chief Hachta and our people," Dahteste said. "Don't shame me, Beaver

Johnson. Your actions will make me look weak among my people, and this I won't have."

"She's right, pilgrim," Rusty said. His eyes were full of understanding. He knew Levi was only trying to protect his own. "I'm afraid you have no say-so in this matter. Dahteste signed up and paid her way, so she has the same rights as us to participate. Heck, maybe she'll knock some sense into that thick head of the Will's. It'll be about time."

It was evident that Dahteste wasn't afraid in the slightest. This was the bread and butter of a war chief every day. She was embarrassed by Levi's actions, though. But at the same time, she knew she would have been disappointed if he hadn't acted like he did. Being in love was a challenging change for the young war chief.

Now, she was discovering her husband's world, and she was finding it fascinating and confusing simultaneously.

LAST DRAW

THE FREE-FIGHTING COMPETITION HAD BEEN ROLLING right along. Many wounded and banged-up mountain men chose to have a few stiff drinks to kill the pain and watch the rest of the matches just the same. Just because they lost the fight didn't mean that they lost interest. Now, they were rooting for one friend or another as the betting continued to skyrocket into the day. Those who already had fought and lost watched as they ate and sipped on free whiskey.

Nobody was seriously troubled they had lost. They all knew different men had different skills. Still, even the losers knew they were special simply to have participated. Not every man west of the Missouri River would chance a fight with a frontiersman of this caliber. For a chosen few, it was an opportunity to rub elbows with the ruggedest of men in the country and for just a moment, be one of them.

Dahteste slipped through the slats of the ring and to her corner. She was bursting with energy and eager to have her turn in the match. She had won her first fight and planned to win the second too. Of course, these men were the best of the first batch of forty, so none of them would be daisies or weak of heart. Levi followed, and Rusty was waiting with a wooden box and a canteen. Angus had a foothold on the first rung of the pen as he leaned over and gave advice nobody could hear.

The Crow war chief sat and focused on the man across from her. Of course, she barely knew Captain Will Forrester, unlike the other mountain men. No matter what they said, she didn't trust an army Indian fighter, no matter how good a man they said he was. Too many of her people had fallen from the sabers of men like him. As far as she was concerned, they were all greedy men who felt their government was entitled to every piece of land they claimed, no matter who the actual owners were.

Dahteste flinched when someone behind her rang the bell, and the match was on. She sprang to her feet and instantly began searching for her opponent's weaknesses. The obvious one was his missing arm, so she led his weak side and went south-paw. There were more fragile points to every man, which she knew for sure. This wasn't her first battle with a capable enemy. Some she had in the past had been to the death. She wasn't afraid of what could be the outcome. She was a war chief.

She knew other weak points were there. She just had to find them in time to be able to turn the tables and take advantage. She knew she couldn't deal with his size and doubted a US Calvary officer would be a piece of cake, either. Most were cold-blooded and didn't shy from the sight of blood but were more lured to the curiosity. Some men like him could smell the claret even before they saw it.

The captain's blue eyes were vacant of anything but insane gloating and the urge to kill. He let out a scream as terror flashed in his eyes, and he rushed the woman warrior. It sounded like a wounded animal. It obviously didn't matter to him if she was a woman or a man. His attack was vicious and lightning-quick. The captain fell into a free fall descent into chaos, malice, and self-destruction.

When Forrester slammed his fist into her chin using all his weight, her big brown eyes rolled backward as a stream of blood poured from her bottom lip, then she sagged onto the ground. The fight had only begun, and she was already floundering like a fish out of water.

"Stay down," Forrester growled. "I don't want to kill you, but I will if you make me. You won't be the first Indian warrior I've killed. It don't mean squat to me that you're a woman. You would kill me if you had the chance, wouldn't you? I feel just the same."

Dahteste silently begged her hands to stop trembling. His brain went blank. She shuddered, shutting her eyes as tears threatened to shed. She already knew she was in too deep to get out alive. She was lying beaten before an Indian fighter in the flesh. The look in Forrester's eyes scared the dickens out of her. Tears flashed in her eyes, but she wiped them away with her sleeve before they touched her cheeks. She had to do this, and she had to do it now! Electrical currents of fear jolted through her body, and she used that energy to launch another attack.

She screamed as terror flashed in her eyes. A trickle of blood ran down her olive-colored chin. Without

warning, a second blow came, even harder than the
first. She hadn't even seen it coming, and the man only
had one hand. When his fist slammed into her head, it
rattled her so bad tears welled up in her eyes, born from
frustration and confusion. Her heartbeat was full of
dread.

The captain's heart suddenly started to pound
between his ears, his thoughts becoming clear.
Forrester's voice came like daggers in Dahteste's ears.
Levi and Rusty overheard what he said. Shock showed
on their faces. An uneasiness rippled through the
crowd. Somehow, everybody knew things were just
about to run off the rails.

"I'm going to kill you if you get up again, woman,"
the captain spat. "STAY DOWN!"

Levi Johnson saw Dahteste move, and he let out a
loud sigh of relief—she was still alive after such a devas-
tating blow. But just as quickly, his relief instantly
turned into rage. He ran to his wife and leaned forward,
taking her slightly trembling hands in his giant paws.
He squeezed them in his own and said, "I'll get even,
darlin'. I'll set this fool straight once and for all. Nobody
is gonna treat my wife like that."

Dahteste was still seeing stars from the two punches
the captain landed. Frustration burned in her eyes, but
she couldn't bring herself to look at the man. She didn't
know if she could control her feelings if their eyes
locked. He was the boogie man the Indian camp
mothers and fathers used to scare the children with
when they were naughty. She saw something wicked in
there and didn't want to look again.

The captain had no redemption, no sense of what
he'd done with no contrition. He would make them beg

and cry before he killed them. This was a vow he made
to himself. He watched as the big mountain man who
claimed to be his best friend tended to the woman. He
wondered how he felt about it all, but like before, he felt
nothing. It was time to end the history between the two.
The captain knew the man the Indians called Beaver
would insist and try to bring back a memory long lost.
Forrester was not inclined to pursue the issue further.
He felt these memories wouldn't improve his life, and
he didn't want the additional baggage.

The captain's blue but distant eyes grew slightly
more interested. Now, he was to fight a man of his capa-
bilities. He towered over him. Levi pushed back a strand
of hair, shaking his head, pushing his lips into a tight
line. His feelings for Dahteste made him run past fear,
worry, and dread. What Levi Johnson had just seen sent
his heart through his chest and his mind spinning like
a top.

The captain's look was lit with elation and vindica-
tion. Levi got up and sighed, looking over his shoulder.
He helped Dahteste from the ring as she trembled, then
he focused his attention on his new enemy. Now he
knew the captain wasn't the same man he was when
they came to the Rocky Mountains. His fall and the
bang on his head had changed the man for life.

Then again, maybe he'd always had that mean
streak in him. Perhaps it was just waiting there all that
time to come out. Johnson didn't recognize any trace of
the old Will Forrester in the officer who now stood
before him. He knew then and there that he had to kill
him. He was too full of hate to be allowed to live
because he could endanger Levi's family again.

When the two young mountain men went at each

other, it was in a sudden burst of energy. They raced
from their corners to the center of the ring and crashed
into each other chest to chest as their arms flailed. The
sound of their first impact was loud. The captain was
clearly out for blood and didn't intend to allow Levi to
walk away from the fight alive. The sounds of fists
making heavy contact with flesh sounded so loud it
almost seemed artificial. The men thudded their fists
into each other like they had been waiting for this fight
all their lives. It sounded like prize fighters punching
sides of ham.

Blood spatter covered both men as noses broke, and
ears were nearly torn off from the flurry of blows. Still,
they hammered on each other like they were born
mortal enemies. Body shots weakened them both as
their kidneys screamed in pain, but they bit their lips
and fought on, regardless of the piercing bolts of agony.

Dahteste nearly broke free to help Levi, but Rusty
grabbed her arm and shook his head. A calm look in his
eyes made her stop struggling and settle down. There
was a wisdom there that she instantly trusted. She was
torn between her honor and calm reserve and near
panic, seeing her new husband be beaten to a pulp,
maybe even killed. Still, so far, she couldn't see who had
the advantage. It looked like they were thrashing each
other to death, punch by punch and kick by kick. Still,
they didn't slow down even though they huffed to
gobble air. They ignored the discomforts and fought on
for all they were worth.

They both knew there would be no end to the
round, and there would be no time to catch their breath
and recuperate. This match would be finished when
one of the two was dead, if not both. This was as violent

as fighting matches get without weapons. Despite the lack of guns, one could quickly die that day.

All it took was the wrong kind of bang to the head or even a ruptured kidney or damaged liver. A broken rib could puncture a lung, killing the wounded contestant slowly with lots of pain. They knew the rules when they signed up, so there were no questions. They continued to slam their massive fists into each other's faces and torsos.

Despite the quick attack and severity of the aggression, somewhere back in Levi's mind, he wondered if he could kill a man who had been such a close friend. Then again, he knew if he hesitated, he would be the one to die. When he looked into the captain's eyes, he saw tombstones. Maybe they were the reflection of his own eyes.

"It's gonna be all right." Rusty moved his lips silently. "It is what it is." The crowd roared on, making it impossible for everyday conversation.

As usual, Rusty had a fatalistic view of things. If things were to work out badly for both men, they could end up dead, but who was he to question the actions of another or their destinies? He sat and calmly watched. The click of a hammer came from under Rusty's legs. The barrel of a pistol was just visible. He was ready in case his worst fears materialized. It was against the rules, but sometimes they were there to be broken. If he had no choice, he would do what he had to.

In their final clash, they wrestled each other to the ground. Levi was on top thrashing on the captain, then the officer tossed him off, jumping on top, and began hammering Johnson into the ground. The fight was brutal; for all appearances, both men were out for blood and prepared to take each other's lives. The captain landed a blow that would break the jaws of most men. Johnson's eyes tried to crawl back into his head, but he knew it was his last chance. If he faltered now, he could lose the match and his life.

He shook his head and drew back his fist, but suddenly, Forrester had a large rock in his hands. It had worked loose from the ground. He raised it over his head and began its downward trajectory, right for Beaver's face. Johnson knew he didn't have time to dodge and couldn't block the blow, so he waited for the end. "*Our Father who art in Heaven...*" In fractions of a second it would all be over, and he would be dead.

Dahteste raced across the ring from Levi's corner, ripping away from Rusty's grasp on her arm. In one smooth motion, she picked up a large stone from the ground and drew it back. She stood behind Will Forrester as he raised the large rock to kill her husband. She slammed the rock into the captain's temple with all her might. He fell over like a crumpled stack of cards in a sudden downpour. His eyes rolled back, and he dropped the stone while falling on his side. A long chatter of breath left his body, and he went limp. Blood seeped from the torn skin on the side of his head. His blond hair was stained red.

The chunk of boulder landed right beside Johnson's head. He rolled out from under the captain, panicked. The army officer looked like he was dead.

"I think you killed 'im," Levi said incredulously as he unsuccessfully tried to gobble enough air to slow his heart down. He looked from Dahteste to his old best friend, whose body was motionless.

"I meant to kill him," Dahteste replied as she stared

at the body of the maniac. How could this man ever have been her husband's best friend? "He had to die. Can't you see he lost his mind? He might have come after us if I hadn't killed him."

"Don't count your chickens before they're hatched," Rusty said. "I seen his boot move. It might be a twitch of death, but we best make sure." Steel pulled the pistol from under his leg and aimed at the motionless body as he drew back the hammer.

"You can't do that, Rusty," Levi said. "Killin' him like that would make you just as bad as the captain, and then again, you might just be shootin' a corpse. Remember, once he was a good man. And iffin he is dead, do ya wanna have that on your conscious? Killin' a man twice? Why, ya might as well stab 'im and hang 'im too."

"You can drop that stone now," Rusty said as he lowered his gun. "I think he's dead anyway."

Dahteste still had the blood-stained rock in her hand. Her white-knuckled fist relaxed, and she dropped it to the dirt with a thud, creating a little puff of dust. A drop of claret fell from the tip of her finger, only to vanish as soon as it hit the dirt.

DISTANT DREAMS

THE SAME STRETCHER THAT HAD TAKEN THE DYING LITTLE
Bull away removed the unconscious captain from the
ring too. They lay him in a cot inside one of the smaller
tents. When Doc Black checked him out, he found his
breath barely detectable. Sure, he was busted up as bad
as Levi Johnson or maybe worse, but the horse doctor
couldn't find any life-threatening wounds. Time would
tell if he came around and wasn't spitting up blood.

Then again, that last blow with the rock might have
scrambled his brains, and he might never wake up
again. There were too many ifs in the equation for Doc
Black to formulate a plausible diagnosis, especially for a
horse doctor. At that moment, he was out cold somewhere deep inside his consciousness. Could the captain
break through the dark veil, or would he never awaken
again? It was impossible to say. Levi wasn't so sure if he
wanted him to come around or not anyway. If he just
died, it might be simpler.

"I think this fella is gonna live after all," Doc Black
finally said as he held his hand on the unconscious

man's brow. "His fever's already broken, and some color is comin' back into his face. His heart's faint, and his breath's shallow, but he ain't dead. At least not yet, he ain't. Now, that don't mean that he'll come to, though, with such a bang on the head; he might have jumbled his gray matter, so many things might not work anymore. In that case, he'll just slowly die. I'm sorry, but that's the best I can do with what I've got to work with. I'm afraid I can't tell ya anymore."

Levi had a look on his face that was a mix of puzzlement and relief—pain and danger. He was glad the captain hadn't died though he didn't really know why. Still, he couldn't believe he would kill him—his old best friend. It was a close call on all counts. Now he wanted to get away from the man. He knew the new Captain Forrester wasn't somebody he wanted to be around. It could cost him his life, and even worse, his wife's life.

He wondered if the captain would want revenge for Dahteste's interference in the match. She had cheated. Under the house rules, Forrester had every right to bash his head in, and Dahteste had no right to interfere. The only rules to the game were no weapons. Nobody ever said anything about rocks, stones, or even fence posts.

Maybe it would be better for everybody if the captain never regained consciousness. If he did come around, Levi had no intention of furthering the discussion about their lost friendship. As far as he was concerned, that was long dead and gone. Sometimes, things in life changed, and there was nothing a man could do to turn it back to what it was. Nobody could turn back time.

Lucky for them, Bobby the Baptist had only disqualified them, considering the circumstances. He didn't want to make an enemy of Rusty Steel either. He already knew how dangerous that could be—not to mention his young apprentice and Crow wife. One could be more dangerous than the other. So, he let them go. Of course, they had to forfeit their bets. It cost Rusty and Angus each a dollar, and they were put out. They only liked to make what they considered large bets like that on a sure thing.

Rusty dug deep into his pockets when it came time to pay up. He pulled them inside out, and they were both empty. He looked at his partner trapper with a puzzled look.

"Ain't ya got any money left?" Angus asked.

"No, I'm broke flatter than a snake through a wringer," Rusty admitted. "Cover my dollar until we sell our furs, pard."

"I should have known better than bet cash-money with you," Angus growled. "You never pay your gamblin' debts."

"Maybe you should work on your people skills, you old fool," Rusty retorted.

"My people skills are fine," Angus retorted. "It's my tolerance of idiots that needs work, so I don't need to control my temper. I need folks to stop tickin' me off."

"Oh, shaw," Dennis grumbled. "Y'all are as stupid as bean curds. Now, stop actin' like a couple of teenagers. It ain't becoming to grown men."

Dahteste opened the flap and entered the tent. Her angry glare flashed at the captain's body. But when her eyes grew wide, she couldn't stifle a smile. All the men's stares were drawn to the beauty. She curled her hair with her finger, feigning shyness. She batted her eyelashes.

"Is he dead yet?" Dahteste asked. She hoped he was. She would never admit it, but she was still scared of him, even unconscious. She felt he was like a rattlesnake, always ready to strike at the least expected moment.

"No, he ain't dead yet," Doc Black said. "And that's no way for a lady to talk. Especially right in front of the patient. Just because his eyes are closed doesn't necessarily mean he can't hear ya. That's what they call one of them mysteries of science. Nobody knows what's goin' on in the brain of a man out cold."

"Do you mind if we wait for a spell?" Levi asked. "I don't really know why I feel like sitting and waiting, but I do. You can run along iffin ya want, darlin'. There's no need for the both of us to stay."

"I'm not leaving you alone with the captain no matter what you say," Dahteste vowed as she fingered the handle of her knife. "What would have happened if I had not interfered in the fight? You would be dead, darlin'." She held her hand to her lips and snickered.

"You sure are right there," Levi replied. "I saw death knock-knock-knockin' on my door as clear as daylight. I was already sayin' the Lord's Prayer with my mortality at hand. Had you been half a second later, I'd have had my brains scattered in the dirt right now."

"I don't know what y'all are talkin' about, but you must keep your voices down," Doc Black said. "As you can see, we have several patients here, and they all need some peace and quiet."

"Why, most of 'em are dead drunk, is what they are." Levi chuckled.

"Just the same, you are currently in my domain, so I

must insist that you do as I say. You can stay only if you both be quiet." Doc Black gave them a stern look.

————

FORRESTER'S MIND raced through the pages of his life like a book in the wind. His eyes darted under his eyelids as he continued in a deep, unconscious state. It was like he was trying to fight his way out of a maze of veils. His fingers and toes occasionally twitched. Doc Black didn't know if it was a sign of life or an imminent death. At this point, anything could happen.

Everyone but Levi and Dahteste had left to get something more to eat and to check on the boys and the beaver pelts. The theft risk was still present—at least until they got their furs sold and the money in gold coins and on their persons. Johnson didn't know why he felt compelled to wait to see if the captain awoke. He unconsciously drummed his fingers on his pistol's grip. Like he was ready to pull and shoot him at the slightest move or provocation. Was it that he was afraid? he asked himself.

He knew if Will did die, it was not only his own fault, but it would also be the fault of Johnson and his wife, Dahteste. Maybe he still felt he bore some smidgen of responsibility. Maybe some tiny amount of loyalty to a friend that was no more.

The captain continued to breathe such shallow breaths it concerned the doctor. Dahteste expected him to stop breathing from one minute to the next. She crossed her fingers every time there was a lull in his breathing, hoping it would be his last. Still, he continued to fight for his life, although silently.

An hour later, Levi and Dahteste sat behind the doctor dozing off and on. The captain hadn't moved, but still they waited to see if he regained consciousness.

"Well, howdy there, Captain," Doc Black said, surprising everybody in the room. "It appears that you've come back with us to the living after all." He removed his hat, put it over his chest, looked up, and said, "Thank ya, Lord, for sparing one more soul on my watch."

"Where am I?" Forrester asked in a croaky voice. His eyes were confused. "And who are you?"

Levi heard the voice from behind the doctor. His head filled with dread when he did. When Dahteste heard it, it hit her like a lightning bolt, and the bottom fell out of her stomach. She, too, felt the dread.

"Why, you're at the Rendezvous in the Rocky Mountains. I'm Doc Black, and I've been tendin' to your injuries." He chuckled. "Yours and everybody else's in the tent city. I've been busier than a cat in a room full of rockin' chairs. You're a lucky man, Captain."

The doctor grabbed some medication, filled a large glass syringe, gave the captain a shot, and moved to one side. The captain looked up, and his eyes spread wide. Johnson and his wife were standing behind the doctor.

Will Forrester blinked his intense blue eyes and said, "The doc reckons I'm lucky, Levi. What's he on about, and who hit me in the head? I feel like a team of eight-horse wagons has run over me."

"Where does it hurt?" Doc Black asked.

"It'd be easier to tell ya where it doesn't hurt, Doc," the captain replied. "And what happened to you, partner? You look like I feel. And why the funny face?"

"Now, don't go pushing yourself, Captain Forrester,"

the horse doctor said. "You've had a bad bang on the noggin', and it wouldn't do to move too fast for a spell. You're likely to go under again, and I can't guarantee you'll come back."

"And you say I got a bang on my head?" Forrester asked. "Why don't I remember anything?"

"That's the gospel truth, so help me, God," Doc Black replied. "As far as you not rememberin' anything, I'm afraid you and I have just met, so I know about as much as you do."

Everything started to fit together like bees and honey. All the pieces began to fall into place, filling in the captain's memory. He even remembered what had happened since the first fall, when he lost his horse. It came rushing back like a smack in the face in early morning. His chin dropped to his chest when he looked back at Levi Johnson.

Levi looked at the captain, and for the first time, he saw him with clarity, saw what he was feeling. Where all this had been leading from the start. This was purification in its purest and most elemental form. Their friendship had been put to the ultimate test, and still, after all was said and done, it had apparently survived.

Levi moved his mouth like a fish out of water, but nothing came out. Will Forrester's words came like rain after a long drought.

THIEVES

THE FULL MOON HUNG IN THE SKY LIKE IT WAS REELED OUT on a string slowly dropping to the horizon. A blanket of stars twinkled overhead, as white, cotton-like clouds floated between the heavens and the earth. The lunar glow cast silvery shadows on the countryside. The temporary tent town was nearly as busy as it was during the day, but the part set aside for the trappers to camp was cast into deep shadows. Most of the fires had burned down, and all that remained were orange glowing circles like small craters. It was the early morning hours, just before the first light would appear on the eastern horizon. This was the time of night for predators and thieves.

They could see the big dog's eyes even in the dark. Its black fur blended with the night, so he was only partially visible. The canine lay beside its master, waiting for the thieves to show. It emitted a low growl from somewhere deep inside, warning them somebody was lurking out in the early morning shadows. They believed it was just a matter of time. Everybody at the meet knew who had the best pelts and did expert curing. It was Rusty Steel and his bunch. Now, they had twice the number of furs as ordinary trappers, and mountains of bundles circled the sleeping men.

Four members of the compound hid, waiting from places hard to see with the naked eye. When the first rustle was heard in the bushes outside the clearing, the trained ear could hear the sound of clicking hammers. But the thieves weren't professionals. They were merely other trappers who had fallen on hard times themselves.

Many people came to the Rocky Mountains in search of making an easy buck. But when they arrived, they realized their dream of easy money was only a dangerous illusion. They often found out too late, costing them their lives. Or maybe somebody stole their furs, and they chose to replace what was stolen from them over going home empty-handed.

Rusty, Angus, Levi, and Will lay motionlessly, watching and waiting for the first bandit to step foot into their campsite. Until they crossed these boundaries, they couldn't do a thing. They had to catch them in the act for any justice to be served in the distant valleys below the peaks of the Rockies.

Finally, three shadowy figures crept near the camp from the north side and three more from the south. With the bright moon, they could make their way with little difficulty. It was nearly as bright as a cloudy day. Finally, the moon dropped off the world's edge, and they tumbled into utter darkness. They had picked this very moment to strike and steal as many pelts as they could carry on the mules waiting just outside the clearing.

The thieves' eyes shot all around, looking for some-body awake, but there apparently was no one. They moved deeper into the camp until they came to the first bundle of beaver pelts. Each one was worth a small fortune. So, the more they could steal, the richer they would be. The only problem with their plan was that dead men couldn't spend money.

The first thief suddenly froze on the spot. Rusty dug the gun into the back of his skull. His fingers had just wrapped around his pistol grip as he felt his insides gnash together in alarm. He knew he would get his head blown off if he pulled now.

"Come on, over here," Levi whispered as he wagged his pistol at him. "I figure we've separated the chaff from all the wheat. Now, don't you dare call out to your partners, or I'll feel obliged to blow your brains out. Do you understand?" The small-time thief nodded.

Rusty came from behind and thumped the thief in the head with a heavy barrel. He gave Johnson a cross look.

"We don't want any of 'em gettin' strappy and trying to fight back," Rusty said as he swung his barrel across the night, squinting his eyes into the dark. "Sometimes, you're just too dad-gummed soft, Beaver."

"I figured we could tie and gag 'im," Levi replied.

"Now, you're just wastin' time. Come on, there's five to go," Rusty said and instantly vanished into the dark.

The next two thieves didn't know they were so close to danger. The captain squeezed the trigger, and the chunk of lead blasted a hole in the first man's knee from not two feet away. For an instant, the muzzle flash lit up the night. The impact shot off his kneecap as he jumped on one leg, howling while clutching the other. Bone was visible through the ragged hole.

The man beside him turned to run, but he didn't see the rifle stock in the dark until it was right before his face, and it was too late. His nose bent to one side as his cheekbone cracked, and he went down. The winged thief continued to wail. The wounded man tried to reach for his gun, and Dog attacked. He clamped down on his forearm with jaws like a steel vise. Skin and muscle were ripped to pieces, and bone broke under the pressure of massive jaws.

By then, Angus, Mountain Dennis Breed, and Portland Pete hung from a low limb. They had ropes wrapped around their arms, and as soon as the last three thieves walked under the tree, they looped their heads and dropped to the ground, lifting the outlaws up by their necks.

By then, the whole camp was awake, and men were building fires and lighting torches. Every mountain man and trapper feared losing their hard-earned money to thieves—men who were too lazy to do the hard work and schemed to steal what others had labored and risked their lives to earn.

Three men kicked their feet as they struggled to free themselves from the ropes around their necks as they wildly twisted their bodies. Time slowly ticked by until they finally strangled and accepted their deaths. Then they took the next three men, even though two were barely conscious and the other was still howling from his blown-off kneecap and damaged arm. They hung them with the same three ropes as their partners.

A crowd of a hundred mountain men watched and cheered on the executioners. There was no room in their lives for men who took that which wasn't theirs. They were the only law they had so far from civilization, and they knew they had to send a strong message too.

"Does anybody recognize the bodies?" Rusty asked while standing on a whiskey barrel.

"Them's two of the Squirrel brothers with their cousins," a voice said. "They come from the Squirrel clan. I've heard tell they have kin back in Kansas."

"Well, we ain't takin' 'em to Kansas, that's for sure," Rusty said. "We best get to diggin' a half dozen graves. I hate to leave a man unattended. I'll make the crosses, and don't worry—I'll keep it simple. I'll carve Squirrel somewhere on one of 'em so their kin knows it's them iffin they come a-lookin'."

TRUE FRIENDS

"I'D FEEL SAFER IF THAT CROW WOMAN WAS IN JAIL. CAN'T anybody think of somethin' to detain her for? You'd need a company of soldiers to take that woman alive." The captain laughed at his joke.

Dahteste curled a grin and said, "Everybody says that."

Virgil had finally found the captain after looking for him for hours. The last place he expected to find him was in the hospital tent one of the fur trading companies provided. When he located him, he was with his friend Levi Johnson.

A scruffy mountain man stood a little wobbly after taking the last slug from a labeled bottle. Then he fell flat on his face, and everybody in the camp exploded in laughter. Rusty laughed until he got a stitch in his side. He caught his breath and pondered on his life.

"Becomin' old is the dumbest thing I've ever done, and it's comin' at a really bad time, too," Rusty lamented. Hanging the men had made him look hard at himself, and he wasn't sure if what he did was right or wrong. He wondered what he'd be asked on the judgment day and if he'd have the correct answer.

"Now that we caught the thieves, I reckon we'll be safer than a tick on a dog with no legs." Angus chuckled.

Levi pulled his head out of the water barrel and shook like an old dog, sending water spray everywhere. Dahteste watched and laughed.

Captain Forrester sat next to Virgil and listened and smiled. His friend Lovejoy marveled at the change in the officer. The man he had met had been angry and bitter, but the soldier that was friends with Levi Johnson was a soft-spoken man who preferred to listen more than talk. He sat as calm as a summer breeze, enjoying close friends' company. Lovejoy couldn't have imagined him so different had he not seen it with his own eyes. He had almost given up hope on the captain, but it turned out deep inside he was a good man. Patience, indeed, was a virtue.

Levi and Dahteste lay on a blanket and whispered secrets into each other's ears. She threw her head back, laughed, and punched her husband on the arm. They seemed happy everywhere they went but had to suffer the hardships Mother Nature dished out in the most remote places of the Rocky Mountain wilderness.

Angus McFarlin and Rusty Steel continued arguing over whose fault it was for losing two dollars on a bet.

"You make me so angry I could smoke a pickle," Angus grumbled.

"Hang on a minute, maybe I can find ya one to smoke, stupid," Rusty growled.

When he wasn't looking, Rusty smiled. He needed Angus to wind up and entertain him. He wasn't meant to live alone. Of course, none of them were meant to live with such a number of people as those attending the Rendezvous. They were fine in their compound, even though it looked like they would have a new member in their small home. Virgil, Will and Levi planned to build a cabin for them and Dahteste. Living in a tipi in the middle of a Rocky Mountain winter was very restricting. The four began planning to construct a large cabin with a separate room for the newlyweds.

Before, they might have had a problem extending their compound, but since the new building would house a Crow Indian war chief from Hachta's tribe, there would be no problem, especially not after selling all their furs for top dollar and securing a gun or two.

Dennis Breed had a drink in one hand and food in the other, no matter when or where you saw him. When edibles and refreshments were free, he made sure he never stopped ingesting either. He doubted he could eat and drink himself to death in two weeks, but he was going to give it one heck of a try, and he couldn't think of any better way to go—with a full belly, his boots on, and a whiskey-filled mind.

More men rode into the Rendezvous. Some of the new arrivals were heavily armed. It seemed like more and more people joined the already disorderly crowd every day. Levi wondered when the flow would stop and begin to go the other way as people started to leave. Still, the meet had just started, and who knew what entertainment would pop up next? It was as close to a circus as any of them had ever seen, but if they wanted to sell their furs they had to be there. Angus and Rusty wouldn't miss it for the world.

With five hundred drunken mountain men,

anything was possible. They wondered how many men would make it the whole two weeks and survive. At the moment, the numbers grew and grew with each passing day. Where would all these people go after the fur trading companies had taken down the tents and pulled up stakes? Most of the attendees didn't ponder what might or might not happen in the next twelve days. They were there to discover the unexpected and they were not to be disappointed.

"Well, we're two days into the Rendezvous, and we're all still alive." Rusty laughed. "I figure either we ain't havin' enough fun or we're getting old, and I don't fancy it be the latter."

"Let's pull straws to see who has to stay with the pelts," Bob said.

"Don't worry, boys," Captain Forrester replied. "Virgil and I'll keep an eye on them. There's enough entertainment right here for me. I don't need any more excitement for the day. I think the last month was about all the commotion I could take."

The captain winced when his split lip opened again, and blood dripped to his chin. He had two black eyes; his nose wasn't as pretty as it once was, and his face was severely bruised. The black and blue marks were turning a hue of yellow. Every time he laughed, which was often, it made pain shoot from fractured ribs. He wondered if Levi felt as battered as he did. He was just happy they were both still alive, and he wondered what the Rockies would throw at him next.

Mayhem on the Oregon Trail

Levi Johnson Mountain Man Scout 12

This book is dedicated to my old mates: Bob, Charlie, Albi, Stewart, Doc John, Ian, Drummer Dave, American Dave, and Gary, but especially to you, John Duffy. I look forward to our gatherings on the odd Friday.

"There is no hunting like the hunting of man, and those who have hunted armed men long enough and liked it, never care for anything else thereafter."

Ernest Hemingway

INTRODUCTION

The last Rendezvous was held in 1840 in Daniel, Wyoming, and brought more than five hundred trappers to the meet to sell their cold-water beaver pelts. Everyone expected it to grow with each coming year. With the sudden loss of interest in the top hat market and its decline the following year, the prices dropped, and a new skin came into favor. This, combined with the near extinction of beaver, changed the Rockies forever.

Its replacement was the buffalo hide, which was pliable, odorless, and durable, used for coats and blankets. This change brought the sudden end of a fifteen-year custom exclusive to the Rocky Mountains—the Rendezvous. The beaver business went under from one season to the next, and many mountain men were forced to search for new ways to make a living.

The first people to cross what was to become known as the Oregon Trail were missionaries headed for Oregon City. The first was Minister Jason Lee, a Methodist. Then came Elijah White and finally, Marcus and Narcissa Whitman. Henry and Eliza Spalding accompanied them, with others. Their destination was Walla Walla in the Columbia Valley. The Indians called it Many Waters, which is now part of Southern Washington State and Northern Oregon.

Joseph Rutherford Walker was an explorer, mountain man, trapper, buffalo hunter, and Indian fighter born in 1798 in Roane County, Tennessee. In 1819, his family migrated to Missouri, and in 1820, he traveled to Santa Fe, which was under Mexican rule. He was said to be one of the early Taos trappers in Alta, California. He worked on the Santa Fe Trail before returning to Missouri, where he was appointed sheriff. Always interested in exploring the western frontier, he joined expedition after expedition, finally discovering new routes to California from the South Pass. His gravestone says he slept in Yosemite in November of 1833.

In 1840, Walker and a band of followers made the first known north-to-south crossing of the eastern Great Basin by European Americans. From Brown's Hole along the Green River, crossing the Wasatch Range, then traveling the upper Virgin River until it reached the Colorado River. Then across the Mojave Desert to Los Angeles.

ORANGE MOONS

As soon as Angus McFarlin saw the moon, he instantly felt it had some special meaning. It sat over the horizon like it was frozen in time. It appeared to be so big it dwarfed the mountains before it. As the frontiersman turned his head toward the heavens, orange glowed on his face and eyes. Stars twinkled from one end of the earth to the other, casting everything in a rusty glow.

He wondered to himself what it meant. He was on guard duty with Captain Will Forrester. Rifles and pistols filled their belts. A long saber hung from the officer's side. He pushed back his long blond hair and brushed his mustache with his knuckles. They had a small fortune in beaver pelts and didn't want to risk another attempted robbery. Bales of furs were stacked high behind the men on watch.

Angus thought about his Crow wife back in the Indian stronghold high in the Rockies. He wondered if Pine Needle would be waiting when he returned. The tall, gangly man tugged on his long gray beard as he stared into the night.

Thousands of bats flew across the sky between the earth and the moon. They silently raced into the distance like a long serpent, snaking through valleys, down ravines, and around peaks, heading for tonight's feeding grounds. Wolves howled at the pumpkin moon, as goose bumps spouted on McFarlin's leathery skin. He was wrinkled like an old dog, but his eyes were alert and danced with a spark of wonder.

Will's gray-blue eyes locked with Angus's. They each saw the edginess in the other's. They felt like anything could happen tonight and knew what the other was thinking without speaking a word. The air was charged with electricity.

Despite the fact they were at the Rendezvous, and over five hundred people were attending, they still knew they were in the wilderness. Regardless of their numbers, somebody was always ready to risk everything to steal what others had worked a year to earn. If not the Indians—who claimed the furs had been stolen from their creeks and streams by trespassers—then by the men who wandered the mountains searching for people to rob. Some were outlaws hiding out where no lawman dared venture. Others were simply wicked people with evil minds.

Some of the mountain men had agreements with the local Indians, like Rusty Steel and Crow Chief Hachta. Their presence was beneficial for both the trappers and the Indians. The mountain men were allowed to make a living, stay on Crow land, and live the life they chose in the wilderness. In turn, the Indians had a guaranteed supply of tobacco, coffee, steel tools, knives, and black powder. The occasional rifle was frugally supplied for hunting. All the mountain men knew these same guns could be used against them one day, so they traded them sparingly.

Then there were the highwaymen or out-and-out bandits. Wherever there were large amounts of money involved, even city slickers traveled hundreds of miles to harvest the unsuspecting frontiersmen's valuables. From fortune tellers to men claiming to have maps to secret gold mines, they all gravitated to the Rendezvous like a giant magnet pulling in people with ill will.

Rusty Steel, Levi Johnson, and his wife, Dahteste, snored lightly close by in peaceful slumber. The rest of the men from the compound slept on the other side of their cargo. There had already been one attempt to steal their pelts, but the attack was thwarted, and the six thieves were hung forthwith. Dozens of coyotes spoke to each other in the darkness. The captain tried to penetrate the long shadows cast by the moon but with no success. Then they heard a rustling in the bushes, and Forrester's knuckles turned white as he held his rifle in his fist.

The fires had burned down again, and orange craters dotted the campsites as trails of black smoke snaked into the sky, disappearing just over the dying embers. Again, it was that time of night when both Indians and thieves were bravest, just before the crack of dawn. A big black dog lay beside the snoring Rusty Steel. His long tongue hung out the side of his mouth as his ears shifted, and he subconsciously listened for warning sounds in the night. The dog's legs twitched, and he whimpered as he ran in a dream. His snout rested on his master's leg.

More than forty campsites were filled with mountain men in bedrolls. They had come down from their
homes to trade their beaver pelts for supplies and gold.
Some trappers only had a bundle or two, but others, like
Rusty Steel's people, had theirs and all the Crow Indians' furs from the stronghold. That was every cold-
water beaver pelt they had trapped during the long
winter months lost in the Rocky Mountains. In all, the
bales of furs represented a small fortune.

Some trappers had already been robbed but not by
bandits. They had had their furs plucked from them by
clever trading companies. That, or they lost what they
had earned during the long hard winter playing poker
and games of chance in the temporary tents that dotted
the area. That was what all the free whiskey was for: to
grease the gears in the frontiersmen's and Indians'
heads so they would be more pliable and even more
manageable when it came time to bargain for their
hard-earned furs.

The local thieves knew there would be plenty of
money where there were trappers selling their goods.
The Rendezvous had been the yearly meet for nearly
twenty-five years and had grown with each passing
season. The demand for beaver pelts continued to grow,
and the furs became more valuable back East and even
more so in Europe. Top hats were the rage of the
wealthy back in the big cities. Thieves tried to rob the
trappers coming and going to the meet. Every flimflam
man and con artist within five hundred miles showed
up for the Rocky Mountain Rendezvous. Some even
came from greater distances, including across the
Atlantic Ocean.

Flies buzzed in the air, hovering around McFarlin's

nose and ears. He unconsciously swatted at the bugs, but they continued to pester. There was some sort of electrical current in the air. It raced through the mountain men's bodies, making their hearts throb between their ears as they waited with dread and anticipation. The air had a distinct heaviness like the unexpected would come at any second.

"I don't know that anybody in their right mind would try to steal our pelts after we just hung the last six culprits that tried," Forrester whispered, but he knew it was wishful thinking. Of course, many men in the wilderness didn't think twice about taking what belonged to others for themselves. "It would take a bunch of fools to hit us so soon after we made such a statement, but then again, stupid people are abundant west of the Missouri River."

The captain's eyes traced their way across the tree line. He knew just beyond that lurked men who dreamed up schemes to steal whatever they could. Not just Rusty's and the Crow's furs, but every skin that wasn't sold was up for grabs if somebody became too lax and didn't pay close attention. Personal items vanished at the speed of light, and even cumbersome bundles were spirited off as if by magic. The captain unconsciously patted his empty sleeve.

In the past, the local Blackfeet Indian tribes had made it clear they didn't like the meet to be held on land they considered theirs. They had attacked two Rendezvous, but that had been when the trade fair was smaller. Still, they were always a risk. It all depended on the size of the war party. Usually, they used hit-and-run tactics, hoping to scare the intruders from their land, but the mountain men were used to dealing with hostile

Indians just like they dealt with grizzly bears, mountain lions, and poisonous snakes. It was all part of the deal if you wished to live, hunt, and trap in the Rocky Mountains.

———

JACK SQUIRREL SAT in the shadows of tall bushes with three of his many cousins. Their hats were covered in leaves and branches, making it harder to spot their heads as they popped up over the edge of a large boulder at the tree line. There, they could spy on the men with the furs and still have suitable cover in case they were spotted. The mountain men's camps littered this part of the Rendezvous set aside so the trappers had their own place to sleep. Supposedly, the fact they all made camp in the same spot should make it less likely that the Blackfeet made a blatant attack, but you just never knew. In the past, they had done worse to people they liked more.

The other local tribes called a temporary truce and used these two weeks to make their business and have a rare, close-up look at the White men. Of course, the trading companies took advantage of the Indians whenever possible too. They made it easier by filling their bellies with liquor. That was something that didn't mix well with the local population, primarily as they weren't used to the effects of alcohol. Indians who had drunk too much lay scattered along the sides of the main path through the maze of people and tents.

That didn't mean the loss of three brothers and three cousins would go unavenged. At this point, the Squirrels were more focused on restitution than on turning a profit. The whole family was a vengeful lot, thus the constant feuds. Then again, if they made money, too, that was fine. Now, it mattered little to Jack if they got the beaver furs or not. His primary intent was to get even for killing their kin. The Squirrel clan had a half dozen feuds running all the time. Some stretched back for more than three decades. These were primarily back in Tennessee, although a couple still simmered back in Missouri.

When somebody wronged a Squirrel somewhere down the line, they would have to pay for their aggressions. Jack intended to get even with the men who had killed his brothers, not to mention his first cousins. If you killed one of their family members, they would all come and get you and administer revenge, but as the leader, he felt he had to draw the first blood. It would make clear their commitment to restitution and send a signal to all those who opposed his clan.

They were outraged when they found out six men of their coterie had been hung for something as little as theft. They hadn't even intended to steal a horse or kill a man, which would be a hanging offense. Jack knew for a fact that they had done nothing more severe than stealing a few furs from the crazy mountain men who lived lost in the wilderness—men who apparently made their own law, court, and jury right there in the forest.

The Squirrel clan believed the Indians to be a sub-human race that should be abolished, and that White people like them should take their place. The land they claimed as theirs should be taken away from them, and the tribes banished to small plots of land far away from their homes. Surprisingly, at the time, many men and women had similar beliefs and thought the Army should kill or herd them all to someplace where they could control them, so they wouldn't interfere with the acquisition of their property. Apparently, nobody noticed the land had belonged to American Native tribes for thousands of years before the European American settlers made their way westward.

"There're only the two guards awake right now," Stan Squirrel whispered. "Still, I reckon we best wait until we bring a few more of the family. It'll be too risky to start a gunfight with just the three of us. I like to have better odds, especially with seven more of 'em sleepin' in plain sight all cozy-like around those cursed beaver skins. I doubt their guns be far from their bodies. I know I sleep with mine under my saddle."

"Whatcha mean, wait, fool?" Jack spat. "Them's the devils that hung your cousins. You know they've all gotta die."

"Of course, they've gotta die, but we don't have to die with 'em," Stan Squirrel replied. "These mountain fellas be mean sorts, for the most part. Now, I'm not sayin' they can best a man from Tennessee, but we still need to have a plan. What if somethin' goes wrong, and we have to get away?"

"You just keep the fact that we come from Tennessee to yourself, cousin," Jack retorted, then looked over his shoulder. "Remember, we hail from Missouri. We're all wanted for murder back home. If you keep flappin' that big mouth of yours, we might have somebody decide they wanna earn some bounty money. Iffin I hear you say Tennessee one more time, I'm gonna break your jaw."

"Who's gonna mess with us way the heck out here anyway?" Stan asked. "We're in the wilderness, for Pete's sake. Why, there ain't a city within five hundred miles, and that ain't much more than a town. How do ya think the mountain men got away with hangin' our kin? That's 'cause there's no law up here. We can do what we want just like them. I ain't seen no badges among the folks that have arrived so far."

"I ain't leavin' tonight until I kill me one of them fools," Jack spat. "Then, we'll figure out how to get to the rest later today. Maybe we can pick 'em off one at a time or figure out some way to draw 'em into a trap."

Jack laid his rifle across the rock, resting the heavy octagon barrel on a rolled-up blanket. He licked his thumb and brushed the sights. He drew back the hammer until it clicked. Then they waited until it got light, and he had a clear shot. After the kill, they could vanish into the forest. There were so many people at the Rendezvous that they could disappear in plain sight.

As Jack Squirrel slowed his breathing, the first signs of light touched the eastern horizon. He aimed for the mountain man's camp with all the bales of furs. A few people began to stir as they rekindled their fires, but the campsite nearest them still lay in slumber. He could only make out the two guards, but they had good cover. It would be a lucky shot to get one of them. If he missed, it would be for nothing, so they continued to wait for their golden opportunity. He was only going to take a shot for the kill. There was no room for error.

Jack and Stan didn't have to wait long. One of the mountain men sat up in his bedroll and rubbed his eyes with the heels of his hands. Then he stretched his arms over his head. Jack traced his movements with his rifle barrel. Of course, he couldn't tell one of the group's members from another, but he knew where they slept. It didn't matter which one he killed as long as one of his brother's murderers died before he slipped back into the cover of the forest and the foothills. If they were lucky, they might get another one later that day, but before they left, Jack Squirrel planned to let his new enemies know he was there and who he was. He was the man and the family they shouldn't have messed with.

The edge of the earth turned a fiery red. It looked like the end of the world, but it was the beginning of a new day. As the sun crept into the sky, it flooded the land with light. The pumpkin moon began to slip behind the western horizon. It slowly neared, but just as it touched the earth's edge, it quickly vanished. Long shadows stood tall along the provisional village and trappers' camp.

The crack of a heavy rifle shot—a chunk of lead rushed out the barrel, followed by a flame and a puff of smoke—then silence. An aging mountain man with a drooping gray handlebar mustache, scraggly hair, and beard was walking toward the two guards. He smiled, then suddenly frowned, and stopped in his tracks, looking down at his belly. A stream of blood and viscous liquid sprayed into the dirt as he slapped his hands over the hole, and he dropped to his knees, blinking back the pain.

Jack was just close enough to be able to confirm the kill shot. He wouldn't be dead yet, but he was going to die just the same, and it would be painful as hell, just as the leader of the Squirrel clan had planned. He'd hit the target exactly where he aimed. A smile curled on his lips, and he turned as he and his cousins slipped into the mass of trees and bushes. They vanished immediately. The alarm was heard in the camp in seconds. Still, nobody had seen the shooter or knew where the bullet came from. Jack had made sure the guards were looking elsewhere when he took the shot.

In seconds, they vanished into the vegetation and in minutes, were at their horses. If they hurried, they wouldn't be caught. Now was the time to advise the family and get reinforcements prepared for another attack. This one would be the real deal. Jack Amble Squirrel didn't intend to let a single mountain man live. Those who committed crimes against his family would suffer a horrible death.

THE SQUIRRELS

THE SQUIRREL FAMILY CAME FROM TROUBLE COUNTY, Tennessee. Some thought it an odd name to call a town, but those who lived there ensured the village lived up to its reputation. From as far back as anyone could remember, the Squirrel family had populated one part of the county or another. They had always been numerous due to the family tradition of having up to a dozen children per wife. Some of the Squirrel men had two or even three wives and families. Of course, even in Tennessee this practice was illegal but not uncommon.

Men across the West were sometimes accused of harboring such practices, so nobody enforced the law—especially if they didn't reside in the same town. As a rule, the Squirrel women had their first child with the arrival of their first menstruation and were kept pregnant for the next decade, if not more. The head of the clan, Jack Amble Squirrel, preached the word of God but by his own interpretation of the Good Book and the laws of the government of the United States. The former had many of its words and messages distorted or misinterpreted, and the latter they believed wicked and ignored.

During the last years, the Squirrel family had constant run-ins with the law, and finally they were driven out of Tennessee by US marshals and fled west. They were wanted for the murder of several opposing clan members over the years. Their feuds were known statewide, and their notoriety forced the local law to act. For the next decade, they traveled aimlessly like Romanian Gypsies, eventually moving farther and farther toward the wilderness. Everywhere they went, they shortly found themselves unwelcome. Their customs and beliefs were too radical for most Americans.

When they were run out of Missouri by the sometimes mountain man, Sheriff Joseph Walker, they pushed farther west toward the Rocky Mountains. Eventually, their travels brought them to the Yellowstone Valley. It was so rich with game that they had no problem providing healthy diets for all the clan members, who now numbered well over a hundred. They were so numerous and well-armed that they were seldom preyed on by hostile Indians—even if most of them were women and children. Even the women were taught how to shoot to better defend their perpetual wagon train. That, and the fact that they never stayed in one place for very long. They were as nomadic as the American Plains Indians they despised.

The Squirrels lived in the wagons they used to transport themselves daily farther west. Every time they found a place where they wanted to stay, something happened; a local died, and they once again had to flee. The Squirrel clan had lived in a perpetual loop of discovery and escape since they were forced to leave Trouble County. The name seemed to follow them like a curse, and they had been on the run ever since. At least until they discovered the foothills of the Rocky Mountains and beyond. It was isolated enough that the skeletons in the family closet wouldn't come to haunt them, nor would they be told what to do by any government.

As far as they could see, there was no law or government at all in the Rockies. It was the precise type of environment they were looking for. Someplace they could raise their many rafts of children, make their own laws, and follow their interpretations of the scriptures.

Jack sat on the bench seat of the covered buckboard wagon as it bounced down a rut-riddled, snaking trail beside the Green River. Three young green-eyed girls sat beside their father. He drove the lead wagon of the clan. They had found a small, isolated canyon to camp in not far from the Rendezvous. Fifteen wagons pulled into a tight circle, and instantly they were busy with activity getting the camp ready for the night; in what seemed like a few minutes, they had built a small place of their own. They lived just like the people they wanted to eradicate—the Native American Indians. Both were experts at moving their homes at the drop of a hat.

Jack Squirrel pulled the team of horses to a stop, set the brake with his boot, and jumped down. Wagon wheels creaked and jolted as they rounded up the wagons in a defensive position. Brown dust rolled off the wheels as the spokes appeared to spin backward.

"Jenifer, you tend to the children," Jack said over his

shoulder. The clan leader had eighteen children in all, and his three wives were all currently pregnant.

The difference between the polygamy the Squirrels lived and that of others was they all lived with their wives like one big happy family under the same roof. Jack's spouses were aged sixteen, twenty-two, and thirty. The latest wife was the same age as some of his children from his first spouse, Jenifer.

Stan pulled up behind Jack, spat a half yard of brown juice off the side of the wagon, and wiped his mouth with the back of his hand. He jumped down, his boots making puffs of dust. Stan wasn't a tall man, nor was he particularly good-looking. As a matter of fact, the whole family was somewhat homely—tall, gangly men and women and all with black hair and green eyes. They looked like somebody rubber-stamped copies of their fathers and forefathers before them. Jack's newest wife was also his first cousin.

"Get the men together," Jack whispered as soon as they were out of hearing distance of the women. "We've got to have a talk about what we're gonna do next."

The Squirrel men never allowed the wives, mothers, or daughters in on the older males' secrets. The women were so accustomed to their way of life they hardly noticed and were too busy taking care of the girls and a handful of young boys who couldn't work yet. They did heed the words of the Holy scriptures Jack preached each night at the dinner table. Jack especially liked to preach about all the pain and suffering that would befall them if they didn't follow his interpretation of the Bible. That, and all the evil men that populated the earth.

The clan leader used religion to control and cower the women into being docile like sheep. He made it sound like everybody in the world was mistaken and wrong, and the only ones on the truly holy path were them. He assured them that was why only they would be saved when the judgment day came.

He preached to his family that they had to find a place just for them, isolated from the rest of the world. Somewhere they could make their own small settlement, which would only be composed of members of the Squirrel family, and everyone would follow their peculiar Christian beliefs, albeit far from the actual messages in the scriptures. In short, Jack Squirrel would make his own set of laws and woe to those that interfered or didn't follow accordingly.

As the men gathered down the trail into the canyon, they talked while waiting for their leader, Jack. Everybody was talking about the same thing—the hangings. They had all seen firsthand the graves of their brothers and cousins. Someone had marked the site with a wooden cross that said SQUIRREL, so those who did it knew who they were.

At the Rendezvous, they had heard all about it as soon as it happened. They found out quickly but not fast enough to stop the lynchings. It appeared the mountain men didn't linger when it came to stringing up men they didn't like by the neck. They were told it only took a matter of a couple of minutes from the beginning to the end—hardly enough time for anyone to interfere.

"Them fools that killed our kin must have been waitin' on 'em when they went in to steal the pelts," Jack said. "Heck, it should have been as easy as rollin' out of bed as I made the plan myself. They were supposed to get in and out as quick as spit. They had the mules waiting a short distance away, but something tipped the mountain men off. I wonder what it was?"

"Still, taking a few furs ain't reason enough to hang six fine men," Stan huffed. "I heard they didn't even get near the pelts before they were on 'em. These mountains are full of wicked men. But like you say, they were waiting on 'em for sure."

Dark thoughts started to worm their way into Jack's brain. His mind had gone from thinking of ways to steal the furs to getting revenge on men who dared question their ways.

"I can assure you all that vengeance will be ours." Jack grimaced as he walked to the head of the crowd. He had a scowl on his face as he bunched his fingers into fists.

Twenty heavily armed Squirrels stood, giving their clan leader their full attention. They all thought Jack was blessed by the hand of God. What other explication could they have, by his cryptic interpretation of the Bible? He was their leader because he was the chosen one picked to understand what was truly written and, in turn, explain it to them so they, too, could be saved. And it all made complete sense to them as soon as Jack explained. The head of the clan called it reading between the lines.

Jack raked his fingers through his ear-length black hair. He rubbed his green eyes and pouted with puffy lips. He scratched his hooknose with his knuckle and rubbed his cleanly shaved face with a calloused hand. He stood on top of a wooden vegetable box somebody fetched from the wagons so he could be seen. He pushed his five-foot-seven-inch frame up with a hand on his knee, then towered over the men before him.

"You all know what those mountain men did to our brothers and our cousins," Jack said with hooded eyes. He looked like he was going into another one of his trances. "Now, we have to let 'em know we're here. I just killed one of 'em. That was the rifle shot you heard."

"I've been hearin' rifles go off all day long," Riley Squirrel said. "I'm afraid we couldn't tell one from the other." He pulled his belt tight. The heavy pistols he wore across his skinny waist drooped under the weight. He used the back of his fingers to flick his greasy, limp hair out of his face. The trace of a mustache shadowed his lips as they curled cruelly.

"Jack shot 'im right in the gut so he'd live long enough to suffer. I figure right about now he be sufferin' mighty bad." Stan snickered. "I figure if he lasts tonight, we should hear 'im a screamin'. You boys should have seen it. Blood poured out of 'im like a water fountain. He watched his life spill onto the dirt." He shook his head. "The look on his face."

Stan laughed until he got a stitch despite the dirty look from Jack. The laughter was contagious, as it often was when nervous men made dangerous decisions. Soon, they were all anxiously snickering as Jack fumed and forced himself to be patient. They were his family, after all. After what seemed like an hour to Jack but was probably a few minutes, the men settled down and stared at their leader, waiting for instructions.

That was when they all heard it. The screams Stan had been waiting for came loud and clear. The gut-shot mountain man wailed like a shot-up wolf with its leg in a trap. It even made some of the Squirrel family nervous; goose bumps sprouted on their arms, and they cringed.

It came like music to Jack's ears. "What'd I tell ya, boys? I'm feelin' better already."

More snickers rippled through the group of angry men. Their courage was bolstered by their leader's actions and his bold words.

"This is just the beginning, cousins." Stan Squirrel grinned. "We can even kill the Injun woman. Maybe enjoy her for a spell before we end her life."

The backhand surprised some of the younger men but not Stan. He knew he had gone too far the second he said it, but he couldn't stop the words from coming out of his mouth. They walked right out on their own. He knew the boss hated Indians just as much as he did, but Jack didn't tolerate rape and a series of other mortal sins he pointed out in the Bible. Jack said they would be no more than the heathens they were trying to eliminate if they did such things. As they moved westward, they killed as many Indians as they could find.

Riley sat on the wagon tongue, popping blackheads and wiping them on his shirt. He didn't even notice the disgusted look Jack shot him. He was oblivious to others' opinions. He found that as long as he followed his leader, everything seemed to always work out. Even in the settlements where they got into trouble and ran out, they escaped quickly. One moment they were there, and the next, they had pulled up stakes and disappeared. Their leader seemed to sense trouble just before it arrived.

Of course, they were all well-trained to depart on a minute's notice. They had been run out of settlement after settlement, village after village. Even the cities and larger towns caught on to their ways too quickly to spend much time in civilization. Now, they searched for something different away from the rest of the population in a place that would be like their own country. Maybe Jack would make himself king and name the new country Jack Ville.

GRAVEYARDS

ANGUS MCFARLIN HAMMERED A WHITE WOODEN CROSS into the ground with the flat of a shovel, the same shovel Captain Forrester had used to dig the hole. They were the men on night guard, so they felt it was them that let their friend down. Nobody from their compound had ever died of natural causes or been killed, so it shocked them all when they lost one of their own. It made it so personal that it hit them like a bolt of lightning.

Virgil Lovejoy had his Bible in his hand, but his eyes didn't see the words on the pages as they stared at the freshly painted cross. He had the scriptures memorized. The cross stood over a mound of soft dirt. None of them wept because it wasn't their way, and Dahteste would never betray her fierce façade by allowing tears to stain her cheeks. Only the black man shed a tear—for someone he didn't know.

Still, they could all see the pain in each other's eyes. Some suffered more, and others less. Yosemite Bob had been the eldest of them all. He was a constant in their lives, even if his ways were quiet. He was a born follower. He had been there in the compound in the Rockies nearly as long as Mountain Dennis. Years ago, when he arrived at the cabins, he was lost and confused, so the mountain men adopted him and took him into their fold.

"It's a shame we couldn't bury him at home," Syracuse Sam said as he unconsciously rubbed the scar on his head. A Blackfoot Indian had scalped him, but he survived.

They were all as hard as any mountain men they had ever seen, but now, they felt their mortality. Before, they'd felt indestructible, but now, they knew it was just a matter of time before it would be their turn to go.

"Amen," Rusty said, slipping his hat back on his woolly head. They all stood near the tree line at the edge of the gathering for the Rendezvous. They buried him near the trail so that when they returned, they could pass by and visit. "The trail behind us seems to be stretchin' out far, and the trail before us appears to be gettin' shorter all the time. Don't you worry, Bob. We'll be meetin' up with ya sometime in the future."

"It's gonna seem strange back at the cabins without Bob," Portland Pete added. "He sure did play a mean game of checkers."

Strangely enough, the most affected was the newest member, the captain. The frontiersmen had taken longer to side up to Forrester than they had Levi. Of course, Johnson was already a trapper from the young age of eight, so he had more in common with them than a West Point officer. Beaver was famous back in his home in Southeastern Indiana. He was called Trapper Boy by his family and friends and was known for inventing traps for most small game in the forest. He was a natural outdoorsman, and nobody was a better shot, not even the captain, except maybe Rusty Steel. Who was best was to be determined at this year's sharp-shooting match.

They had all watched as Bob died a slow, painful death. His screams finally unnerved them all. In the end, Rusty gave him a cocked gun, and they walked away. After a brief spell came a single gunshot. He had ended his agony like a gentleman. It was the way of the mountains. They all knew a wounded member of the party would slow them down were there the need to flee —especially when it was clear he was going to die anyway.

When the pistol shot rang out, Forrester flinched like the bullet might find its mark in him. He had thought all the men that lived in the compound were beyond defeat, but now he knew different, and from that grew a terrible need to defend his friends, especially with what he had unknowingly put them through.

The episode with amnesia had obviously shaken Levi, Rusty, and the others. For him, it was all foggy and difficult to see clearly. It was like his mind wandered in a fog even though his memory was back. Only the time he was under the effects of a damaged brain was unclear. If he were honest, it was mainly due to the fact he didn't want to look too deeply at who he was then or what he had seen in himself.

Now, Forrester felt he was a different man than before the fall. But he also felt the change from soon after the fall to now. The injury sent his mind through a transition, and he wondered if it was over yet or if it would be never-ending. The damage was obviously there, although it seemed to have healed or at least changed. But would it be forever, or would it be a fleeting condition out of his control? Will Forrester waited to see what different changes would become apparent with time.

They all knew somebody had killed Yosemite Bob from afar, but the old trapper hadn't made any enemies in the last couple of days, and they couldn't think of anybody else. Then they all thought about the same thing simultaneously: the clan of men named Squirrel. They had been told they were all cousins or brothers but had assumed they had hung them all. Six members of the same family should have made a dent in their males. Now that they knew what the threat was, they needed to know where it came from and whether it would come again in the immediate future.

The captain suddenly pulled a pistol and turned to cover their backs. They were all facing the grave, so they were open for another ambush. There were people everywhere, and he didn't know where to look. Then there was the trail back toward the Rockies. His stare hardened as he removed his hat and used it to block the sun. He looked at Levi and nodded.

"I think we're dealing with trash with no moral code," Forrester said over his shoulder. "We better watch our backs from now on."

"I never imagined there would be more of the Squirrel family," Levi said. "I wonder how many there are."

"I reckon there be enough of 'em to bushwhack poor Bob and not run away. Numbers make men brave," Rusty grumbled as he fingered his mountain lion claw necklace under his long gray beard. Two bear canines clicked on a leather string around his wrist. "That means it ain't just one or two, for sure. Now, we have to watch the furs so they don't get stolen and find the scallywags that killed our pard. That'll be stretchin' us pretty thin if they're a serious threat."

The murder had happened on the captain and Angus's watch, but a shot in the dark could have happened on anyone's shift. It was evident that whoever did it had taken a shot at the first one that he got a bead on. He had to have seen Forrester and Angus, but they always kept watch from good cover when possible, especially when they were expecting company. Was it random when they killed Bob? The mountain men didn't think so. They believed they had been chosen for revenge by however many Squirrels were left alive.

"They got Bob easy because we never expected to find such lowlifes here at the Rendezvous, but they won't get us again," Captain Forrester promised. "We're getting lax living in the mountains. Nearer civilization will always be more dangerous for us than in the wilderness. Your skills aren't as valuable in a town or settlement; in a big city, they're nearly worthless. There're other worlds out there that all of us aren't built for, but I am."

Nobody understood why the captain took it upon himself to personally get even with the killers. Sure, he had gone through a hard time losing his memory for so long, but he had changed in small ways too. Now, he was less aloof than before and seemed as protective of his friends as a mother hen, even though he and Levi were the youngest, not counting Dahteste. A fire burned in the officer's eyes and got brighter as the hours passed.

"By now, they could have run off to pert near

anywhere," Mountain Dennis said. His two gold teeth shined in the firelight.

"Now, you know as well as I do, they won't go until they've shot the lot of us. After today, I figure they take us for easy targets," Rusty said. "Whatcha think we ought to do, Captain?"

"How about you boys guard the furs from any other clans or gangs that might want to try to rob us?" the captain said. "Levi and I will go into the woods and find the killers before they get lucky and shoot or stab another one of us. You'll have to be our bait if we don't find them on our first venture out of sight. If we move quick, we may catch up to them, but we won't get them all if there's six more."

"What if there're a dozen or more?" Dennis asked. "We may have run into a hornet's nest and bitten off more than we can chew."

"What were we supposed to do?" Rusty growled. "Let them take what's ours? No, sir, not while I'm still breathin'. I reckon we all owe old Bob the effort. We'll do whatever you say, Captain."

"I can track a snake across a river," Beaver Johnson said. "You boys just make sure you don't make yourselves an easy target. Something tells me the shooter was sure of his shot. He waited until it was nearly light. I can't tell exactly how good he was because the distance wasn't great enough, but he's good enough a shot to kill us if we stuck our tails in the wind. I reckon they fired from over there by the brush. There're woods right behind there, so they have their escape. Anywhere else, somebody from the Rendezvous would have seen them. I doubt anybody would pay any attention to another gunshot. Those wild boys sure are wastin' a lot of gunpowder, ain't they."

"Come on, or we'll miss them," the captain said.

"You're not going without me," Dahteste added. "I can track as good as any man. I can track a crow across the sky. That's harder than tracking a snake across a river. For a Crow warrior chief, snakes are child's play." She gave her husband a daring look.

"Now's not the time, darlin'," Levi replied. "I'd prefer iffin ya stayed. I don't want cha to get hurt."

"And I would prefer if you didn't tell me what I can or can't do," Dahteste replied. "Just because we're married doesn't mean I can tell you what to do, does it?"

"But it's different with men," Levi pleaded. "Where we're from, women tend to the house and children."

"I didn't know we had children—yet." Dahteste curled her lips. "Where I'm from, I am a war chief. With Crow Indians, some men tend to the tipis, as do women too. But although most warriors are men, we also have women warriors. It is not rare to find a woman war chief either," Dahteste said firmly. "So, I don't play that game." She winked. She was learning the White men's ways and language almost too fast for Levi Johnson. Despite the fact his six-foot-seven-inch frame towered over his wife, her spirit was so big, sometimes she seemed to be just as big as him.

"We don't have time to bicker, or the tracks will go cold, then neither one of you will be able to follow them," the captain said. "Let's go. I have a feeling you won't win this tug-of-war anyway, old buddy. Let's grab the horses quick. We can't risk it on foot, or we won't catch up. I want to settle this today before any more innocent people get shot. If these fools are reckless enough to fire into the camp at dawn, they may spook and shoot anybody they feel like shooting."

Five minutes later, they were riding bareback into the forest. There wasn't time for saddles. They felt like they were being watched as soon as they got out of sight of the camp. A black stallion, an Appaloosa, and a brown, fourteen-hundred-pound mustang raced out of the Rendezvous and toward the tree line.

"Do you feel it?" Dahteste asked. "We're being watched, but they are not white eyes. Maybe Blackfeet."

"We don't have time for this. If they're there, let them come," Forrester said and nudged the stallion, and it burst forward. Muscles rippled across the animal's legs and chest.

The tracks were easy for the three to follow. The Squirrels didn't appear to be frontiersmen of any caliber. Maybe they weren't there just to steal like most.

"If they're a big family, maybe they're out here lookin' to settle, and we just had the bad luck to have crossed paths," Levi whispered as they brought their horses to a walk. "We don't want to run into a bullet, do we?" He winked at Dahteste, and she smiled a crooked smile.

Levi and the captain were all business and as serious as death, but Dahteste seemed almost too eager to wreak the wrath on their enemies. Maybe it was due to the meaning of her name. In English, it meant Warrior Woman, and she was all of that, from the top of her coal-black hair right down to her beaded knee-high moccasins.

JOSEPH WALKER

STRINGS OF HORSES AND HEAVILY LOADED MULES LINED
the trail. Missouri Sheriff Joseph Rutherford Walker
rode to the head of the line. The sometimes mountain
man sat astride a beige quarter horse with white socks.
Men in black jackets and pants with white shirts and
high collars walked beside the beasts of burden.
Women wore long gray dresses that hung to the ground
and walked behind their men. Their jackets were char-
coal gray and rose to their jawlines, showing little flesh
or skin.

Bonnets covered their heads and half their faces
against the harsh sun, as did long sleeves to their wrists.
These men and women were missionaries on their way
to the new mission in Oregon City, only nine hundred
miles away. The missionaries had paid Joseph the three
hundred dollars they had agreed on back in Montana,
and now he was duty-bound to get them to their
destination.

They'd hired Joseph to escort them along the
sparsely used Indian trails. The final part of the pass

had been discovered by Jim Bridges and Jedediah Smith only the year before. These fine people paid him what he asked, so off they went. There were twenty missionaries in all, with five helpers. The trail was considered too difficult for prairie schooners or covered buckboard wagons, so James had ordered them to purchase mules to carry their cargo so they wouldn't break down and have to make rafts to cross rivers. They were more expensive than oxen, but they were faster and did well on little water. The mules groaned under the weight.

Everything went as planned until the ford on the Platte River crossing Walker knew about. There was word of the construction of a new fort there. It was said it would be named Fort Casper, but that was still an Army project for the future. They hadn't brought wagons, so they could take the mules and horses across without problems. What Joseph hadn't counted on was quicksand all along the riverbanks. They lost five horses and five men before their very eyes. They vanished under the mud in less than three minutes and disappeared, animals and all.

Unfortunately, all five were scouts and helpers Walker had hired to make the arduous journey across what would soon be the Oregon Trail. Now, he was stretched thin for experienced frontiersmen and horses. This jeopardized his travelers, so he had to find a solution. The settlers were his charge, and he understood the responsibility and the damage to his reputation if he failed. The loss of his scouts and their horse had come as a blow. The sight alone spooked the travelers. Nobody had ever seen such big men and their horses swallowed up by the earth in minutes.

When what was left of the group made it to South

Pass, Joseph saw that without more help, he wouldn't make it all the way to Oregon City on the Pacific coast. There were almost a thousand miles to go. He and Rory just weren't enough hands to take care of twenty-five greenhorns with all their supplies—especially if they got hit by hostile Indians. Walker pulled on his coal-black beard, making his face look even longer. He wore a black eastern beaver fur hat with a wide brim to keep the sun off his fair skin.

"I reckon I'll have to ride down to the Rendezvous and see if I can't scare up a half dozen horses, some scouts, and maybe some guns for protection," Walker said. "I've seen lots of Indian signs lately, so we don't want to get caught short of gun hands. These missionaries will be like a bunch of puppies in a mountain lion's den."

"I agree, boss," Rory Breaker said. He leaned to the side and spat into the dirt beside his horse. A fat quid bulged his cheek. "I figure if we can take good cover on high ground, we should be able to fend off anybody that approaches. We've got enough food and water to sit 'em out if they show. These folks ain't used to the wilderness, but they do know how to shoot. That'll deter the Indians, but it won't help much down the road. They are greener than baby pines."

Rory pushed his dishwater-blond hair aside, showing a freckled face. Joe's right-hand man looked ten years younger than he was. Many people mistakenly believed he was a young man or even a large boy. That would be the last time they erroneously angered Breaker.

"Well, even the best can die out here," Joseph Walker said. "At least it wasn't the missionaries that were swallowed up by the marsh. The men that died knew how dangerous the trip would be. They were all experienced trackers, and they made one little mistake, and it cost them all their lives. And they all five knew better too."

"I told 'em not to bunch up in case Indians attacked, but they were gettin' strappy and weren't being careful," Rory Breaker said. "I doubt the thought of quicksand ever crossed their minds. I know it hadn't crossed mine. Some of the mountain men think they're indestructible. There's a thousand ways to die out here, Joseph."

"Overconfidence can take your life as quick as spit," Walker said. "Them boys should have known better like you and me. But it is what it is. Now we'll have to scare up some help. It's mighty lucky the Rendezvous is on now, and it ain't but a hundred miles' ride, so if I go it on my own, I'll get there on the third or fourth day of the meet. There should be five hundred trappers and traders there, so I should be able to scare up a couple or three trackers. If they're mountain men, all the better."

"Try to get four men at least, boss. We've already seen it's better to have more help than less. This land eats people up like a meat grinder. Don't worry about us," Rory said. "I figure if we don't move about, we'll be all right. I won't let any of 'em out of my sight. Don't you worry on my account. You know I can take care of myself."

"You're the only one I ain't worried about, Rory." Walker smiled. "You're as good a partner as I could have ever hoped to have."

The next day, Joseph Walker rode south from Daniel, Wyoming, toward the site of this year's Rendezvous. He rode from an hour before first light until late into the night, using the moon to guide him. He had traveled these mountains and plains more than just about any man alive besides Lewis and Clark, and he was still hungry to know more. He was also looking forward to reaching the fur trading meet. He had been to a couple in the past because he was initially a beaver trapper, so he was well versed in mountain men, trappers, and their ways. He even had a friend or two who should be there if he had any luck.

After a week of hard riding, he rode down the hill until he had the Rendezvous in sight. Joseph was surprised at its size. It had grown double and then triple that of the times he had attended. Now, it looked like a small circus in the middle of nowhere. A smile curled the edges of his lips, and he grew thirsty for a glass of whiskey. Smoke curled from dozens of fires across the area. Men of all shapes, colors, and walks of life mingled in the crowded saloons and provisional trading posts. Everybody seemed to have furs in their hands, even the Indians.

When he rode into the large camp, he was nearly overwhelmed by the presence of so many people. Many more Indians were present this year than had been in the past. Signs announcing free whiskey in bold red letters dotted the meet. He wheeled his horse toward the first sign he came to and dropped down. His horse walked to the watering trough in front of the open tent. It provided shade and allowed a breeze to blow through and chase the flies away. Socks, his quarter horse, dropped dung as he walked.

Joseph R. Walker strutted up to the hewed planks that lay across wooden barrels. A man stood behind the bar, filling tin cups as fast as he could get the liquid out of the barrel. The tap only ran so fast, and the mountain men were clearly impatient. Joseph stood to the side so he could watch the show unravel. The bartender grabbed his cup next and filled it to the brim. When he set it on the table, golden liquid sloshed out onto the bar, but nobody was paying any attention. The only objective that Walker could see was that everyone there intended to get as drunk as they could, and quickly. Some of the men hadn't had a proper drink since last year.

A newspaper had written a short column about Joseph Walker. It stated: "He was accompanied by the wildest Red, White, and Black men they had ever seen. He appeared to have abandoned civilization, married more than one squaw, and preferred to spend his life wandering the mountains and deserts. He carried on an almost nominal business of hunting, trapping, and trading with the fierce Indians. He was a man of great natural ability, prowess, and natural resource."

Of course, a mountain man in the newspapers was known by one and all, but Walker kept his wide-brimmed hat pulled down to shade his face, making him harder to recognize. He preferred to select who he was to speak to and have a drink with. Joseph wasn't exactly unfriendly but was more impatient with ignorant people. He valued his time much more than the average traveler, so they barraged him with stupid questions if he allowed it. His eyes flashed across the tent-covered saloon, but he saw no familiar faces.

He sipped on his whiskey as he inconspicuously eyed the action. There were a dozen men there that suited the bill in size and apparent ruggedness. But that wouldn't be enough for Joseph Walker. He was looking for another man like Rory, who could be left alone and think for himself. He knew he had bitten off a tough end of a hard chew, but he felt confident he could still get the missionaries to their destination. The Rendezvous had saved him, he was sure. He just had to wander around without attracting too much attention, and he would find what he was looking for. He counted on his good wit and selling skills to convince four or five men to ride along for a reasonable price.

He realized that more help would cost him most of the money he had been paid, but that was how things rolled when in the wilderness. If a man could walk away from such a journey with his life, then he had won the battle even if there was no longer a profit. He believed that in the future, this route would provide him with an unlimited supply of work and good money. He just had to get the first bunch of people across to say he did it, and he would be on his way.

Walker had heard rumors from Washington, DC, about soon-to-be-opened territories giving free land to people willing to travel two thousand miles and home-stead it for two years. He knew the keywords there were *free land*. Everybody wanted to have something for free, especially if it was fertile land that apparently didn't belong to anybody.

THWARTED AMBUSH

ONE MOMENT, LEVI WAS LEADING THE PARTY OF THREE and the next, it was Dahteste. The captain just smiled and shook his head. He'd never seen a woman so hell-bent on outdoing her husband. It wasn't to belittle Johnson either. He was sure she felt threatened in some way and was using her show of skills to cover her true feelings. It must be overwhelming to find yourself in the middle of a sea of white faces when you had lived with your tribe all your life. Despite being a war chief, she hadn't ever traveled so far before, either.

The tracks were so easy to follow that Forrester could have found his way by himself, but then again, you never knew what they might run into. When it came to tracking and trapping, he left the job to the experts, and his best friend Levi was the best he had ever met. Even Rusty Steel said so when Levi wasn't around; he just couldn't admit it to his face.

When they came to the river, they wheeled their mounts north against the water's flow. They kept an eye on the far bank, which was only a stone's throw away.

Both sides were covered in dense vegetation, and the edges were soft. A horse could sink up to its belly in some places, but Dahteste and Beaver led them away from all the dangers the captain didn't see.

When Levi and his wife dropped down from their horses almost simultaneously, Will stopped and did the same. They crouched for a moment, listening. The only sound was a choir of insects.

"They're just over the river upstream a bit," Levi whispered.

"How can ya tell?" the captain asked as he looked around. He didn't see a thing.

Levi pointed to his nose and inhaled. Forrester did the same; the faint smell of cooking meat filled his senses. They hobbled their horses and let them graze on string lines. They didn't want them to wander off if there was gunfire, but they wanted to allow them to graze in case they were gone for a few hours. At first, they made their way closer to the riverbank. Each movement was slow and deliberate, like mountain lions stalking their prey. When they got near, all three closed in, crawling on their bellies.

Dahteste parted the brush, and only her eyes could be seen by the trained eye, but there wasn't a trained mountain man in the bunch she saw before them. Looking back over her shoulder, she gave her companions a puzzled look. Levi and his best friend, the captain, slowly parted the bushes where they lay, and their eyes popped wide when they saw so many women and children—the exact opposite of what they had expected. They were settlers, after all, but there must have been four or five women and children to every man, and the whole bunch looked alike. Not like twins, but it was apparent that family genes were flowing through every one of their veins.

They saw over a hundred people preparing food and doing their daily deeds around their camp. The wagons looked like oak, so they were built to last. Covered buckboards made a defensive circle.

"At least they know how to prepare themselves against Indian attacks," Levi mumbled.

"What do we do now?" the captain asked in barely a whisper.

"What do you mean, what do we do?" Dahteste retorted, wide-eyed. "These men killed one of ours, so they must die. That is the law of the mountains. That is the Crow law."

"I think the law of the mountains is the man responsible for killing Yosemite Bob needs to hang or pay one way or another," Captain Forrester said. "I can't see starting a shooting match with all these people. There are too many women and children. It's too dangerous. They sure are a bold bunch."

"Don't forget they were going to steal our beaver pelts," Dahteste said in a hushed voice. It was just over a murmur; they had to watch her lips to understand.

"Yeah, I know, but just the same, how are we gonna find out which one took the shot, and what if all of 'em is mixed up in Bob's murder?" Levi asked. "They may not allow us to make a choice."

"So, what do you want to do?" the captain asked. "I can't see just taking a few shots and putting some more of the Squirrel family down without knowing who's responsible. It just isn't the right way to go about this."

"And what is the right way?" Levi asked. "That's exactly what they did to us. You were on guard duty. You and Angus both said the shooter shot Bob at random. It could have been Dahteste or me just as easy, or even you. Then how would you see it?"

"Lookee over there," Dahteste said and nodded across the Green River where a group of about twenty men had gathered.

One of the men climbed up onto a wooden box and yelled, "Gather around, family!" He waited patiently as he hung from the side of the wagon, and all the men in the group stood around him in a semicircle. It was clear he was the head of the family. Both mountain men and the Crow woman memorized his face. Even from across the small river, they could see his wild eyes and how he gestured with his hands when he talked. He looked like he was preaching a sermon. Maybe he was.

Dahteste raised an eyebrow and mouthed, "And the women?"

They all looked back at the sizable camp hidden in a small gully beside the river. It was the perfect spot to isolate themselves from the rugged men at the Rendezvous. If the mountain men got wind that so many women were this close to the Rendezvous, some of the drunker ones would already have been there pestering them. It wasn't their fault, but some hadn't seen a White woman who wasn't a soiled dove in years.

It was clear that they would be unwelcome. The women at the meet were limited to a few very friendly squaws, a dozen or so mountain men's Indian wives, and a half dozen ladies of the night. They had traveled over five hundred miles to fleece the wealthy trappers. They had small tents the size of a single bed, and there was always a long line standing out front, waiting.

"This is the strangest bunch of folks we've run

across in the mountains," Levi said. "I don't rightly know what they're up to or what to think of 'em."

Dahteste put her finger to her lips and said, "Shush and listen."

Just as the Crow woman indicated, they could hear what the leader of the clan was saying. He had one of those voices that carried and could be heard above the roar of a crowd, and out there by the slow-flowing river, it was clear as a bell. It almost seemed loud.

"We all know what we have to do," Jack Amble Squirrel said in a clear voice. All the family men around him were quiet as mice and had humble faces before their obvious leader. "I know y'all are anxious to build your homes nearby, but we have family business to attend to first. We still have to avenge the death of my three brothers and our cousins. My soul won't rest until we get restitution. This is more important than settling in and building our homes. Honor and justice must come before comfort, or my soul won't rest easy. First, we tend to business, and then we can go and look for the perfect place to live. We can ride into the mountains until our wagons can't go any farther and make our stake. But first things first."

"And what about all of their furs right there for the takin' back at the Rendezvous?" Stan asked. "I almost feel like all of them scraggly men owe us after what they did. Hanging six of our kin for doin' pretty much nothin' but poachin' a few furs. They's unjust is what they are. Look how much they have and how little we have. It ain't fair, is what it is."

As they continued talking, the three watching were shocked by what they heard. It appeared that most of them deserved to die, but they weren't done yet. Just because they were following the words of an evil man didn't mean they were evil too. But now they wanted to steal the mountains of furs stacked high in the trading posts of the Rendezvous and kill the men who'd strung up their family members. They were clearly all prepared to steal and kill again if that was what their leader told them to do. Maybe they were more used to committing such crimes than Captain Forrester chose to believe.

"This ain't over by a long shot," Levi whispered. "Now what cha got to say, Will?"

The captain pursed his lips and frowned. He remembered how he would have dealt with this group of reckless men just a short time ago, and he felt he knew he would kill them for what they did and what they planned. But now, for some reason, he felt like forgiveness was in order—at least until he heard their plans. Now, they weren't leaving any of them a choice.

"When I shot that godless half-man, half-Indian, I felt no remorse because these mountain men are just as unhuman as the heathen Indians that scorn the earth!" Jack Squirrel cried out to the crowd. Even from a distance, they saw how easily he could wind his kin up. "They deserve to die just like the heathens we've killed on our path west. It's our duty as Christians to rid God's land of wicked people and make way for the good and just. That's our duty to the Almighty, my brothers."

When Dahteste heard what the Squirrel leader said, her eyes shot daggers and were full of hate. She gripped her bow in her white-knuckled fist.

"These are the Crow people's enemy, husband," Dahteste said in a gravelly voice. Her hate for Indian killers began to surface. "That makes them your enemy too, Levi Johnson."

The captain could hardly believe what this man was saying. He talked like he was from another planet, and they were due this land, and the Indians who had lived there for thousands of years should perish. He continued his heated speech of hate and violence and all in the name of God. The captain shook his head and frowned. The Squirrel's family leader wasn't leaving the captain a leg to stand on. He would be forced to do something, and it couldn't be put off.

"I do believe they aren't going to leave us any choice, are they?" Forrester said. "And I was hoping we could maybe meet with them with a flag of truce or something. Maybe talk like Christians and work this out. But I've never heard of the Christianity that they're talking about. It sounds like their leader is making things up as he goes. I've never read where God condones genocide."

Dahteste looked at Levi with questioning eyes.

"He means to kill off all the Indians," Levi explained to his wife.

"Eliminate the owners of the land and keep it for themselves?" Dahteste asked.

"No, it's much more than that," the captain said. "They're saying that all the Indians and their tribes should be wiped out to the last man. That's what genocide means. It's a mighty evil word, ma'am."

"I wouldn't trust that wicked fool if he were prayin' in a church," Levi said.

Amazingly, after all the talk about stealing what wasn't theirs and killing the ones responsible for hanging their family, Jack Squirrel led them all in prayer. They bowed their heads and moved their lips to the memorized scripture.

Jack Squirrel took a deep breath and said, "Leviticus 24:19. And if a man cause a blemish in his neighbor; as he hath done, so shall it be done to him; breach for breach, eye for eye, tooth for tooth; as he hath caused a blemish in a man, so shall it be done to him again."

"Amen!" called the men in the gathered crowd of cousins. It was clear that they revered their leader. It was almost like they were in a spiritual trance, but the leader was clearly crazy.

Levi and Will hadn't even noticed that Dahteste had grabbed her husband's gun. The gunshot startled them both, and they looked at her with surprise. Their eyes shot back to the leader just in time to see him spin like a top and fly off the vegetable box he was standing on. His shoulder exploded in blood and bone. His scream echoed down the river. They wondered if the people back at the Rendezvous had heard it. It sounded like a wounded wolf.

"Dagnabit, darlin'," Levi huffed as he grabbed the rifle. "At least ya should have killed 'im."

"I was trying to kill him," Dahteste replied. Her mouth was no more than a gash. "You two weren't doing anything. You heard what that preacher man said. I had to try to kill him before he killed any of my people. I'm a war chief. I can't hear and see what he said and did and walk away. I would be shamed in the spirit world."

"Now, don't go callin' him a preacher man 'cause I ain't ever heard a man of God talk like that," Levi said. "He's plumb crazy is what he is, but he ain't no man of God, and that's for sure."

"Believe what Levi says, Dahteste." The captain

frowned. "This man hasn't got a religious drop of blood in him. He's using the Bible and God to get his flock to do his dirty deeds and protect him when he does his."

"We can't stay here any longer," Levi whispered. "We've gotta move. They'll know who it was with all that *eye-for-an-eye* stuff. Right now, we don't have enough cover and are outnumbered. We best get back and have a word with Rusty Steel. He'll know what to do."

As the group of men across the river crowded around their religious leader and family patriarch, the three spying on them escaped before the others could gather their wits and come after them. There were only three of them against twenty men, so even if they weren't mountain men, they probably knew how to shoot if they'd made it this far.

As soon as they had cover from trees, they jumped up and raced for their horses. Their hearts redlined as they heard the first shouts behind them. Unfortunately, Dahteste's shot hadn't killed Jack Amble Squirrel. It had ruined his left arm, but he was alive and angrier than ever, and now all his family wanted revenge. They had winged the one man the Squirrel family held in high esteem, their religious leader. Now, there was no way they were going to let this go.

The women had heard the shot and their spiritual leader's scream, but they continued their chores like they were programmed to do. They only acted or changed their routine when their husbands told them to, which was always at the order of Jack Amble Squirrel. They happily let the men deal with the danger and hostiles. Still, the women were all trained to shoot, so their response would be formidable if they were attacked.

When they reached their horses, they hurriedly unhobbled them, leaped astride, and wheeled them around to see if they were being followed yet. Dahteste sat astride the Appaloosa. The spotted horse reared and stomped its feet in anticipation. This was a war horse, and it yearned for action. It smelled blood and was ready to race into a fight.

"Not now, boy," Dahteste said to her horse in Crow. "It will come soon, though."

OLD FRIENDS

RUSTY STEEL, ANGUS MCFARLIN, AND VIRGIL LOVEJOY moseyed around the Rendezvous looking for deals and any familiar faces. Every year, the two locals ran into some old friends or rivals. This year, they wanted to get their business done before they started to let their hair down and drink enough to regret it the next day. When they sold their furs was of paramount importance. The prices fluctuated daily with the influx of mountain men to the meet. But what mattered the most was the quality of the pelts.

The best ones would make their way back to New York and Boston, and the very highest quality furs to London, Paris, or even the big cities like München, Germany, and Vienna, Austria. There, they would bring double the American prices. The first days of the Rendezvous were the worst time to sell because most trappers that arrived early immediately got dead drunk and were cheated by the big buyers, so buying prices were low. The day's lowest price would mark the starting bids for the next.

Every day, it was the same thing. Angus did the dickering, and Rusty watched his back. When it came to business, they didn't trust anybody, especially not this year, as the furs they had to sell weren't all theirs. Virgil sat by, sipped on a cup of whiskey, and studied their skills and tactics. He was amazed at how well Angus and Rusty worked together. Angus talked pleasant and soothing to the buyer, acting like he wanted to sell now and maybe even be friends, and Rusty grumbled and swore the whole time, stalling, making it obvious he didn't trust the buyer. Still, they didn't sell their beaver pelts but waited for better prices. They were both as sly as a couple of foxes.

Some men arrived at the meet and immediately sold all their furs so they could spend the rest of the time getting drunk, partying, and losing at the poker tables everything they had earned during the past long cold winter.

Both mountain men had lived in the Rocky Mountains for a long time and knew almost anybody worth knowing. Angus knew that if a man were patient, he would wait and see how the prices fared, especially as they had only the best cold-water beaver pelts to sell, and they had hundreds of them. Every buyer knew Rusty and Angus were at the meet and precisely what they had in the way of furs. All three of the big buyers had spies all over.

Of course, Virgil had never seen anything like the Rendezvous, so he was wide-eyed and followed the two rough old cobs around like a puppy. Like most newcomers, he'd sold his buffalo hides as soon as the meet started. Still, he was happy and believed he had gotten a fair and square deal. He still had more money than he ever imagined having and didn't think a little more would make him feel any better than he already did. He left the gold with his partner, Captain Forrester, who was much better skilled at keeping the money safe.

Virgil relished the freedom to have money and nothing more to do. He was on the first vacation of his entire life. His smile stretched so wide you could see his wisdom teeth. His hunting trip had succeeded in the end despite losing his two helpers.

"You be a bit off your graze, ain't cha, Angus?" came a voice from behind the mountain men. "Last I saw you was back in Kansas just over a year ago. Don't tell me you've given up workin' for a livin' and have turned to hangin' out in places like this."

Angus shot a glance over his shoulder and smiled. "I don't favor talkin' to vermin, but I reckon I'll talk to ya just this once. How ya been, Joseph?" Angus said to his old friend. "You remember Rusty, don't cha?" The friends shook hands.

"Of course I do," Joseph Walker replied as he proffered his hand.

"This here is our new friend, Virgil Lovejoy." Rusty grinned.

"Howdy. I hope you're aware of what caliber of men you're gettin' yourself involved with." Joseph laughed as his eyes crinkled at the edges. "Any friend of these two old thieves is a friend of mine."

"As a matter of fact, I recognize you from somewhere, Mr. Walker," Virgil said.

"Don't mister me, friend," Joseph said. "The name's Joseph. Back in Missouri, I'm Sheriff Joseph Walker. That's where you've probably seen me if you come from the East. Just about everybody that does comes through town."

"And who is that handsome fella?" Joseph asked as he squatted to pet the black dog at Rusty's feet.

"Mind yourself, now," Rusty said, expecting Dog to give him the usual growl. "He might just have a go at cha."

Walker petted the dog's head, and his tail wagged like a broken hinge. He smiled and said, "What's he gonna do? Wag me to death with that big old tail of his?"

Virgil broke out laughing, and it caught on, and soon all three men were laughing like they were crazy, patting each other on the back. Angus cackled with delight, and Rusty grumbled, disgusted.

"My dog ain't usually that friendly," Rusty complained. "I'm afraid he's gone soft on me."

"Don't worry, old pard," Joseph said. "All dogs like me. They know I'm not afraid and don't intend them any harm. That's what makes dogs so brave, ya know. They can smell your fear, and I ain't got none, so they leave me be."

Rusty grumbled, sucked on his quid, and spat into the sawdust floor beside Dog's head. The eyes on the black hairy face looked up, and he growled.

"So, now you're gonna growl at me, but not a complete stranger," Rusty Steel rumbled.

"Ya still tryin' to sell this season's beaver furs?" Joseph asked. "I heard tell y'all have some quality work. How's that workin' out for ya? What if the beaver pelt market falls apart tomorrow? You know as well as I do that it can go any day."

"Yeah, but iffin it does, we won't know about it until

next year, and the folks buyin' the furs won't know until they reach St. Louis or a telegraph. I know what I'm doin'. I wasn't born yesterday, ya know. Good things happen to those who wait for stupid."

Despite the weather, a man wearing a heavy coat walked into the crowded saloon, brushed against Rusty, tipped his hat, apologized, and carried on. Rusty slipped behind him and grabbed him by the collar. He shook him like a rag doll, and stolen items fell from the inside of his coat.

"Lookee here at this, moron," Rusty barked. "Whatcha think you're doin' comin' in here taking what ain't yours? You ain't leaving and not payin' for your goods, are ya?"

He had a small bale of mink furs behind his back in his hands. As soon as the thief was discovered, he pulled a knife on Rusty, who was closest.

Steel's eyes twinkled, and he smiled and said, "Why, I'm sorry, I didn't bring a knife." Rusty pulled his light jacket aside and showed a wide leather belt full of pistols. "Only a dumbass brings a knife to a gunfight."

"Treat me good, and I'll treat you better," Angus said. "Treat me bad, and I'll treat ya worse."

The nickel-dime thief's eyes spread wide when he realized he was caught. He had been stealing small things for the last two days. It had started with a man's pipe. It was so easy he decided to try something else. Next, he'd walked into a camp of sleeping men, pulled on expensive boots, and walked away. On the last day, he had wandered around the large saloons set up by the fur trading companies; he was good at stealing things. He became braver and more brazen with each theft. Nobody challenged him because nobody had seen him, even though he often took what wasn't his in broad daylight.

But now, all that had ended so suddenly it caught the thief off guard. His reflex was to go for his knife. He didn't have enough money to repurchase his gun. He had sold his furs the first day and lost all the money and his rifle the first night playing cards. Now, he was stealing things to sell after he left the meet. If he didn't acquire some money, he wouldn't have food to make it through the winter. Tobacco, coffee, flour, sugar, corn flour, and lard, among other things, cost money.

He looked at Joseph Walker with pleading eyes, but all he saw was laughter in the mountain man's face. Then he turned to the Black man.

"Can ya help me, mister?" the thief asked.

Virgil looked over his shoulder, thinking the thief was talking to someone else. When he realized it was him he was pleading with, he said, "It's gonna take Jesus and another three white folks to keep me from whippin' your tail myself."

"There must be some mistake here!" the thief called out. "I'm not really a bad person. I just fell on some hard times."

"Well, you made the mistake, fool," Rusty spat.

He opened his arms, spread his hands, and began to say something—maybe a plea for mercy. But it was cut short. Joseph took two steps forward, and they saw a flash of hard steel. Four fingers fell into the tobacco-stained sawdust, and blood spurted from the thief's fingers.

"That's just to make sure you don't get sticky fingers again." Joseph chuckled. "Now, ya ain't got no fingers at all."

"You best run over there to them cookfires and shove them stumps into the coals," Angus said as his brow furrowed. "If not, you're gonna bleed to death in a few minutes. Nobody here's intendin' to kill anybody for petty theft, but I approve of the lesson, Joseph. You are a clever fella, ain'tcha?"

Walker squatted and picked up the fingers and wrapped them in his bandanna. He looked up at curious faces.

"Medicine men from the mountain tribes pay good money for things like white scalps, ears, and fingers. No sense lettin' 'em go to waste. He ain't gonna be usin' 'em anymore."

"You ain't changed a bit, Joe Walker." Angus laughed and slapped his knee. "Come on, let's go get us somethin' fiery to sip on while we shoot the gab."

THE DILEMMA

RUSTY, ANGUS, JOSEPH, AND VIRGIL PULLED UP FOUR empty chairs in the corner. They appeared to be the only seats in the tent. Angus wondered how many miles they had traveled to get there and if they intended to take them back when the Rendezvous was over. Joseph rolled a whiskey barrel between them and tipped it up to make a table.

In seconds, tin cups full of whiskey materialized as if by magic.

"So, did ya come all the way from Missouri to see the Rendezvous, or were ya missin' your old pards?" Angus asked.

"Oh, you know I always miss old friends like you boys," Walker replied, smiling. "But unfortunately, that ain't what brought me down here. I have a bunch of city folks in my charge. They be missionaries. I was takin' 'em to Oregon City when I lost five of my six men back on the North Platte River where it meets the South Platte. The folks I'm guiding be green, so I need some real help that won't run away if they see a few Indians and don't expect it to be a party."

"Where are these eastern folks you left?" Angus asked. "By the time you get back, they may well be dead. There're lots of Indians around here right now, not to mention highwaymen. A fair number of trappers are walkin' around with considerable amounts of gold on 'em, which always attracts thieves."

"Nah, they're a hundred miles north of here holed up at the bottom of the South Pass," Joseph replied. "I left 'em on a high ground with good cover and plenty of rifles. We made it that far before I decided we couldn't make it to Oregon with just the two of us. We were sittin' ducks for any Indians. I've got my old pard Rory lookin' after 'em. You remember Breaker, don't cha? He's an able-bodied man. I could use four or five more just like 'im. That's what I came down here for. Lucky for me, the Rendezvous is still on. I wasn't quite sure of the date, but I knew what month it was. My men that died got reckless and rode into a strip of quicksand. They had the habit of all ridin' bunched up while they whispered gossip about the city folks. They were like a bunch of old hens. Now, I reckon they'll be broken of that habit, won't they?"

"You never can be too careful, but experienced trackers should have been looking for quicksand along uncharted rivers," Rusty replied. "That's a fool way to lose your life. Mind you, I've seen some experienced trappers fall in the clutches of quicksand but not five at once. That's some bad luck, that. *Arena movediza*—that's what the Spanish and the Mexicans call it—moving sand. It's tricky business, but iffin ya keep your head, you can survive. All ya gotta do is arch your back like you're floatin' on water until somebody throws ya a rope, but most folks freak out, and the more you move about, the deeper you go. It must have been somethin' to watch, five men and their horses disappearin' like that. I've seen a man and a wife go down together. My-oh-my, how they wailed. Then, once they went under, there was an eerie silence."

"It ain't somethin' I wanna see again, that's for dang sure," Joseph replied. "It shook up the folks I'm workin' for somethin' fierce. We didn't even have anything to bury, so they made crosses for all five and planted 'em as close to the quicksand as they dared. Now, they're scared of everything, and we haven't even run into any Indians yet. That's why I need four or five trackers that can shoot and don't spook. What better place to look than the Rendezvous?"

They ordered more whiskeys all around with some lousy-tasting warm beer. Peanuts in the shell sat in a wicker basket on the table. Empty hulls were scattered over the ground. Smoke hovered overhead like a blanket, running from one end of the tent to the other. Somebody ordered cans of peaches, and they all appeased their sweet tooth. Everybody around them seemed to be talking at once, making the noise level rise with every hour. More and more trappers continued to flow into the Rendezvous. It was like a river of mountain men emptying into a water hole that became a pond and was now nearly a lake.

"Would you call that a herd, a gaggle, or a flock of buttheads?" Levi said in a loud voice as he approached his friends. Then he saw the stranger sitting beside Angus and clamped his mouth shut.

"Excuse me," Levi said as his face flushed red. He

pulled his hat off. "I spoke before I realized you men had company. I'm Levi Johnson, and this here is Mrs. Dahteste Johnson. I reckon y'all be friends. You sure do look to be of the same breed. Excuse me for my poor timing of a bad joke."

"Actually, I like to think of us as a gaggle." The Missouri sheriff chuckled. "Joseph R. Walker's the name, son. I take it you be Rusty's apprentice I heard so much about. Why, your tales are told all the way back in Kansas! And you must be the captain. Whatcha know, Angus? I read about these two in the newspapers. Somethin' about an expedition with scientists and smart folks. Why is it I ain't heard no more about it?"

"You don't say?" Levi grinned, surprised. "You've heard tell of us all the way back in Missouri? We're famous, Will."

"You didn't hear any more about the expedition because most of us were killed," the captain frowned. "We were headed for California. I'm a West Point gradu- ate, and I majored in geography. I was tasked with mapping the best trails to California and finding new locations for more Army forts farther west to protect the coming settlers. But as you can see, that didn't work out."

"Is that a fact?" Joseph said. He winked at Rusty. "Ya say you're a mapmaker, are ya? And you were headed to blaze trails to California? Why, you're a man after my own heart."

"Now, hold on a dad-gummed minute!" Rusty roared as he jumped to his feet. "You don't have a mind to offer my boys a job, do ya? They've already got enough work with Angus and me."

"Whatcha talkin' about, old friend?" Joseph asked

with a sly smile. "I just got here today, and you've already got me runnin' off. I intend to stay a spell. A day or two either way ain't gonna change the next thousand miles for my missionaries."

"I'll go see if I can find some more chairs," the captain said and vanished. By the time he returned, Levi and Dahteste were sitting cross-legged on the floor. Miraculously, Forrester had found more chairs.

"I discovered where the chairs came from," Forrester said with seat backs hooked in his arms. "The fella that runs this place brought ten from Old Fort Boise. They're machine-made and are as light as a feather. I bought the lot for the cabins."

"Well, I'll be. That was just what I was thinking about," Angus said. "The ones we've got are made from trees and weigh a ton. Some of 'em still got little stubs from branches stickin' out. We can hang these on pegs in the wall without worrying about the pegs breakin'. That was mighty kind of ya, Will."

Soon, Mountain Dennis Breed, Portland Pete, and Syracuse Sam located the rest of their friends. Every time somebody else showed, Forrester would bring out another chair. The other three had been shopping on their own for something special to take back to the cabins for the winter. The harsh cold made them stay indoors for a few months a year, so all they had to do was cure furs and play cards or tell tall tales.

"Lookee here," Pete said, holding aloft a box. "I bought us a backgammon board."

"Where is it?" Angus asked.

"It's inside the satchel," Pete replied. He opened the latches on the box with a handle; inside was a brightly painted backgammon board, and in the middle were the black and red pieces in neat little boxes. The new owner was grinning like a possum. "I think it was quite a find."

"I've never seen such a fancy backgammon game." Rusty smiled. "That's gonna make for some fine game time on some cold winter nights. We should buy a couple more. One for each cabin."

"There was only the one game," Pete said. "The owner was a funny talkin' man with a big, hooked nose. He said he brought it from a place named Persa. I think I've heard of a town in Indiana named Persa."

"Persia ain't a town, it's a country, and it's in Asia," Joseph Walker said. "On the other side of Europe, a long way away. Over seven thousand miles, to be exact, so I doubt you've heard of it."

"The design looks Irani," Virgil said to surprised faces. His trace of a mustache looked more like a shadow.

"Why, how is it you know about such things, Virgil?" Joseph asked, curious.

"There was a time years ago when I was a slave, and my rich owner had a collection of backgammon boards," Virgil replied. "Some were fancy, made right into tables with ivory inlay and all. He claimed Persians invented the game. He taught me to play when I was a young man. He said all gentlemen should own one. He never traveled without one of his smaller boards. At night, when I was done with my chores, we played, sometimes well into the night."

"It's kind of like chess, then, ain't it?" Joseph asked.

"My owner, the Englishman Fitzgerald Worstshire III, said backgammon was an even better challenge because, in chess, there were only so many moves you could make to win a game, and the combinations in backgammon were endless."

"Personally, I like checkers best," Syracuse Sam said. "Backgammon is too danged fast, and chess gives me a headache."

Joseph, Angus, and Rusty snickered. It was evident that Sam wasn't the most intelligent man in the room. But he was one heck of a trapper. Each man had his strong points and his weak ones, too, like everybody everywhere.

"Since you are all such good friends and all, I'll talk in front of our new acquaintance," Captain Forrester said. "I'm afraid we'll have more trouble from the Squirrel family, and probably sooner than later. We tracked them down to a ravine upstream on the Green River. They're over a hundred strong. The strange thing about them is there are only about twenty men and maybe five or six boys out of over a hundred. Maybe close to one hundred-twenty. I've never seen so many women west of the Missouri River."

"What are you tryin' to say?" Rusty asked. "I'm not getting your drift."

"That's just it," the captain replied. "I'm not so sure of what we saw either. There are more than a hundred of them, but all but twenty-some are women and girls. It doesn't make any sense. I've read in the newspapers that there is less than one White woman to every hundred men out west, but with this bunch, the women outnumber the men five to one."

"That's a good thing, ain't it?" Sam asked, grinning. "I never mind havin' a bunch of women around."

"And that ain't all," Levi said. "The women seem to act like a herd of sheep, doin' what their husbands want." He stared at his wife, but she just shot him another dirty look. She wasn't budging on her ways.

"What's worrying is what their leader said just before Dahteste shot him," Captain Forrester said.

"Dahteste shot 'im?" Rusty asked. He slapped his knee and laughed. "Boy-oh-boy, does that girl have spunk?"

"The problem is she didn't kill 'im," Levi said. "She winged 'im good so that he won't be usin' his left arm again, but I think it just riled 'im up. The whole bunch seemed to be some kind of cult. He preaches from the Bible, but I figure the words he uses ain't what he's readin'. Now, he's told his people we've all got to die for hangin' his kin. Killin' Bob wasn't enough revenge for this fella. He's hungry for more blood."

"Did you say you know where the Squirrel family is?" Sheriff Walker asked. "That'll be Jack Amble Squirrel and his kin. They're from Tennessee, just like me. They were run off for murderin' a few members of other clans they were feudin' with. I personally ran 'em out of Missouri, so once they find out I'm here, they'll be aimin' to shoot me too."

"So, you know this crazy fella?" Levi asked. "I don't know what he's preachin' to those folks, but they follow him like pups to their mama. They seemed hypnotized."

"Hypno-what?" Sam asked.

Dahteste looked at Levi with questioning eyes and raised an eyebrow.

"Somebody find me a dictionary," Rusty spat. "You know you can't use big words around some of my buddies." He nodded to Sam and Pete. "Some of my friends be as dumb as two marbles in a tin can, but they have grit, can shoot the wings off a fly, and are trapper savvy. In the Rocky Mountains, schooling isn't something that does a man a lot of good, and you're never judged by your fancy handwriting. A man is more respected for his trapping skills than anything else. So, try to use language we don't have to look up in the words of Webster."

"The whole bunch practices polygamy," Joseph said. "That's illegal in most states. At least for White and Black folks, it is. For Indians, I reckon it's overlooked. I know chiefs have several wives."

"Here ya go again," Rusty growled and turned to the barman. "Where's that Webster's dictionary at?"

"Poly-gamy?" Dahteste asked. "My chief has three wives, and they are fine women. Why does the English language have so many words?"

"Why, English is one of the languages with the least words," Joseph said. "Spanish has many more words than English does. I speak it, and it's much more complicated. It's whatcha call a romantic language."

"Why would we want to learn Spanish when we speak Crow and English?" Dahteste asked.

"Believe it or not, twice as many people speak Spanish as English," Joseph said, showing his vast knowledge. "All of Mexico and south speak Spanish, including South America, right down to the very tip. Then there's Spain in Europe, where the language comes from, and they even speak Spanish in the Philippines."

"Where's that?" Sam asked. "I'm afraid I was home-schooled, and my ma couldn't read or write, but she did teach us to sign our names."

"Past Indonesia," Joseph replied.

"Now you're just confusin' me," Sam said.

"Back to the Squirrel family," Sheriff Walker said. "They're wanted for murder in Tennessee and a half dozen thefts in Missouri, plus who knows what'll turn up later. A few folks were found dead under suspicious conditions when they were around, too, but we don't have any proof or reason for those killings."

"From what we've seen, they don't need much reason," the captain said. "They shot Yosemite Bob while hiding in the bushes. I would imagine if you got Jack Squirrel alone, he wouldn't be so brave. He seems to me to be a bully. He sure has all his kin bullied into believing what he preaches—even if that's killing and stealing. I don't know how he explains that in the Bible, but there you go. Everywhere we travel, we run into stranger people."

"Well, ya can't come to the Rendezvous and not expect to run into an odd character or two." Rusty laughed. "You've got a badge, Sheriff Walker. Why don't you just deputize us all, and we'll go and arrest the bunch? That'll end it all, and the women can ride back with the folks from the fur trading companies. They can ride in the wagons with the bales of furs."

"Lord have mercy on those women if the men here at the meet find out they're there," Angus said. "Especially if they're left on their own."

"We'll have to make sure nothing happens to them, then," the captain said. "I'll make it my personal business to see that they aren't harmed."

"In that case, it ain't them I'm worried about," Rusty said. "It's them I'm worried about and you, with them blues eyes and yellow hair. Maybe you'll fetch one back to be your wife." He laughed until his face was as red a tomato.

THE POSSE

WHEN RUSTY STEEL TOLD SHERIFF JOSEPH WALKER TO deputize them all, he wasn't at all serious. He intended it to be more like a sour joke, but Joseph didn't take it that way. He took him up on his offer straight away.

"All of ya, raise your right hand," Joseph said. "I hereby deputize the lot of ya." It was short and sweet and to the point.

"That didn't seem very formal," Cavalry Captain Forrester said. "Mind you, I've never seen a posse deputized, but I expected some ceremony around it."

"Without badges, it's even less formal, but we have to work with what we've got, so I didn't figure it was worth a lot of rigamarole. It's legal just the same," Joseph said. "Now, show me where it is you found the Squirrel family. I figure it'll be better if we find them before they find us."

Virgil was tickled pink. "I've never even imagined being a soldier, much less a deputy sheriff," he snickered. "I wish Joseph had some badges. Could you imagine that?" He laughed loud and deep, pleased as punch.

Ten horses fell into formation as the captain led the way to the Squirrel family's wagon roundup beside the river. Dahteste rode her spotted Appaloosa beside Levi. She didn't have a rifle but had a quiver full of arrows and her bow, and she was clearly unafraid. This wasn't the first time she had ridden into battle. Levi wondered how many husbands could say the same about their wives.

Horses' hooves hammered the ground as a dust cloud followed the riders north. It was ten against twenty, but the smaller force was by far the deadlier. None of Rusty's men doubted how the fight would pan out. They had each killed in violent skirmishes. They all knew they would probably lose a life or two if they were unlucky. But it had gone too far now to turn back. There were dead man to account for, and the law was the law. Just because Jack Amble Squirrel interpreted the Bible any way he wanted, it didn't change the letter of the law or the actual proper interpretation of the Good Book.

Typically, the courts would decide what to do with such men, and the list of accusations would be long. But they all knew the Squirrels would never surrender. At least not as long as their leader was alive. Nobody was prepared to take them five hundred miles to the nearest jail anyway. It would be far too dangerous. Halfway to the circled wagons, the captain and the sheriff saw the first hint of a dust cloud in the distance. Just like Jack, the leader, had told his people, they were coming to get revenge.

As the lay of the land opened, it allowed them to ride wide of each other, making them harder targets and allowing them all to arrive nearly simultaneously at the point of conflict. They pulled their horses into a loose V formation with Captain Forrester at the head of the column of deputized riders. The sheriff rode to the right, just a little behind the captain. At least together, they gave more of an official appearance than buckskin-clad, woolly-haired men alone. Sunlight flashed off Walker's badge. That would be the first thing they would see, and Forrester's saber would be the second.

Joseph was determined to end the reign of terror perpetuated by the Squirrel family across the country, all the way from Tennessee. Their leader, Jack, was obviously insane. He was so far gone there was no hope for him to come back to earth. Hopefully, that wouldn't be the case with the rest. But if the mountain men were put in harm's way, they would reply with a barrage of bullets. The Squirrels were clannish, feud-crazed killers, but the men coming for them were all warriors of one sort or another. They were professionals, one and all. Even Virgil, who was a man of peace but could shoot the thorns off a cactus at a quarter mile.

Rusty Steel pulled up beside the sheriff.

"You're too old to be fightin'," Joseph said over the pounding hooves. His lips curled.

"I'm sure as heck too old to be losin'," Rusty replied. "So, let's make this quick and to the point. These boys don't know what they're in for."

Joseph looked at the captain, who had fallen in beside him, and said, "You might as well get it off your chest 'cause I can smell the wood a-burnin', so don't try to hide it."

"I guess I'm just reluctant to see this happen," the

captain said. "I was hoping for some peaceful way out of this."

"But they killed one of yours," Joseph said. "There's no peaceful solution for murder, son. The only response here is a bullet or a noose."

Joseph gave him the sign, a thumbs up, as he touched his horse's flanks. As soon as the captain saw him move, he shot off out front like always. The cavalry officer rode off like his hair was on fire with his saber in his only hand as he waved it over his head and let out a war cry he had heard from the Comanche, the same Indians that killed his men. His eyes were full of fury. Now, they had done it and pushed the soldier too far, and he was angry as the hell that was coming for the wicked and those who defiled the Bible. The very man who wanted to find a peaceful solution was to be the Squirrel family's worst nightmare.

———

JACK SQUIRREL RODE in front of his disorganized men. Here, there was no orderly column of riders or offensive formation. The men carried a mismatch of rifles and pistols; all of them were dangerous, but some were not as well-suited for their environment as others. Of course, all the Squirrel family knew how to shoot, and many had already killed their first man. But they'd never practiced shooting from the back of a charging horse. They didn't know what chaos awaited them, nor did Jack. He had always been the kind of man who bushwhacked his enemies. He was a master at ambushes and sneaking up on people. Most thieves were.

The difficulty of fighting from horseback never crossed their minds. They probably believed they would find their enemy, sneak up on them and kill them from afar in a safe place with plenty of cover, like always. So far, all their battles had worked out that way. But this was the first time they'd taken on someone that wasn't another feuding family. These men were used to fighting hostile Indians and grizzly bears.

When their leader shot a glance over his shoulder, he could see how fanatical his men's eyes were. He could almost see the zeal in their faces. This made Jack happy, but he wondered if they would hold when they clashed with the enemy. Not one had been a soldier because the Squirrels didn't take orders from anyone but another Squirrel, and they were suspicious of all government and official people—especially sheriffs, marshals, and Indian agents.

When Jack Amble Squirrel saw the dust cloud in the distance, he assumed it was some of the wagons from the fur trading companies. Then he wondered why they would be traveling on this bad trail that led to nowhere. It took him a few minutes of hard riding before he put the mountain men and the cloud of dust together. He was suddenly shocked that they were coming for him. That wasn't in his plans. He was supposed to be coming for *them*.

Jack slapped his horse's rump with the reins and set his spurs, making his mount burst forward. He didn't know what else to do because he didn't have a plan B. The men riding behind him stepped up their pace. Horses' lungs heaved as hooves stamped the hard ground, churning up the earth as they raced ahead. The weeds and earth behind them were trodden down.

When the leader shot another glance over his shoulder to ensure his men were keeping up, he saw the change in their faces. Now, fear showed in their eyes. When he looked back toward the front, he saw the soldier with his sword. When he screamed, goosebumps sprouted on Jack's arms, and a chill went up his spine as the soldier raced straight for them. Another huge young mountain man was closing in beside the soldier with a rifle leveled. He never saw the flash, smoke, or heard the crack of the gun.

Jack was thrown from his horse with such force he flew twenty feet before hitting the ground. That was just when they all clashed. Smoke from black powder filled the air, and bullets whizzed by men's ears, tugged at their clothing, and slammed into their bodies. Now, screams from a dozen sources filled the air until that was all they could hear.

Running flat out, Dahteste dropped to the side of her horse, and from under his neck, she shot three arrows in under two seconds. Three Squirrels went down.

The sun bore down, and rays of light flashed off the captain's sword as he lopped off one, two, and a third head. His tempered saber cut through their necks like a hot knife through butter. Their heads rolled across the ground only to be trampled by the horses. Animals and men all clashed in a hand-to-hand battle. Everyone's fear had passed, and each combatant's only objective was to kill the enemy before they killed them and to survive the day, but the Squirrels failed miserably.

What seemed to take an hour was over in minutes, and the ground was littered with the dead. There were no wounded that would survive. Joseph and Forrester wheeled their horses around, looking for more enemies, but there were none. Still, a crazy fire burned in the captain's eyes.

Levi nudged his horse over to his best friend, reached for the captain's reins to stop his stallion from running off, and softly said, "It's over, Will. They're all dead now, so you can stop, my friend."

Dahteste's horse stood beside Levi's but nervously stomped the earth in anxious anticipation. The woman war chief's eyes were as wild and angry as the captain's.

"You too, darlin'," Levi said. "Settle down now." He looked over his shoulder and asked, "Did any of us get hit?"

Angus was kneeling beside Portland Pete, who was shot in the head. The hole was neat and clean, and he didn't appear to have another mark on him. It must have been a lucky shot. Pete had survived smallpox, which scarred his face, but was killed by religious fanatics from some crazy sect for no real reason.

A short distance away, Rusty sat on the ground with Syracuse Sam's head in his lap. He whispered something to him as he rocked him back and forth like a mother with a small child. The men stood back as the old mountain man ushered his old friend to the afterworld as gently as possible. A tear accumulated in his eye, but he blinked it back and rubbed his nose with his finger as he cleared his throat. He sat like that for nearly an hour, whispering kind things into his dying friend's ear. He held his hand like he was his only brother.

Finally, his lungs chattered, his body shuddered one last time, and his eyes crawled back into his head. Rusty looked up at those left with a thousand-yard stare. Life in the Rocky Mountains was hard on an average day, let alone when a bunch of crazies came to settle. But the Squirrel family wouldn't be settling here. Not anymore, they wouldn't.

"What are you going to do with the women?" Daht-este asked. "In our tribe, when we kill all the enemy warriors, we keep the women to help grow our own tribe. Crow men and even warriors take them for their wives. Only a fool would leave them to die."

The question shocked Levi and Will, but the older mountain men and even Virgil weren't shocked at all. It seemed the practical thing to do but also the most unlikely.

"I don't see these poor sheepy women not dying from fright just by being in an Indian stronghold," Joseph said. "They might go crazier than Jack Squirrel pushed 'em to be. Where is he anyway?"

"He was the first man I shot," Levi said. "I saw it clear as day. I shot him right through the throat, and it knocked him off his horse."

———

JACK SQUIRREL WAS WINGED, and his arm was ruined, but he wasn't dead. Buried in the ground would be the only way he would allow things to sit without revenge. Especially now that they had crippled him for life. He didn't care even if his followers were killed to the last man. It was all for a greater glory. They didn't see the big picture like he did. They were his flock, and he was their shepherd. All they needed to know was to follow him without question, and they would have their passage to glory no matter what happened today.

He stared at the clouds as they lazily floated across

the sky between the earth and the heavens. They looked like strangely shaped cotton balls. He wondered why he couldn't move. He blinked his eyes, but his vision didn't clear. Things were still fuzzy, but he wasn't going to give up yet. He had only just begun to fight and seek more revenge. After all was said and done, he was not after revenge. He was coming for a reckoning.

He dreamed of a land where all the men and women looked like him and had green eyes. They would be happy and would have hundreds more offspring. A twinge of pain pricked his conscience. Now, the women and children wouldn't have husbands and fathers. What would become of them? Then again, they were mere sheep, and if they had to be led to the slaughter for the greater good, so be it. Then he thought again—now he would have even more wives. That was something that he didn't mind. The more spouses and children, the better. He only hoped for one ordinary boy to come out of all this so he would have someone to follow in his steps when the time came.

He clutched at the Bible in his hand. Jack Amble Squirrel had brought it with him all the way from Tennessee. It had his name printed on the front with the year 1828. His grip was slippery, but he didn't know why. He saw angels dance in the sky above him. They had golden wings and hair but also green eyes and freckled faces like the Squirrels. He knew there was a special heaven waiting for them too.

He suddenly remembered that all three of his wives were with child. He wondered if there would be more women or boys born this time too. The few young men they had were strange. One was missing fingers from birth, and another was blind and had a bad stutter, but all the girls seemed as healthy as possible. He wondered if it was because they were inbred. Still, he longed for a normal son to carry on when he was gone. Unless the day of glory came before; then it wouldn't matter anymore. With the Second Coming, he was sure he would walk beside the Lord in all his glory.

His breath chattered like he had a broken windpipe. He couldn't see the hole in his neck. It gave a jagged view into his throat, which was full of blood. It was dark —almost black. He tried to gobble up more air, but his lungs didn't seem to work. They, too, were filling with blood from the wound. Tears filled his eyes as he realized this was the end. The warm feeling he felt was his own blood. He tried to talk, but his mouth opened and closed like a beached trout. He made a long, hissing exhale that seemed to last a full minute but was probably only seconds.

Two men and a woman stared down at his body. There was hate in their eyes, but he didn't recognize them. More people's faces appeared and looked down on him. Some shook their heads, but no one cried or even frowned. Their mouths were hard lines.

He tried to hold their stare and moved his mouth, but no words came. His pupils dilated and then disappeared leaving only the whites of his eyes visible, and his body went limp. He fouled himself when his muscles relaxed, and he died. A stench came from the body as blood pooled beneath him.

The last thought that crossed his mind was a question. He knew it was so important it could change the world's way of being. He reached for the words, but they eluded him. They knew he was grabbing for them. There he would find the secret to it all. But it slipped away from him just as easily as his life slipped away from his body that very moment. He couldn't even remember if they had killed all the trappers or not. A dark veil covered his brain. Somebody spat. It splattered on his forehead. That was the last thing he felt. The smell of tobacco was strong, and that was the last thing he smelled.

The last thing he remembered was the Army man riding right at them like he didn't even know what fear was. Jack could see he had all that soldier crammed inside him, burning to bust out. Why did he only have one arm, and why was he covered in blood? Jack also remembered seeing the flash of his evil eyes and his saber as it took off the heads of men that fought for him and their way of life. The very men they meant to strike down with the wrath of God had come for them like the devil incarnate. Jack never expected a ten-man charge. Nor did he expect the mountain men to be such good shots. He didn't hear a single shot from their guns without one of his men falling off a horse. He watched it all play out helplessly from the ground. Then his world went black.

RUNG TO HELL

LEVI BEAVER JOHNSON SET HIS FOOT ON THE SHOVEL'S step. It was the first rung to heaven or hell. He pushed the blade into the ground and tossed the dirt aside as he began to dig the second grave. Will Forrester was already digging the first—two six-foot-deep holes to bury their dead friends. They had gathered rocks and stones from the river to put on top of the mounds of earth to keep the varmints from digging them up. A big black dog lay in the shade and watched everything that moved.

Rusty Steel and Angus McFarlin were busy carving names into a pair of crosses. The white paint was still tacky and stained their hands. Virgil held an open Bible as his finger traced under the words, and he quoted a verse to stay busy so he wouldn't cry until he was alone.

Lovejoy said, "John 11:25. Jesus said to her, 'I am the resurrection and the life. The one who believes in me will live even though they die.'"

Three crosses stood before three piles of dirt and stones. Half the original members of Rocky Mountain compound lay buried at their feet. They hadn't come to the Rendezvous ignorant of the dangers. But this had come from an unexpected source. This new enemy hadn't lived in the Rockies. They all wondered how the constellations collided for such a thing to occur. Would there be other settlers with like minds and crazy leaders?

Everybody felt something big was just about to happen in every place west of Kansas, but they couldn't pinpoint what it was. The only one that believed he knew what was coming was Joseph R. Walker. He stroked his long black beard as he stared into the fire and thought about the future. Orange coals reflected in his eyes.

Nobody cried but Virgil Lovejoy, and he silently cried for everybody. Forrester was envious of his friend. Crying was something he had dominated because it was unbecoming of an officer. Right then, he felt he could cry a river, and the other mountain men felt the same. They were all accustomed to death, although not those of the compound's members in so short a time. They laid them to rest beside Yosemite Bob, three friends, side-by-side forever.

Each man passed by the graves, removed his hat, and said goodbye to old friends. Rusty was hit the hardest of the men from the cabins. He had almost felt like their keeper, and now, he had let them down. Life was always hard in the mountains, but now the settlers were moving west, and some were more complicated than others, but none of them were good for the mountain men or the local Indians.

When they finished, they made a fire beside their dead friends. The sun blushed orange on the horizon as it silently set. A blanket of stars rolled out across the dark blue sky, making millions of tiny, sparkling dots, light years away. Crickets chattered in the dark.

"So, what are we gonna do with the women?" Forrester asked. "There must be eighty with the girls and boys, if not more."

"That's another can of worms we still have to open," Rusty said. "I imagine Jack Squirrel left a few men back there to guard the women. So, this ain't quite over. They won't know what happened to their cousins, brothers, or whatever they're supposed to be. But they'll know who we are."

"Did anybody count the Squirrel bodies before we left the killing fields?" Levi asked.

"I checked if they were dead, and they were," Rusty said. "That was the only thing important to me at the moment. We didn't want any of 'em to pop up and shoot us in the back."

The captain frowned and shook his head. How could he have forgotten such an important detail?

"I totally forgot to count the bodies," Forrester lamented. "I believe I was somewhat consumed with the battle and wasn't myself. Normally, I'd never miss such an important detail. If nothing else, to notify the law."

"Yeah, and I'm the law you were supposed to notify, so don't feel too bad," Sheriff Walker said. "I plumb forgot as well. These people put me off my feed. I just can't figure 'em out—can't get my arms around how they followed that maniac."

"Maybe you will have a chance to find out tomorrow," Dahteste said. "Maybe the men left to guard the women will talk to us and not try to kill us. Just maybe they can live. Crow Indians rarely kill every enemy left, or the few survivors will live for revenge. It is important to leave them just enough people to continue and be responsible for providing for the children."

"I have no intention of lettin' a single Squirrel continue to go anywhere other than the end of a rope and a grave," Joseph Walker growled. "Too many men have died at that family's hands to let even one live. They stained the great name of my home state, Tennessee. No, I ain't havin' any of it. This has got to end now."

"That's harsh, ain't it?" Virgil asked.

"This is a harsh country, brother," Joseph replied, then he fished his quid out of his mouth and spat into the dirt.

"Yeah, it'll be too risky to try to walk into their camp at night anyway," Angus said. "That's a surefire way to get shot."

"We can walk the horses in first thing tomorrow with a white flag, so they know we wanna parlay," Rusty said. "At the same time, we can show our numbers, so they'll be intimidated." He looked around, but nobody stupid and with a small vocabulary was left among them. He shook his head and said, "We don't need that dictionary anymore, either. Anyway, nobody's gonna hang anybody until we hear what they have to say. Too many men have died already."

"I still don't know what we're gonna do with all the women," Angus said. "Even if we took one each, that'd still leave like seventy or more."

"I know a few warriors in the Crow camp who would love to have a yellow-haired woman." Dahteste laughed.

"No, that ain't gonna work," Rusty said. "Settin' that many White women on Chief Hachta would surely end our friendship." He laughed until he got the hiccups. "Despite the violence, life still goes on. The road behind us is much longer than the one before us, so we might as well do our best with what we've got left. Sam, Bob, and Pete just showed us we're only mortal. At least for us men gettin' on in age."

"Now, I'm the oldest one left," Dennis said, blinking. His chin hung to his chest.

"On the brighter side of things, now Will, Virgil, and you two love birds don't have to build a new cabin," Rusty said. "There's one vacant as of today. I doubt Chief Hachta would have taken kindly to buildin' another one anyway, despite you bein' married to his war chief and all, Levi."

"I reckon we can build a small room on the side for Dahteste and me," Levi said. "Maybe even put the smallest fireplace in there. That'd work out just fine for us. All we need is a little privacy."

After a little small talk, they all went silent. Everybody pondered what had happened earlier that day. Fierce battles like that only happened a few times in a lifetime for men like them. In the end, maybe they hadn't come out so bad after all. Twice as many would have died had the Squirrels been better shots.

THE WOMEN

"KEEP ON THE LOOKOUT FOR VULTURES," RUSTY SAID AS he scanned the sky. "I've got a bad feelin' about the rest of that bunch. I reckon we might just be riding into another hailstorm."

Before they even got close to where they'd seen the circled wagons the day before, they saw the birds of prey high in the sky. There must have been a hundred. Below them were clouds of black smoke. When the sheriff and his posse rode to the edge of the clearing before the circled wagons, they all had their rifles with the stocks' butt plates on their thighs, their hammers cocked, powder horns and patch boxes full but with the barrels pointing toward the heavens.

They hoped to enter peacefully but were ready for another fight if that was what it came to. Fire flashed in the captain's eyes again as his heart began hammering in his chest, and his mind began to twirl out of control as he filled with fury. The electricity passed on to his black stallion as it hammered its hooves. The spark seemed to ignite in seconds. Levi gave him a worried look, but Will didn't notice. Rusty and Will's long guns had white bandages tied to the ends of the long barrels —the sign of a parley. They all wondered if those left alive would believe their intentions or even notice. Dead bodies littered the ground between them and the wagons.

They could see women with rifles in the distance. Half the wagons were burned, and two were still on fire as smoke snaked toward the sun. Fearful eyes spread wide and stared back at the posse. The fires crackled as flames lashed out. One wagon collapsed as the dry wood burned quickly. Indians and women alike lay haphazardly scattered at the edge of the circled wagons, dead or dying. The children were nowhere to be seen. Only a handful of females were visible. The vultures overhead circled lower and lower to get a better look at the feast they would have at their next meal.

"Easy now, ladies," Joseph said, carefully nudging his horse forward. "I be from Tennessee just like y'all, so don't worry. As you can see, I wear a badge. We're here to save ya. I'm gonna step down from my horse now, so don't shoot me, please." Joseph smiled as he slowly climbed off his horse. The curled edges of his lips trembled slightly. "Now, I'm gonna put my rifle down so I ain't no threat." He laid his gun on the ground. "All right, now, who's in charge here? I don't see any of the Squirrel menfolk."

Nobody said a thing. The terrified women just stared at the mountain men and blinked like frightened does in a hunter's gunsight. They could see their grips tighten on their rifles. Would they shoot Joseph? They sure were scared enough. Captain Forrester rode right up between the armed ladies and Sheriff Walker and saluted the woman hanging over the seat with a rifle in her white-knuckled fists. Her face was red with blood, but it didn't appear to be hers.

"Ma'am, I'm Captain William Forrester of the United States Cavalry, at your service. It appears that you have had hostile Indians attack your small wagon train. Can you speak, ma'am?"

The woman looked confused, unsure what to do or say. She began to drop the barrel, but her hands were shaking. She was still terrified. The captain wasn't sure if she was going to shoot or not.

"You don't have to drop that gun barrel if you don't want to, ma'am. You keep it pointed at me if it makes you feel better. All I want to do is have a chat with you and see how we can help you. Do you understand?"

She nodded, then dropped the gun anyway and began to sob. The sudden truth settled in, and her eyes spread. They could see the terror and confusion. She glanced around. Dead bodies lay everywhere. It was a miracle any of them had lived.

"They're almost all dead!" she cried. Blood speckled her dress and face and smudged her hands. "Jack Amble didn't leave us a guard like he usually does. He was afraid of the men who had hanged his brothers, so he took every man we had. I don't know what he was thinking."

"And why would someone want to hang his brothers?" the captain asked, even though he already knew.

She looked behind her as if making sure their leader wasn't there and whispered, "Because Jack Amber

Squirrel told them to steal. He even told them all to kill the mountain men; they weren't the first. He killed one of his cousins because he wanted his sixteen-year-old wife."

"But you know that's against the law, don't you?" Forrester asked.

She nodded. "Us wives aren't allowed to speak our opinion, or we get a whipping. But we have more education than the men, and it wasn't hard to figure out what was really going on. We were trapped like those beavers you hunt, but the trap wasn't steel. It was psychological and physical fear."

"Now that I'm here, you can talk all you want," the captain said as his lips smiled a mouth full of white teeth. It was just enough to put the woman at ease. "May I step down, ma'am? I want to check the rest of you to see if I can help."

When Dahteste surprised the woman by jumping the wagon tongue and wheeling her horse behind her, she screamed.

Before she could swing her gun around and shoot the Crow woman, the captain grabbed the gun and said, "She's with us. She's...our translator. She won't harm you. We're all deputized by the sheriff here. See his shiny badge? And I'm with the Army. See my saber and my cavalry hat?" The woman didn't notice the blood dripping from the end of its sheath.

When the ladies left alive saw that these men and the Indian woman weren't there to kill them, they welcomed them gratefully. The relief swept over them like an ocean wave, and they all gave a deep sigh. Some still silently sobbed, and their shoulders shook, but at least they had stopped crying. There were no more tears left.

"I didn't think we were going make it out alive. My name is Betty Crockett out of Limestone, Tennessee—at least I was before I was captured and forced to marry my husband. I'm kind of the unofficial leader of the Squirrel women. The Squirrels captured me like they did many women here. That was back in my home. I had no say in the matter. Have you seen our husbands?"

The mountain men looked at each other, wondering what to say and who would say it. An uncomfortable silence followed. Nobody said a word for the longest time.

"Did something bad happen to them?" Betty finally asked.

Nobody knew how badly they would take the news.

Kansas Sheriff Joseph Walker walked up to Mrs. Crockett, laid a hand on her arm, and said, "I'm afraid we have some more bad news for ya, ma'am. I'm sorry to tell ya they're all dead to the last man. Jack Amble Squirrel included. He was the first one shot when they attacked us head-on. They had no idea of what they were getting themselves into. It just couldn't be helped. There wasn't any other way. They came at us with guns blazing and left us with no choice. They even killed two more of our friends."

They all held their breath, expecting the usual cries of pain at losing a loved one. But that wasn't what came out of Betty Crockett's mouth. She began to laugh. At first, it was a snicker, then a chuckle. Finally, it was full-blown laughter, almost like she had gone mad. Most of the men looked at her, puzzled. Only Dahteste and

Virgil understood. Some of the other surviving women snickered through their tears too.

"My friends back home who come from other tribes were traded for horses," Dahteste said. "Those dead Indians are Blackfeet warriors. They intended to take all you women. Where are the children? We spied on you yesterday, and many little ones were with you."

"When the hostile Indians showed up, we sent the children running off with two of my friends. We thought they would be after the women to rape and kill, so we sacrificed ourselves for the sake of the children. But they seemed more interested in stealing us than murdering us and killing us. Most of us would rather die first, so we fought anyway. Still, many of those who resisted perished." Betty looked at a dead friend whose body lay on the ground inside the circled wagons. She had two arrows protruding from her heart.

"You should have never separated the children from the wagons," Dahteste said as she clicked her tongue and shook her head. "The Blackfeet will already have the children who knows where. They will have spies all over here too. Some will still be out there watching us now, but we are too many with guns. They will know who we are too. There are few secrets among the tribes in the Rocky Mountains. Indian gossip is rampant."

"How is it you speak English, and you're a Blackfoot too?" Betty asked.

Dahteste spat on a dead brave and said, "No, I am not Blackfoot. I'm a Crow war chief. My name is Dahteste. I am Levi Johnson's wife." She nodded at Beaver, who still sat on his horse like the rest of the men, surprised into silence. "Come on then. Let's see how many women are left alive. Then we have to bury the dead. The Blackfeet will have to be sent a message." She looked at Levi and then Rusty.

Her husband didn't know what she meant, but Rusty Steel did.

"Angus and I'll get to scalpin' the braves right now," Rusty said.

"What?" the captain demanded. "We can't do that! That will make us just as bad as them."

"That's bold talk from a man who lops off heads like they were clumps of grass," Joseph retorted.

"If we don't scalp 'em just like they'd scalp us, and have already done to some of these women, we won't send a strong message," Rusty said. "This way, they'll know they're messing with warriors, not normal settlers. They'll think twice before they follow and try to capture the few of you left."

In the end, only eight women survived, but all of them were so scared Joseph figured a few would never be the same as before the attack. At least they had been saved from the Blackfeet, who were known to be cruel masters.

"Them men you call your husbands seem to be slavers themselves from where I'm standing," Virgil Lovejoy said. "Trading flesh for cattle or horses is pretty much the same that happened to me until I was set free. I understand how ya feel, ma'am. But freedom is a funny thing." Lovejoy stared hard into Betty Crockett's eyes, so he was sure she understood. "It heals all wounds inside and out. Mark my word. From now on, you few left alive will have a better life where you can make your own choices like I hope to do myself."

"Why, freedom is why we live in the mountains," Angus said. "We make our own laws, and only the just and fair survive in our environment. Freedom is worth it all. It's what the world is about."

It took all day to bury the dead women and clean up the eight that survived. One petite lady was so far gone they had to gag and tie her in the back of a wagon, so she wouldn't run off alone and get caught.

"I reckon the women are gonna be grief stricken if we don't bury their leader separately, instead of throwin' 'im in the hole with the rest," Joseph said.

"Grief?" Angus asked and snickered. "Betty looks like we're buryin' her mother-in-law."

They knew the Blackfeet wouldn't be far away and would pick off any strays they could find. So, they put all eight women in one wagon. Rusty and Angus sat on the bench seat, Steel with the reins and McFarlin with a rifle primed and ready to fire in each hand.

The riders rode at six points around the wagon—to make a statement as much as for protection. Dahteste and Levi rode out front. Nobody among the group was as good as the Crow war chief at spotting her tribe's worst enemy, the Blackfeet. Joseph and Captain Forrester took up drag and shot looks over their shoulders every few moments as Virgil and Dennis rode the wagon's flanks.

Walker knew that it should be over, but things hadn't been working out like usual since his departure from Montana. For him, since they hit Casper and lost the men in the quicksand, things had had a life of their own. Still, they had seen no sign of Indians. He wondered if the yearly Rendezvous was such a good thing for the mountain men and especially the Indians. Maybe it was getting out of control, and more bad men would come each year, and there would be more killings.

At the end of the meet, men were always found dead. Most had drunk themselves to death, and others died in suspicious circumstances. They were hastily buried unless their friends or kin were close enough to contact.

BARTERING

When they arrived with the surviving women at the Rendezvous, it appeared that everybody there had already heard about what happened with the small wagon train and its occupants. So many people knew of Rusty Steel and his group that the gossip shot through the crowd as fast as the clicking down the wire of Samuel Morse's telegraph.

Of course, exaggerations were raging all over the meet. Although the mountain men always commented on and even criticized the rampant Indian gossip, that couldn't hold a candle to the frontiersmen's tales and lies. The number of women saved already was said to be a thousand.

When the wagon rolled into the mountain men's camp, the waiting mountain men were disappointed there were only eight women still alive. So, many men cursed the Blackfeet for their actions, and they swore revenge. Their reputations were enough to make the hostile tribe leave the area, and they vanished before five hundred mountaineers tracked them down and turned on them for denying them the chance to charm a new girlfriend or wife.

Despite the mountain men's grizzly appearance, when proper ladies arrived at the Rendezvous, most men treated them like royalty and were on their best behavior. More than one fancied heading back home into the mountains with a new wife, and many of them had the fortune to provide a good home and a happy future. Some even had pockets full of gold.

It would all depend on what the eight women wanted to do. Did they want to return to Kansas or even back to Trouble, Tennessee, or continue westward with Joseph and his charge of missionaries? Or maybe some of them had traveled far enough looking for the land of milk and honey and wanted to settle down and make a home right there.

Many mountain men took Indian wives, but others found the differences too great and preferred to live alone rather than with one of the tribes. Even though there were only eight women left, many men at the Rendezvous fancied an opportunity to offer them a fine home, land, and a husband that didn't misinterpret the Good Book and would take care of them and treat them kindly. Time would tell if any of these rugged men got lucky before the meet was over and the women were taken back somewhere safe, where civilized people lived and there was no threat of hostile Indians.

They walked into the meet and wheeled their horses behind Rusty Steel. He seemed to have a plan and to know where he was going. None of the others had any idea of what they were going to do with eight terrified women.

Scared or not, they were rugged to have made it this

far, especially since they were the ones doing all the work as they crossed the plains. The Squirrel men treated their women more like servants than proper wives. Most of the women had to share their husbands with other spouses too.

None of them liked this fact, but none of them dared complain, or they ended up stripped to the waist and given twenty lashes by their leader, Jack Amble Squirrel himself. All the women there bore scars on their backs due to punishment for one rebellious act or another, but none as many as the handsome Betty Crockett. She'd made frequent visits to the whipping post. The chunk of wood was so often used that the Squirrels uprooted it when they left Tennessee and took it with them everywhere they went. It bore the blood and sweat of many women and even a few men. It was part of their heritage—at least until now.

The wooden post had a dark significance, and Jack had used this threat successfully with most of the women. It was a wonder Betty was still alive. It was only her beauty that saved her from death. Unbeknownst to her now-dead husband, Jack had had designs on her too. He enjoyed it when he whipped her until her back was bloody. Each scar on her skin was his, like he had made his signature in leather. He had always expected that one day he would finally tame her, kill her husband, and take her for his fourth wife. He would make her sleep with him shirtless, so he could enjoy the view—not of her full breasts but of her crisscrossed back.

"Head for the fur trader that we've been barterin' with for the last two days," Rusty said as soon as they reached the meet. "I think now's the time to make that sale we've been puttin' off for so long. They're already watchin' our furs for us until we get back, so maybe we'll give in and sell to 'em for the favor and maybe a couple more. We could do worse."

They arrived at the Rocky Mountain Fur Trading Company and pulled the wagon to a grinding stop as dust fell from the wheels. Rusty Steel and Levi Johnson went in to talk, and the rest of the men stood guard all around the wagon. A wake of dust trailed their moccasins toward the trader. They all had their rifles cradled in their arms. A big black dog followed Rusty into the fur trading company's tent. It growled as it passed the guards at the entrance.

The women in the wagon looked scared again. Their eyes were spread wide in fear as their lips trembled. Some ducked low and peeked over the edge, and others hid behind the canvas cover. The only one that refused to cower was Betty Crockett. It was clear that she was one of a kind in this strange group of misfits. Her mature beauty hadn't been lost on Captain Forrester either. He spied on her out of the corner of his eye, though he hid his interest. When women were involved, he wasn't the bold officer he was while in battle. He was almost shy.

Suddenly, the women found themselves surrounded by hundreds of wild, hairy-looking men with rifles, knives, and pistols. Everyone seemed to be armed to the teeth. It looked like they were all ready for war. The women didn't know which ones looked more frightening, the mountain men or the Blackfeet Indians. But in minutes, they felt friendliness and saw they were more timid than frightening. They neared the women like they were almost scared and were tempted to dart off.

The women's initial thoughts couldn't be further from the truth. The men were even timid before women they didn't know and who were clearly more refined than them. Angus chuckled at how the younger frontiersmen spit on their hands as they slicked back their hair and smoothed down their beards, trying to look their best. He even smelled patchouli oil in the air. Angus cackled, and it echoed.

In minutes, over fifty admirers were standing in line with their hats in their hands, and one and all were grinning like possums. They all hoped for a moment to speak with one of the women. If that was all they got, they believed it was better than nothing. Maybe they would have the opportunity to hold a lady's hand. They weren't even picky and found them each desirable, despite their long, horse-like faces. That was the last thing the Squirrel family would leave behind—that, and all those green eyes.

The mountain men in charge of the Crow Indians' and the compound's pelts walked up to the bar, and the trader poured three drinks. They clicked glasses and tossed back the harsh liquor. Fred Country slammed his shot glass on the bar top.

"So, have ya made up your mind, Rusty? I reckon Levi will do whatever you say. Am I correct?"

"Yep, we're pretty much always in agreement, Fred," Rusty said. "And I thank ya kindly for watchin' our furs while we were out savin' those women. I'm afraid we could only save eight. Over seventy of 'em perished or were captured back there, not to mention the twenty scum we killed who called themselves their husbands." He sucked on his quid and spat a stream of brown juice into the tobacco-streaked sawdust at his feet.

"Well, I can't pay you two bucks a pound like you want," Fred said. "In today's market, it's way too much. You have to let me make a living too, pilgrim."

"But two bucks is the market price here in the Rockies," Rusty grumbled. "I won't take less. I know what the prices are. I was here when you were still back suckin' on your mama's teat, so don't take me for a fool. I ain't Angus McFarlin. I ain't a push-over."

"You know as well as I do that the prices at the Rendezvous are always a little lower than the market price," Fred pleaded.

"And the only reason that's so is because you talk these poor fools out of their furs for a kiss and a promise. You ain't just dealin' with anybody. You're dealin' with me."

"A pelt is a pelt, Rusty. It's worth what it's worth and no more," Fred replied.

"Yeah, but these are the best-cured furs at the whole danged meet, ain't they? You know as well as I do that nobody can beat Angus at curing furs. Especially beaver pelts. Two bucks a pound it is. You owe me two thousand two hundred dollars." Rusty proffered his hand.

"Dagnabit, Rusty, you know I have to make a profit too," Fred whined. "You're not leavin' me any room to wiggle."

"Make it an even two thousand, and I'll make up the difference with Chief Hachta," Levi said. "I'll hunt for 'im this winter or somethin'."

"You're spreadin' yourself pretty thin, ain't cha, Levi?" Rusty said. "Iffin ya take on too much work, you ain't gonna do anything right."

"Then it's a deal," Fred said as he spat in his palm and stuck it out to shake.

The mountain man grumbled for a moment, then looked at Levi's pleading eyes, spat in his palm, and shook.

"Oh, there's one more thing, Fred," Levi said, grinning like a mule. "When ya head to market, we need ya to take the women that don't wanna stay here or head on with Joseph back with ya."

"But that wasn't part of the deal," Fred said. "I watched your furs for ya. I had an armed guard on 'em the whole time you were gone. If it weren't for me, they'd have been stolen."

"After we killed the twenty thieves that already tried?" Rusty retorted with his feathers ruffled. "I doubt there be a man here that would dare to take our furs iffin we set 'em in the middle of the camp and walked away at night."

"We'll make it up to you next year, Fred," Levi said. "You know we're good for it. I have an extra mouth to feed nowadays."

"Speakin' of mouths to feed, I'm sorry about Pete, Bob, and Sam, boys." Fred frowned. "They were fine mountain men, they were. May their souls rest in peace. You boys have done enough to make the man upstairs happy for a spell. Just 'cause trouble comes a visitin' don't mean you've always got to offer it a place to sit down. Tumbleweeds are best left to themselves."

"Somebody had to stop that fake preacher," Levi spat. "He was as evil a man as I've ever laid eyes on."

"The best sermons are lived and not preached," Rusty said.

"For the moment, this is a law-abiding enough place without the Squirrels," Levi Johnson said.

"Yeah, I've been the law abiding this place almost

every day since the meet started," Fred laughed. "These mountain men may not be evil, but they get into more mischief than a bunch of youngins."

Fred reached under the bar and dragged out a heavy metal chest with a large padlock on the side. He fumbled with a ring of keys until he found one and opened the box. Levi's and Rusty's curious eyes tried to peek inside, but Fred was fussy and kept the contents hidden with the lid. Then he slammed it shut and clicked the lock back into place.

Shiny coins and a bag of gold nuggets exchanged hands as men with pistols stood guard. Levi opened his palm, and gold coins reflected sunlight, making his eyes look resplendent yellow. His lips parted and showed white teeth as dimples appeared just above his beard.

"We did it," Levi whispered. "After all that work, we really did it."

"It ain't done and over until we get out of the Rendezvous alive now that we're rich." Rusty cackled.

"Keep your voice down before everybody at the meet hears ya," Levi said as he looked toward the tent flap and the exit.

"After what we just did to the Squirrels, I doubt there be too many strappy thieves left that want to take on the likes of us." Rusty chuckled. "I was talkin' about gambling or losing money at the poker table.

"I've never seen ya gamble, Rusty," Johnson said.

"You've never seen us with so much money." Steel laughed.

Levi shot a questioning look at his mentor as he fingered his bear claw necklace.

THE RAFFLE

ONCE LEVI AND RUSTY MADE THE DEAL FOR ELEVEN hundred pounds of beaver pelts, they turned their attention to the remaining eight women and their own imminent departure back to the compound with three cabins and a tipi high in the Rocky Mountains.

Rusty Steel climbed the wagon wheel spokes, sat on the bench seat, pulled off his hat, and turned toward the ladies inside. Levi was so big that from the back, his head nearly touched the top of the canvas cover, and he was so wide he blocked out the light. He smiled and listened. All the women knew these two men were involved in their rescue, and they trusted them with their lives.

"Betty, I reckon we can start talkin' with you first as you be these fine ladies' leader," Rusty said. "I imagine you've been discussin' what ya wanna do next. We have but three choices, ladies, and I am afraid that all of them will take some brave women to face."

"And those choices are?" Betty asked with raised

eyebrow. She had a hypnotizing stare that kept a man's attention despite her apparent beauty.

"One is to sit out the meet and return with Fred Country and the Rocky Mountain Trading Company's furs. It'll be over in a few days and the men will be takin' the pelts they bought back to market. He'll be headin' for St. Louis. You've already done the trip before, so ya know exactly what to expect, but you'll be safe with the traders 'cause they'll have plenty of guards with 'em to make the cross safely."

"We've all made that trip, Mr. Steel," Betty said. "You did say there were three options, didn't you? I person-ally don't fancy covering ground I've already traveled. So, what are the other opportunities that await my poor friends and me?"

"The second choice is y'all can go up north with Kansas Sheriff Joseph Walker and travel with his missionaries on to Oregon City," Rusty said. "That's a thousand miles or so from here. Now, I can't say how that journey will go because I won't be with you on it, but I've known Joseph Walker for quite a spell, and he doesn't suffer fools or foolish treks. I reckon if Jedediah Smith, Marcus Whitman, and Robert Stuart made the trip when they discovered the South Pass, it must be worth the journey, and I'd feel safe in the hands of old Joe here."

Rusty sat quiet for a moment as he pondered how to propose the last choice. He wasn't sure the ladies were going to like it, but to him it was the obvious and most practical thing any of them could do. At least that was what Rusty Steel and Angus McFarlane believed. It remained to be seen if the women felt the same.

"Or, for those of you who are too tired to continue to

travel, we have selected a list of acceptable mountain men who would be happy to be one of y'all's husbands." Rusty grinned. "Oh, I know this may come as a shock to some of you, but if you consider the practical side of things, you may see my point. You won't have to travel nowhere but up the mountain to home, and you'll have a good provider and a solid home to live in. What more can a woman ask, especially in these conditions? I know it's a tough choice, but I've lived up there for decades, and the Rocky Mountains have been good to us."

The women before them cackled like a flock of hens. They acted like a fox had just snuck into the henhouse. All of them were surprised at the prospect, and some even seemed appalled at first, but after much discussion, they all came to an agreement. Finally, after an hour of chatter the ruffled feathers settled, the squawking stopped, and everybody calmed down.

"Seven of us will stay if we find a suitable man," Betty Crockett said. "Most of our former husbands didn't love us anyway, so for most, just being treated like a decent human being and not whipped at a post will be enough to make us happy. The love can come later if it's meant to be. Today, we must be practical, as you suggest. They don't want to travel any farther. The men must also have money to guarantee their future, so only the successful trappers, please. This was my idea, and they all agreed. I give you my word they will make excellent wives if not mistreated."

"If there's any mistreatin' to do around here, it'll be done by us and to the mountain men who marry 'em and not them poor women," Rusty growled. "Ain't that right, Levi? They've already been through enough, and the suitors have been warned."

"You betcha, boss," Levi Johnson replied. "Now, let's get those women into Fred's tent so we can get this sorted out. That'll stop everybody from gawking at 'em. Now, he'll have but the one woman to take back. Ain't that right, Betty?"

Betty Crockett used her fingers to flick her blond hair out of her face, showing her sparkling eyes. There was a vitality in there that wasn't present in the other women. She had naturally red, pouty lips that made her stand out among the others for her beauty. The rest of the women were no more than handsome with the long Squirrel faces, but Betty was a true beauty and aware of the fact.

"I'm the woman who chose not to stay," Betty said. "I will be going with Mr. Walker north to join the missionaries on the trail to Oregon. I heard the earth is so fertile there, crops grew on their own. That was my original destination, and I don't like to backtrack to where I have already come from."

"Excuse me, ma'am," Levi said. "But you wouldn't be kin to Davy Crockett, who died at the Alamo a few years back, would ya?"

"As a matter of fact, I am—or was. Poor Uncle Davy. He was quite the explorer and politician. My father had eight brothers and sisters. You can see for yourself that a successful and intelligent man can come from the wilderness, just like my uncle. Some of these men here will be important members of society one day too. Mark my words."

"Well, then, prepare yourselves for your new suitors, ladies." Rusty cackled. You could hear it for a mile.

A line of men ran out of the tent, onto the trail, and halfway out of the mountain men's campsite. Joseph and Virgil sat at a makeshift table, taking down names and giving out chits with numbers written on them. The men waiting wore their Sunday best. Some even sported white shirts, shoestring ties, and spit-shined boots rather than the customary moccasins. They wanted to present themselves as civilized as possible, hoping to be one of the seven chosen by the waiting ladies.

Outside, Rusty walked up and down the line of anxious frontiersmen, inspecting them for rejects. He squinted one eye as he looked the men up and down with a snarl. Dog followed him everywhere, and his canine growled every time he stopped. If Rusty grumbled and told them to scat, Dog snapped at their heals as they left. Apparently, there wasn't a man in line ready to talk back to the well-known mountain man and his massive black dog. He was famous for his intolerance of sass.

"Why, you ain't got a tooth in your head nor a pot to piss in," Rusty growled as he kicked one of the mountain men in the butt and sent him packing, with Dog on his heels. He came to a Frenchman, and Rusty asked, "Do you even speak English? Your problem is your brains have been picked like chickens in a barnyard. You should know better than to stand in this line."

The little Frenchie tried to reply, but Rusty pulled him out of the line by his ear, and his scream drowned out what he said. He, too, was sent packing for not speaking proper English as Steel went up and down the line and rejected one prospect after another. He would only offer the women the pick of the crop, as unruly as they appeared. He had been on the mountain long enough to have heard of half the men there. Any of them with the slightest stain on his reputation was dispatched forthwith.

The captain rode up and down the line to ensure no violent protests. But all the men at the Rendezvous had heard the stories. They knew he was the cavalryman who lopped off heads, and they didn't fancy trading theirs for a woman. Many men who knew they weren't up to the mark stood down of their own accord before they were scorned like the rest.

"Remember I said eligible bachelors only!" Rusty yelled. "Iffin ya got mud in your ears, you won't do. I don't want no illiterates either. Iffin ya can't read and write at least a hundred words and add and divide, you can move along right now. We don't ken to fools."

Seven women stood behind the long bar Fred Country had loaned to Rusty and his bunch of trappers and hunters. They timidly sipped on anisette in small crystal shot glasses. They were all nervous, but you could also see their resolve. They had gone as far as they were going to go, and now, they knew they had to pay attention as they selected their men and secured their futures. They had lost everything, many even their children, but so much life had been lost that these poor souls valued this opportunity.

Angus mixed the numbered chits in a hat and held it high while Forrester pulled out the numbers one at a time. Out of the fifty who wanted a wife, only twenty were chosen. It was factored in if they were too ugly, had lice, or hadn't bathed since last summer. Once the selection was complete, the captain, Virgil, and Joseph herded the large men in one by one. They were allowed to speak for a moment about their attributes and why one of the interested women should want to live with them.

Some of the burly men stood there, too surprised or intimidated to speak until prodded by Angus and Rusty. The finalists were good, but that didn't mean they had remarkable personalities or were terribly bright. They were looking for solid husbands and not inventors or scientists. All that was required was that they provide a home and a solid source of income and live in peace. It was all the Squirrel women had ever dreamed of. Now, a few of them had the opportunity to change their names and start anew. None of them wanted to retain the surname Squirrel.

Their cousins lay back in the circled wagons, buried in the ground. They were lucky to be alive, and any extra blessing was welcomed. Despite the pain, they all knew if they didn't make sound decisions, they would soon join their cousins, and they believed that the land of glory that Jack Amble had promised was a hollow dream based on theft and death—everything that was against what the Bible represented. They knew they had to not only change their lives but also had to make amends.

The women behind the bar listened and wrote down numbers and things they liked and disliked about the men on display. Some even chuckled at the way the men were nervous and shy. It made them all the more attractive after being treated like a herd of sheep living with other wives of the same man.

"It's funny how that worked out." Rusty said. "My-oh-my, it's a strange world, and it just seems to be gettin' stranger every day."

"I'd have never believed the whole story had somebody told me," Levi replied. "I can see the women not wanting to carry on, though. This is as good a spot as any to pick to live. I love it here and plan to have children in our compound one day. What better place to raise children? That's how I was raised, and I didn't turn out so bad."

Angus and Rusty both cackled in delight.

"Does that mean we're gonna be uncles?" Angus snorted. "Soon, we'll have a bunch of rug rats runnin' around the compound. Who would have ever thought?"

Once the selection was made and the lucky winners were informed, the weddings were held right there in the Rocky Mountain Fur Trading Company tent. Since there was no preacher present at the meet, the captain had to do the honors. The grooms nervously waited as the brides smiled, and all breathed a sigh of relief. Maybe they had a chance to live a normal, everyday life after all.

"But I've never married anybody before," Captain Forrester fretted. "Come on, Levi. You've got to get me out of this."

"I'll help ya with the Bible verses." Virgil chuckled. Seeing the captain out of sorts was so rare, his new friend couldn't help but poke fun.

"You're the only captain we have," Levi replied. "We've got no choice. I can't do the hitching. It wouldn't be legal."

"But I'm not a ship's captain," Will grumbled. "They're the ones who marry couples when a pastor isn't available, not an Army captain."

"Rusty used to be a ship's captain on the Missouri River, weren't cha, pard?" Angus said. "That'll make the marriages legal and all. The sheriff can certify the act and write it down on paper for the register. That'll give the new wives all the rights they deserve. That's about as good as we can do, Miss Crockett."

Rusty wiggled his eyebrows and gave Betty a mischievous wink. There was a strange look in his eyes.

As soon as he'd heard the pretty woman was kin to Davy Crockett and was single again, Mr. Steel had turned on the charm. Until then, she was just another one of the damaged ladies. Sure, she was a looker, and the rest were more homely, and one was downright ugly, but the mountain men weren't the most handsome specimens in the West either. Everybody had to take what was most practical and suited them the best.

"I appreciate the attention, Rusty." Betty giggled. "But I have other plans. I just got out of one marriage and don't intend to jump into another. I still feel like I have some of this vast country I want to see yet. I'll have to pass on the handsome offer, but I think I'll head to Oregon and take my chances there. Some lucky woman will come along for such a fine man like you despite you being a few years my elder. With such a handsome man, that shouldn't be a problem."

"Shucks, ma'am," Rusty whispered.

She kissed him on the cheek, and his face blushed like a red rose. "It'll be a lucky woman who makes such a fine catch. Why didn't you offer your hand to one of the other girls? I'm sure one of them would have jumped at the chance. Especially since you saved us all."

"I only fancied you, ma'am," Rusty said as he looked at the toe of his moccasin and dug a little hole in the dirt. "I appreciate the compliment just the same."

The seven weddings were held in unison. A few quotes from the Bible were read as Virgil added his two cents to the ceremony. He wanted to make it a sermon, but Angus cut him short at ten minutes.

"These men are dying to get home with their new wives, and you want to huff and puff and blow the house down all day long." Angus snickered. "Close your Bible and let the folks get on with their lives."

Finally, riverboat Captain Rusty Steel said, "Now, y'all may kiss the brides."

It was as strange as it was magical. To be in such a rugged and dangerous place having something so normal happen as a wedding. Seven mountain men went home happy that night. The following day, all the new grooms headed out for the higher part of the Rocky Mountains, eager to get started on their surprise new future with their surprise new wives.

Everybody spent the next day talking about how they barely missed snatching one of the lovely brides. Nobody talked about anything else. It was one of the strangest things to ever happen at the Rendezvous, which had its yearly oddities. All in all, it worked out well in the end and made a few of the attendees happy as a pig in a wallow.

SIDEKICKS

"NOW THAT WE'VE GOT ALL THE BEAVER FUR BUSINESS and the stranded ladies out of the way, how about we celebrate?" Rusty said. "We've sold our pelts for top dollar and don't have a thing to do until we head back home. That is, exceptin' Polecat Jack's sharpshootin' contest."

"I fancy a two-pound steak." Levi grinned as he rubbed his belly. "And a pound of mashed potatoes with a dozen ears of corn." At two hundred and twenty pounds, he could eat a bear.

"So, what's new about that?" Dahteste asked, snickering. "You eat as much as a grizzly before hibernation."

They all headed to the only so-called fancy restaurant at the Rendezvous. The fancy part was because they had more than one thing on the menu, and not buffalo meat or tongue. They had all eaten enough buffalo to last a lifetime. Here, they changed from hard liquor to some supposedly European wine. The bottles even had labels and sold for a dollar apiece, but today they intended to splurge.

"Have you ever had wine, Levi?" Will Forrester asked. "I doubt you'd like it. They say it's an acquired taste."

"What's an acquired taste supposed to mean?" Johnson asked.

Dahteste looked at the captain, as puzzled as Levi.

"It means you probably won't like it the first time you taste it, but it'll get you drunk just the same," Forrester laughed. He looked at the label. "Here, it says it's from Istanbul. I've never heard of wine from Turkey, but I reckon anybody can grow grapes."

"I don't particularly like the taste of whiskey, either, but I like how it makes me feel all fuzzy inside," Levi grinned. "I have yet to drink liquor I like, besides my first cold beer back in Kansas City. Now, that was something worth tryin'."

"Too bad you boys didn't know me when you passed through Missouri. I work on the border with Kansas. With me being sheriff and all, I could have steered ya to all the right places," Joseph said. "There, we have real restaurants, though they'll cost ya an arm and a leg."

When the waiter came, there wasn't anything fancy about it. Somebody had scribbled the short menu down on a piece of parchment with a two-bit pencil, and it was carried from table to table. They offered elk steak, wild boar, rabbit, and quail. They also served mashed potatoes, boiled corn, sliced carrots, and green beans. For dessert, they had apple and cherry pie.

"Well, well," Levi said. "Now we're gonna feed my fancy with some cherry pie."

"Why don't cha put some of everything on the table, and we'll go to eatin' until we're full." Rusty laughed.

"Bring a few bottles of that dollar wine too. When I cele-brate, I don't hold back."

"And I want a whole cherry pie, just for me." Levi Beaver Johnson grinned.

"Would you also like a coffee with your dessert after the meal, mister?" the waiter asked Johnson.

"No, sir. I want the pie right now, and then I'll eat my meal." Levi grinned. "You said we were gonna have a party, didn't cha? Then I'll have my dessert first, and I reckon a whole pie will do it."

When the food arrived, two bowls of steaming gravy sat in the middle. For dessert, the rest had big slices of apple pie.

Not a word was said for over half an hour as every-body ate until they were so full they had to loosen their britches. A few stifled burps slipped by, but they were mountain men, after all. Once done, not a scrap of food was left on the table, and ten dollars' worth of wine bottles sat empty. Everybody pulled out ceramic or corn cob pipes and stuffed them with tobacco twists. Rusty cut a fresh plug from the twist and stuffed it in his cheek.

Matches sparked to life with the smell of sulfur as they puffed smoky bowls to life. Clouds of blue smoke floated before their faces. Angus blew smoke rings while Rusty Steel patted Dog's head under the table. The massive canine's wagging tail hit the floor like a hammer.

"Have any of you fellas ever thought about going out exploring for new trails?" Joseph asked. "Sure, I know you've all climbed the Rockies and lived the life of a mountain man, but have ya thought about what's beyond that? This ain't the end of the wilderness, you know. Not by a long shot."

"I wandered off to see new country just last winter," Rusty said. "I didn't come back until spring. The captain took a similar trip, but that one didn't pan out as well as mine. In the mountains, you just never know how it's gonna go. I found my dog on my last journey into the wilderness, and I saw places I'd never seen."

"The fact is, I really need four good trackers who can shoot as good as me or better," Joseph said, dead serious. "You all know why I came down to the Rendezvous. Sure, I like visitin' my old pards, but I have a bunch of folks in my charge. And they're as green as fresh-cut pine. I'd be mighty obliged iffin you younger folks would consider riding along. I can't make the rest of the journey without good help, or I'll be walkin' these folks to their graves. You'll all be home again before you know it, and I'll give ya fifty bucks each. Now, I know y'all just got rich with sellin' all of them pelts, but a man can always use an extra fifty dollars, can't he?"

"Why, I don't know, Joseph. I can't leave my wife," Levi said.

"I'll pay Dahteste just the same as the men," Joseph said, laughing. "From what I've seen and heard, she's probably worth more than all of ya anyway."

"W-well, maybe if Rusty thinks it's all right," Levi stuttered. "W-w-hat cha say, boss?" He looked at his mentor with big puppy eyes.

"Don't look at me like some moonstruck pup," Rusty growled. "Go on and go with the old fool iffin ya want. I'll get what's ours back home with Angus. We can sneak through the woods and make our way unseen if we go on foot. If needed, we can pay somebody to help

Mountain Dennis bring the horses and mules up. Nobody knows these mountains and woods like Angus and me. Not even the Indians will know we're there."

"You'll pay me the same as them?" Virgil asked.

"And why not, amigo?" Joseph asked. "There ain't no slavery out here, friend. We've left what's loosely called civilization hundreds of miles ago. It's just us humans and wild animals out here now. You've shown your worth, so you'll be respected as such."

"Well, I'll be," Virgil said. "First, I'm a deputy sheriff, and now I'm a scout on a wagon train. I wonder what's gonna happen next. I've even got money in my pocket that I don't know what to do with. Of course, a man can always use another fifty bucks. I know I can."

"Be careful what cha wish for," Angus said. "Ya just might get it in spades."

"It ain't gonna be no piece of cake taking them missionaries from the South Pass all the way to Oregon City," Rusty warned. "I doubt there even be much of a trail. I know them fellas, Louis and Clark, discovered the way looking for something that didn't exist—the Southwest Passage. I think it's been done a few times since, though."

"Why, I've all but done most of it while workin' for the government searching for trails to California. I ain't found a way easy enough for wagons yet, but I assure you I will. Now that the government knows how to get to Oregon, they wanna be able to head farther south. If that land grant goes through, everybody and their mother will want six hundred and forty acres. Even single men without a family get three hundred and twenty, and all they have to do is live on it for two years. Now, that's a deal if I ever heard one. I might take 'em up on it myself if I ain't too busy shiftin' folks back and forth.

"Yep, that's what I've heard, although it's not official yet. When it hits the newspapers, you just watch what happens. Folks will be movin' across America like poop through a goose—lickety-split," Joseph said. "Yes, sir, I've got a feelin' these missionaries I'm takin' now will be just the beginning. There'll be half of Europe on our doorstep in twelve months. And who are they gonna need to take 'em across all that wilderness? Yours truly, that's who."

It was evident that Joseph R. Walker fancied himself as quite the businessman. It was unusual for a man to be skilled at both city life and that of a mountain man, but Joseph was one of the few who were.

"You've got it all figured out, don't ya now?" Rusty growled. "And all them people are gonna come across here and ruin it for all of us livin' in the mountains."

"I wouldn't worry too much." Joseph chuckled. "I reckon a good part of 'em will die on the way. Maybe one in ten, even. It's about as hard a cross as I know, especially the part I call the Great American Desert. Now, iffin you young folks ain't up to it, just let me know, and I'll understand. It ain't the kind of work for every-body. Anyway, the closest the trail will come to your compound is some hundred miles north of here. That, then there's the trek into the mountains. You boys will be long dead and gone before settlers come this far, if ever. Everybody ain't cut out to live in the Rocky Moun-tains. Most European folks won't want to live with grizzly bears and wild Indians."

"Now, it sounds kind of risky," Virgil said. "At first, it

sounded like a journey to some promised land, then ya went and spoiled it with deserts and wild Indians."

"That's why I'm payin' so much, friend. I was only paid three hundred dollars to make the whole trip, and now I've got to pay you four two hundred of that. I'll be lucky if I end up with ninety bucks out of the whole shebang, but I'm lookin' at the future. Just think what a man could charge to take fifty wagons all that way—or two hundred for that matter. I'm tired of standin' in cold rivers and shootin' dumb animals. I figured it was time to leave the sheriff's job for a spell and set out on a new adventure."

"A new adventure..." Levi repeated, like the words held some deep magic secret. "When ya say it like that, it sort of sounds excitin'—even mysterious. Whatcha think, darlin'?"

"I think you have already decided that you are going to go." Dahteste laughed. "You know I won't tell you what to do or not to do, just like you don't tell me. But who will look after my husband if I stay behind in the Crow camp? It would be too easy for you to get into trouble without me to watch over you. I know you are a mountain man, but you're still White, and that's not such a good thing in the wilderness. You can't blend in like an Indian."

Dahteste laughed, and it was contagious. Some laughed from nervous energy, like Forrester and Levi, and others at the folly their friends were just about to embark on. Still, it felt good to laugh after losing three of their best friends. In the wilderness, life went on despite who you lost. If you didn't stay focused, you could lose your own life in the snap of your fingers.

Everybody at the table roared. The wine helped.

Dahteste had proven herself as a warrior and was also quite witty. They all knew Levi had a handful on his hands, but they seemed to be made for each other despite their differences and their different ways of life. Now, they, too, would embark on a new adventure. Angus and Rusty knew this would be hard, but that made it more interesting. They knew it could make or break a man or even a Crow woman. Time would tell when they returned and told their story. It was obvious that they would go. If Rusty and Angus were twenty years younger, they would go too.

"So, are ya gonna come along too, Will?" Levi asked.

"Don't sit on the fence thinkin' about it for too long, because I plan to leave the day after Polecat Jack's long-gun contest." Walker smiled. "Of course, I wouldn't miss that shootin' match for the world. But besides seein' my friends, the Rendezvous has gotten too big for me nowadays. It's a far sight from what it was ten years ago."

SPARKS FLY

"COME ON THEN," LEVI SAID. "WE'RE BURNIN' DAYLIGHT. The early bird catches the worm. We ain't gettin' nowhere sittin' around here on our laurels. We've only got today to explore, and I've got a special treat in store for ya. Tomorrow, we'll be long gone and so will the boys, so make it snappy."

"What bird? Worms? You mean snakes?" Dahteste looked at her husband, puzzled. He had a canvas bag strapped around his neck. She could smell fried chicken. He had a cane pole in his hand and a bundle of string. Two water skins hung from his neck.

"What do you want?" Dahteste asked. "Can I have a piece of chicken? It smells good."

"Not yet, ya can't. We're goin' on a picnic," Levi said. "This is about as American as apple pie, girl."

"Apple pie? A pick-nick? Girl? I'm not a girl," she said slowly. She still didn't understand.

"No, a picnic with food and somethin' fresh to drink. I've got a little keg of cooled tea too. We can leave it in the river for a spell to chill. That's what all couples do back where I'm from in Indiana. They go for a ride into the country and have a meal and go fishin' with their best girls."

"Darling? Indiana—are those Indians?" Dahteste blinked her big brown eyes and asked, "Did you have a woman back where you come from, Levi Johnson?"

"No," Beaver replied, smiling. "I reckon I was too young, and there weren't many women about when I was growin' up. We lived in the forest, but there weren't no mountains, only rivers. That's where I learned to trap and hunt. You're the first woman I've ever known well or been with. If the truth be known, even when we met, I wasn't lookin' for a wife. I was far too busy tryin' to figure out where I was goin'. I reckon gettin' married was the farthest thing from my mind. It certainly did put my direction right." He laughed.

"You are my first...boyfriend. Is that the right word?"

"No, I'm more than a boyfriend." Beaver grinned from ear to ear. "I'm your husband. That's a whole lot better than bein' your friend. There's a lot of huggin' and a kissin' that comes with being married."

Levi laughed, but his wife still looked a little confused. She was slowly getting used to living with a White man, but he still did unexpected things. However, she trusted her husband and knew he only had her best interest in mind.

"Come on. I've rented a buggy. We can head for a narrow stretch in the river. I saw a place where the river bends and a big old oak stands at the water's edge. That'll give us plenty of shade. I've got a blanket in the back. It's been a long time since I've been on a picnic. Way back when my ma and pa took me. It's a family thing, too. At least it was back on the Ohio River."

Ten minutes later, they were bouncing down a trail on a buckboard wagon. Levi had laid the food in the bed behind them, and he held the reins, with his rifle across his lap. Dahteste was snuggled up against him with her arms wrapped around his muscle-packed arm to avoid being thrown off the hard bench seat. Dust curled behind the wheels as they headed for the river and solitude.

At the Rendezvous, it didn't matter where you went, there were people everywhere. After being accustomed to living in the compound where they wouldn't see a strange face during the winter months, it was a shock to be around so many people. At the fur trading meet, they were nearly overwhelmed by the nearness of so many other humans.

Finally, there was nothing around them but green mountains in the distance. The prairie was covered in flowers in a multitude of colors. There wasn't a cloud in the endless sky or a single sound other than the rumbling of the wagon's wheels.

When they pulled the horses to a stop under the shade of the oak tree, a choir of peeper frogs that sang from the river's bank suddenly stopped with the intrusion. When they pulled up, Dahteste found herself squeezing Levi with both her arms and her head pressed tight against his broad shoulder. Johnson dwarfed his Indian wife, but her spirit was so big you only occasionally noticed the difference. She smiled the best smile he had seen all day.

They had the blanket out in minutes, but they left the food for later. Right now, they lay in each other's arms and felt the wonder of being in love. It was like their feelings and emotions had a life of their own, leaving them with balls of nervous energy in their stomachs, slightly dry mouths, and a little breathless.

"Levi?" Dahteste said.

"Uh huh?" Levi brushed his hand on his wife's cheek as he stared into her eyes.

Her voice caught with emotion. "Show me how White men kiss their women," Dahteste whispered, like it was taboo or a well-kept secret. At the same time, he could see mischief in her eyes.

She smirked at herself as her heartbeat nervously ticked, and her pulse raced. Beads of sweat popped up on her brow as she raised an eyebrow in question. Their eyes met in a lingering second of anticipation.

"Like I said, I ain't no expert, but I'll give it a try. C'mere...I really need a good kiss anyway." Levi smiled, and it reached his eyes. His heart hammered in his chest, and his palms became sweaty.

When he hugged Dahteste, her arms nestled around his waist as her eyes pooled and twinkled like little stars. He opened his mouth, and his tongue explored hers. She was startled at first, but then she realized she liked it. Electrical currents of emotion and desire raced through their bodies. Waves of heat came over them like molten lava as strangled whimpers could be heard from deep inside Dahteste. The sun of a new life began to dawn inside them as a fire burned.

The kiss seemed to last forever. When it did end, Levi whispered, "Promise me you'll never stop kissing me like that. I never thought a kiss could be so good. By golly, I think we need another one."

Levi kissed her again. It was another kiss that lingered. He just couldn't help himself. He held her close so she could feel his excitement, and he felt her heart patter in her chest too. Johnson's smile looked like it was a mile wide. Dahteste caught Levi staring at her and returned his rosy grin.

The Crow woman giggled and then slapped her hand to her mouth to stop, but her eyes still laughed. They didn't say anything for the longest time.

"Do you have any regrets marryin' a White man?" Levi finally asked after a long comfortable silence. He bit into a chicken leg and took a sip of tea.

She pushed her lips together and shrugged. She gave him a held-back smile. Her beautiful big brown eyes twinkled, divulging her true feelings.

"No. At least most of the time. Sometimes I am surprised by White men's customs. Why is it that Virgil Lovejoy is brown, the captain is white, and they are friends? Most Indians don't like White men, and we rarely see black men, so we are..." She searched for the words.

"Ignorant to others' customs?" Levi smiled. "Ya see, some folks can't see nothin' but the difference in their color of skin or how they dress or smell. Then there are others, like the captain, that don't see a man's color. All he sees is his soul. I reckon that's a fine quality in an Army officer. They have all kinds of men in the ranks and treat them according to how they behave, how brave they are, and how much they deserve that respect."

"We, too, have such beliefs. But the Crow Indians hate the Blackfeet, most White men, and many other Indian tribes in the mountains and the plains. We don't like much of anybody but our own people. Sometimes, we made peace with the Flatheads on the Great Plains, but that always ended up in bloodshed too. For us, disliking people of another color or language is normal, especially if we don't like how they smell." She broke the serious note and laughed. "We also trade with the Nez Percé, Kutenai, Shoshone, and Kiowa. But we only tolerate each other. When buffalo hunting season comes, we are all enemies again, fighting for the first herds." She smiled. "Don't you find that *in-te-rest-ing*? Is that right?"

"Soon, you'll be speakin' English better than me." Levi laughed. He was as happy as he could ever remember. "Come on and help me fill these skins with water. Then, I'm gonna show ya how folks from back east fish."

Levi Beaver Johnson made a big fuss stringing a line on his cane pole while Dahteste searched for a pronged branch. By the time her husband had found a worm and tossed the fishhook into the water, his wife was wading ankle deep, searching the surface for small wakes of fish under the murky water. In no time, Dahteste had speared a fish and tossed it onto the bank. It flip-flopped as its mouth opened and closed. She turned her eyes again to the river.

An hour later, Levi was nodding off with his fishing line slack. His nightcrawler had disappeared from the hook. While he sat on the steep bank, Dahteste was running a thick string through the gills of a half dozen fish to take back to the camp.

They napped in the shade of the great tree as the water rippled over rocks. Levi lay on his side, and Dahteste spooned into his body, grabbed his hand, and wrapped it in hers under her chin. She was like a little stuffed toy in his arms. The peeper frogs resumed their choir, and dragonflies floated on air just over the bubbly surface. In the shallows, tadpoles with tiny legs scampered across the bottom. Woodpeckers hammered on the tree above them as finches laughed among the leaves.

In the far distance, gunshots could be heard. The Rendezvous was nearly over, and everything was beginning to wind down. Even there, by the river, they couldn't escape all the noise. It because louder as darkness approached.

When Johnson stretched and sat up, he saw lightning bugs flashing off and on far in the distance.

"Come on, darlin'," Levi said. "We've slept longer than we should have. It's best if we get back before dark, with so many shady characters runnin' around the Rendezvous."

On the way back, they felt sleepy after a long day of doing nothing. The nervous tension had finally worn off and left them tired but content. Fish on a string splashed in a wooden bucket in the wagon's bed as spoked wheels bounced down the trail. Dust corkscrewed behind the wagon as the sun crawled toward the end of the world, turning the sky into a prism of colors. Crickets began to chirp, but soon they would be back in the safety of the Rendezvous. In the wilderness, there was safety in numbers.

POLECAT JACK

POLECAT JACK RAN THE SHOOTING MATCH LIKE THE previous years' competitions. It was one of the last events during the Rendezvous due to its popularity. The bidding could go sky high during some of the shootouts. Rusty Steel and Levi Johnson had a grudge match, waiting to see who was the best shot after a year in the mountains. The line of men for the shooting competition was matched only by the men hoping to get married.

Sharpshooters from all over the mountains came to the Rendezvous, and a few traveled five hundred miles from the nearest civilization. It was renowned across the wilderness and as far east as the Missouri River. This year, three men had come all the way from Kansas City. They stood out in the crowd of the locals. They wore fancy boots with sharp spurs, and expensive pistols stuck from their belts. Their rifles were from Europe and said to be of the best quality. But the boys back in the compound trusted their Tennessee long guns above all the rest for reliability and accuracy, both imperative for survival in the mountains.

Joseph stood in line behind Angus with Rusty behind him. Levi and the captain held back to scout the competition. They weren't in a hurry anyway. Everybody there was going to get their chance. Johnson liked to wait for the best of the best and not waste black powder and lead. When the three fancy-dressed men came to the line, they walked to the head and tried to push one of the locals aside. The stranger laid his hand on his pistol when the mountain man protested.

To the city slicker's surprise, they suddenly found every man around them with a rifle in their hands, aiming at their heads. They had picked the wrong bunch to try to bully.

"Get in line like the rest or get your tails out of here," Polecat Jack growled. "We don't cotton to bullies, do we, boys?"

"Are you dumb and stupid, or ya just bein' ornery?" Rusty asked, then he spat. "Now get around back down that line and mind your manners; you might just be treated with respect."

"Be careful, Rusty," Angus said. "They look like the kind that'll sneak up on ya when you're asleep."

"These fools make so much noise they sound like bulls usin' snowshoes wearing cowbells," Rusty snickered.

The city slicker felt the blood rush to his face as his anger boiled just under the surface.

"Be careful what cha do next, mister," Angus said with a nudge and a wink. "That old fella is harder than a sixteen-penny nail."

"Well," the city slicker snarled. "What's it gonna be, big mouth? Lead or money? Just you and me, old man."

When the blow came, it was totally unexpected. The Kansas City dandy was looking at Rusty snarl, not at the massive man behind him. He saw the slightest trace of the fist from the corner of his eye, but it was too late for him to move. When the fist hit, his face seemed to deform with the impact of the massive paw. Broken bones sounded like twigs breaking, and teeth flew out of his mouth like white bullets. He did the crazy walk for a few steps, struggling to stay on his feet. On his fourth attempted step, his legs buckled under him, and he went down like a tub of lard. Levi stood over him, opening and clenching his fist.

"Ain't nobody gonna call my friend an old man but one of us," Johnson said.

The unconscious man lay with his head up against a barrel. Spittle ran from his mouth and down his chin, finally dropping onto his shirt. The wet spot grew and grew.

"Now I'm gonna finish this," Levi said as he grabbed the man's greasy hair in his fist and drew back to give him a mortal blow.

"Hold on just a dad-gummed minute now!" Angus shouted. "What's the matter with you? You can't kill a man for smellin' bad and callin' my pard old. That should be Rusty's job."

"Now just stop, son; that should be enough," Kansas Sheriff Walker said. "I can't let ya kill 'im right in front of me, Levi."

Levi only listened to what Dahteste said. The rest was all clutter. "Stop!" she yelled in the Crow language.

"He's too filthy to dirty your hands on, husband. Let him go. If Rusty wants to kill him, let him do it."

Johnson blinked his eyes, coming out of the violent trance. The bloodshed from the day before still made the younger men nervous and quick to anger. Lucky for the city slicker, Dahteste was there to save his life. The captain stood right behind his friend with his hand on his saber. The next man to make a move would lose a limb.

"I-I-I don't know what got into me," Levi said, seemingly surprised at his own actions. "It's just that I've been nervous as a dog with no legs and a dozen ticks on its neck. Maybe all this Rendezvous stuff is gettin' to me. I'm not used to bein' around this many people."

As the match proceeded, the local marksmen continued to dwindle down to the few best shots. As their numbers were reduced by losses, opponents shot two at a time; the one who missed first or was farthest from the bullseye was eliminated. Polecat Jack was sharp as a tack, and he and his bookies kept track of every bet that went down. Even the ones the house didn't bid on had to pay a percentage to Jack even to play, but nobody complained. It was the best event of the year and was always well organized.

Levi was paired up with one of the three city slickers when they came to the last shooters. The one he hit had yet to wake up, and when he did, he was going to be in a world of pain with all those broken bones in his face. Johnson could see the man's friend wanted to beat him so bad he could taste it. His intentions were revenge for what he had done to his friend. But Beaver wasn't the kind of man who baited easily. He turned the tables and began to bait him.

"That sure is a fancy rifle you've got there, mister," Levi said as he eyed the stranger's weapon. "I bet that's one of them Belgium guns I've heard so much about."

"No, it's not," he retorted. "It's English. They make the best guns by far, in my opinion. Anyone that speaks French has more hot air than skills."

"But who makes the best shooters?" Levi laughed. "The big city or the Rocky Mountains?"

"Why don't you make a decent bet and find out," Mr. City Clicker said with a sly smile. He was the Kansas champ and was sure a bunch of hillbilly mountain men were not up to his standard of shooting or weapon.

"All right, I'll betcha rifles," Levi said. "Or maybe you ain't all that sure of your rifle or your shootin' skills."

"What do you mean you'll bet me rifles? You mean that chunk of steel and wood you have in your hand against an expensive weapon like mine? Don't be ridiculous."

"So, which is it? Ain't ya sure of your gun, or is it your skills you're worried about? It's gotta be one of the two. There's something there makin' you too scared to make a bet. Why, iffin you're so danged positive you can outshoot a hillbilly like me, I don't see why you don't teach me a lesson."

"You are a sassy sort at times, Levi." Rusty laughed. "It would be mighty nice if somebody taught him a lesson and chopped that mouth of his down to size. It's far too big. Maybe you can do an aging fella a favor, mister."

Angus cackled as Steel grinned from ear to ear.

"All right, then," the second city slicker said. "Gun for gun it is."

"Well then, by all means, be my guest and have the

first shot." Johnson chuckled. He winked at his friend Forrester.

The first rounds went well for the man from Kansas, but on the eighth shot, he missed the bullseye. Levi looked at the angry man and winked. He took the shot, and it was perfect—dead center.

"Whoops." Levi laughed, shrugging. "I must have gotten lucky. I can't ever remember shootin' so well. I sure am gonna have me a good time with that fancy English gun. Then again, maybe I'll just sell it back to its old owner. How much ya wanna pay me for your gun?" Levi laughed so hard his belly hurt.

"What do you mean, pay for my gun?"

"That's just the point." Levi smiled. "It ain't your gun no more, no more; it ain't your gun no more."

At last, came the final two shooters. This was the match that all the men had been waiting for. Of course, it was between Levi Johnson and Rusty Steel. The crowd went nuts, as they shouted out higher and higher bids. The bookies had their fists full of money as they yelled back and forth while frantically writing down numbers. People tried to reach over the barrier to encourage the shooters and pat them on the back. Whistles and catcalls rang out until the shooters were finally ready, then the crowd fell silent. You could hear a dime drop, it was so quiet. Nobody wanted to spook their favorite shooter. All their eyes were glued to Beaver.

A rifle hammer fell, the cap sparked, the gun fired, and a lead slug flew out of the barrel, followed by a flame and a puff of smoke. The crowd's heads swiveled their eyes to the target.

"Bull's eye!" roared the counter. "Levi Johnson, twenty-two bull's eyes in a row!"

The pressure was on for Rusty, but still, he didn't show it. Both men were trying to unnerve the other. They both knew that was the only way one of them could win. If they kept their cool, they never missed a shot. They were both proving to be such expert shots that it was hard to tell who the better marksman was. Several times, they put lead slugs in a bullet hole previously made in another round. This just confused the bidding crowd and forced the counter to be extremely careful since so much money was on the table. At the moment, the odds were even as they continued to plug away.

Nobody was in a hurry since this was the last round of shooters. Still, it continued to linger on when they reached thirty, and neither one had made the slightest mistake. The match looked like it could go on all day. They passed forty shots each, and still no winner. The day began to tire, but not the riflemen. They were focused and had nothing else on their minds but the little round dot in the middle of the paper target.

When they reached sixty shots each, they took a break. Hot gun barrels were cooled with fresh water as sweat dripped from the shooters' noses and chins. They laid their guns down and were offered drinks of whiskey, wine, and elixirs, but all they wanted was water. Both men were becoming dehydrated. They say when a man begins to dehydrate, he instantly loses fifteen percent of his concentration and focus. Both the shooters were aware of this fact and knew that whiskey would only make them too comfortable and lose more focus, so they drank their fill from their goatskins and rested for ten minutes before continuing.

"You can give up at any time." Rusty snickered. "You

know I'm gonna beat ya in the end. I have more mental stamina than you do, you young whippersnapper. Age counts for somethin', ya know."

Levi ignored his mentor and sent another round into the bullseye, then turned his eyes to his friend. "How do ya like them chickens?" Levi laughed. "Sixty-one bull's eyes in a row. Come on then, match me, and let's keep it movin', or it's gonna get dark before it's over."

Levi waited for Rusty Steel to shoot.

"I can't even see the target anymore," Rusty spat as he squinted to see in the fading light.

He fired, and the counter yelled, "Bull's eye for Mr. Steel!"

"What do we do now, Jack?" Rusty asked as lightning bugs began to appear scattered across the night. "It's too dark to shoot, and Levi's leavin' in the morning with Joseph Walker. He's taking his wife, the captain, and Virgil, so what don't get done today ain't gonna get done."

"In that case, we'll have to call it a draw. I won't let one man claim what the other ain't earned," Polecat Jack said. "For this year, Rusty Steel remains the leader but has to share the spot with Levi Beaver Johnson. And that's the final word."

Many of the men booed even though they could hardly see in the dark. Fires lit up across the Rendezvous as black smoke snaked into the sky. A couple of fistfights broke out over some unpaid bets, but the debtors were soundly thrashed, and the money taken from them. In the mountains, there was no sheriff or marshal to solve your problem, so the locals took care of things themselves. Still, there was a code of honor prevalent throughout the mountains, although there were always exceptions. There were always a few rotten apples in the basket to pass the rot on to others.

THE MEET ENDS

MULES, HORSES, AND EVEN OXEN CRAWLED DOWN THE trail like a long snake. All the animals of burden were carrying men, women, and cargo. The wagons were loaded down with thousands of pounds of beaver pelts. The fur trading companies left the empty whiskey barrels for the remaining men who were to return to the mountains. They didn't have room for anything but the valuable furs.

Dozens of vultures circled in the sky, waiting for the people to leave so they could pick bones clean near the cooking stations. The odd dead body lay in bushes or beside the river. After every Rendezvous, there were a few dead. Some from excess whiskey and others from foul play. Still, each year the trappers and hunters returned. It was the biggest people magnet in the territories and was in newspapers around the world.

Men and women, Black, White, and Red, rummaged through what the businessmen, mountain men and fur traders left. Items lay scattered over a few acres of what was the Rendezvous the day before. Nothing would remain the following day. Everything found would be used for one thing or another. Even though many things were discarded and abandoned, nothing was wasted in the end.

This year, the fur trading companies had made a bonanza. There was also a record turnout for the Rendezvous. It had grown and grown for twenty-five years. This, in turn, meant the trappers did exceedingly well too. Now, the buyers couldn't get their pelts to market fast enough. Nobody ever imagined the market would soon come crashing down and the beaver hides would be reduced to a fraction of their current worth. The demand had already exceeded the supply to such a degree the beaver would soon come close to extinction anyway. Either way, the future market for beaver skins was doomed.

When the balance of nature was affected, changes came down like stacked dominos and, in the end, affected every living creature struggling to survive in the wilderness. Little did they know they had just experienced the last real mountain man meet in the Rocky Mountains ever. With the drop in prices, the meet ceased to be needed, and Indian and trappers alike were abandoned from one year to the next. Now, they would have to sell their hides and furs elsewhere and buy their coffee, black powder, and tobacco at higher prices.

The next rage would be buffalo coats. The animals were already being killed in the thousands, but soon they would be slaughtered in the tens of thousands and later the hundreds of thousands as demand for the hides grew. Their use spread from blankets to rugs and clothing. The buffalo's cured skin was pliable, odorless, and durable, so it would soon be the hide of choice. The future was always in a delicate balance in the wilderness, especially in the Rocky Mountains. This would also affect all the mountain men's way of life. More significant changes were in the future than any of them ever dreamed, and one way of life was about to end only for another to be born.

The captain, Virgil, Levi, Dahteste, and the tagalong, Betty Crockett, followed Joseph Walker as he rode north, heading toward the South Pass and more of the unknown. Another adventure had them all excited, looking forward to distant lands, and nervous, knowing that things often didn't work out in the wilderness as planned—especially Levi and Dahteste.

This was their first big adventure together into the unexplored. None of them had any idea of what to expect. Only Joseph knew the hardships that lay ahead before the wonder of such a fertile land as Oregon. Would the married couple's differences make them closer, or would their façade crack and chip away, bringing yet another change?

They were all in it for the adventure and, of course, for the fifty dollars each. This may well be their future means of survival. For now, they embarked on a new journey and could only hope they would soon return to Rusty, Angus, and Dennis in the compound in the Rockies. Their friends waited anxiously for their return and the tales they would bring with them. As the three remaining old frontiersmen stayed behind for the first time, they would have to settle for experiencing the new adventures secondhand when their friends returned.

Betty Crockett was just happy to be rid of the Squirrel family and especially Jack Amble. She knew for some time he'd had designs on her despite—or possibly even due to—her belligerent nature. She knew he would eventually have killed her husband to take her into his fold. Her dead husband had not loved her, nor had he even professed to. All he had wanted were children, of which they had none despite the fact he forced himself on her often. She thanked her lucky stars she was even alive and free, so the trip would be a luxury for her despite any hardships they encountered in the days to come.

She, like Jack Amble, believed her husband to be infertile and not her. Or at least that was what Jack had convinced himself, even though Betty wasn't so sure. She could only thank her lucky stars that no child had come of their marriage. If one or more had been born, she now would be among the other mothers grieving over their children lost to the Blackfeet Indians. It was too late for them, but it wasn't too late for Betty Crockett. She was like her uncle and never gave up despite all odds. From now on, she would be the one who determined her future, not a Squirrel male.

Now, she looked forward to arriving in Oregon City to see if the land was as fertile as she had read and heard. And if what Joseph said about the land grant became a reality, maybe she would find a man and settle down on six hundred and twenty acres of healthy land. Who knew what would limit her future when the sky was her new limit? A long time ago, she used to be a schoolteacher. Maybe she would have the opportunity to resume her trade and teach reading and writing to the needy and illiterate, of which there were plenty.

Every time Levi and the captain left the compound, they complicated their lives, but that was what these rugged individuals lived for. To live with the wildest of animals, off the land, like the local natives. What made these men and women who they were was unknown. Still, these chosen few ventured into new journeys as most people changed into a new pair of pants. The unknown was their passion, and they were willing to risk it all for adventure and their chosen way of life.

Angus McFarlin and Rusty Steel lit out on foot in the middle of the night, so nobody saw them leave the meet. The fewer people who knew when they left, the better. They vanished instantly into the dark, using the shadows cast from a silvery moon to navigate. They were so good at sneaking through the brush they didn't make a single sound as they disappeared. The gold from all the furs and hides was in leather purses around their necks. But if nobody could see them, then nobody could rob them.

Once they were in the compound with Mountain Dennis and their guns, it would be hard to get in. The cabins were built like small fortresses with walls two feet thick and heavy timber shutters and doors, and they all had gun slots. The only dangerous element nearby was the Crow Indian stronghold; the chief was Rusty Steel's blood brother, and Dahteste was a member of their tribe like her husband, Levi Johnson.

For the Oregon-bound group, they only had themselves to care for the first hundred miles, so travel was easy for the bunch of hardened frontiersmen and women. They enjoyed the plentiful game the first days, but soon the plains became more barren and stretched so far it seemed unreal. The horizon appeared to be so far away it seemed unreachable. Horses and two mules trotted across an endless prairie, dragging hooves and leaving small puffs of dust in their wake.

At night, they collected buffalo chips to burn in their fire. The dung burned hotter than wood and was never scarce on the plains, as firewood was becoming. At the end of each day, as they passed land where the grass was eaten to the nub, they found thousands of chips, so they never had to carry firewood.

The night sky seemed even bigger than high in the Rocky Mountains. Stars stretched from horizon to horizon in a never-ending blanket of twinkling dots light years away. Their eyes shone orange in the light of the campfire as they made the second meal of the day. Later, Levi and Dahteste lay in the same bedroll, using their bodies to keep off the night chill. The other men donned robe blankets or curled up beside hot coals to sleep the night. Virgil had given Betty a buffalo skin to keep her warm. He had saved the best five he'd skinned, and now he saw how they would be put to good use. Miss Crockett was delighted with the gift.

The morning seemed to take all day to come and the sun to rise into the sky. It stood there like a yellow disk of fiery light as waves of heat appeared in the distance, making everything appear to move. The long grass where the buffalo hadn't grazed blew in the wind and constantly moved like ocean waves. A stiff breeze was a constant from the early morning until just before dark. Coyotes sang their nightly chorus of an evening, and small animals scurried through underbrush.

On the fifth day, Joseph said haltingly, "Hush and get down as low as ya can. Come on and follow me into that gully over there. No need to make our presence known to anyone if it can be avoided."

"What's the matter?" the captain asked. "Who is it? Did you see somebody?"

"I saw a few silhouettes on the horizon, and I don't want them to see us," Joseph said. He took off his hat and raised his head, but they were low enough that they couldn't be seen. "I only saw their shadows, so I don't know precisely who or what they be."

"And what if they're friendly?" Forrester asked. "Maybe they don't intend us harm, and you're worrying for nothing. They aren't necessarily hostile Indians. We did just leave the Rendezvous. It could be other travelers like us."

"All right then, Captain. I'll wait right here while you go and ask 'em iffin they be friendly or not," Joseph snickered. "When you don't come back, I'll have my answer. Here, we don't just have Crow; we've got Blackfeet, Bannock, Shoshone, and Gros Ventre, but like always, the Blackfeet are who start most of the trouble. And, of course, they could be White men too, but like as not, they be as dangerous as the Indians. They could even be a group of bears. We ain't in the Rendezvous anymore.

"Like it or not, most of the scoundrels behave when at the meet 'cause they don't wanna be banned next year. Everybody wants to return to the Rendezvous. But the same characters out here on their own could be a different story. You just watch. If you make it to my age, you'll find yourself being more careful too. If I can sneak my way around a fight, I'll do it every time. I didn't make it to forty because I'm stupid and haven't learned anything over the years."

"The other Indians are from tribes my Crow people trade with," Dahteste said. "If we run into them, I can try to talk to them to let us pass without a gift or fee. Sometimes, if they catch you, the tribes charge for crossing their land. If they don't see us, like Joseph said, all the better. But if they are Blackfeet and see us, we have to fight. And it is always best to kill them before they kill us. They are the enemy of all the tribes."

"Well, there ya go, Captain," Joseph said. "So, should we hide like good little boys and not get into trouble, or should we go out there and let every Indian and thief on the plains know we're here?"

"I get the point," Forrester said. "It just seems like we have to kill half the people we run into wherever we go."

"If they don't know we're here, they won't want to kill us, and we won't have to kill them." Joseph smiled.

"That's just because they are trying to kill us," Levi said. "We ain't started scrap one since we set foot in Kansas."

"It's better them than us," Virgil said. "I don't see any welcome signs out here nowhere, so I figure the land belongs to someone, don't it? And I know for sure it ain't us. So, we're always gonna be trespassing on somebody's property. Even back east, that's the way things go. It's just out here, there are no fences or lines marking off the property, and the land is vast, so it's hard to tell when you've gone from one Indian's land to the next. But Indians' land it is; we can be sure of that."

"It has been this way for thousands of years," Daht-este said. "I know someone is always trespassing on Crow land, and they always will. That is the way of the Indian warrior and hunter. We always think the game is better on our enemy's land. That is why we are warrior people. We fight to protect our land and our buffalo and keep others out."

Forrester frowned, but he took the hacking in stride. He was man enough to know when he was wrong. Will didn't even know why he suddenly wanted to be friendly. He had never been overly amicable before, and sometimes he was downright frightening. At times, the things he did scared even him.

"The Indians call it the Great Medicine Road," Dahteste said. "This trail you talk of has been here for much longer than the White man. You are discovering paths we made hundreds of years ago."

"Be that as it may, we have to find a good enough trail that we can bring two hundred covered buck-board wagons across and not have the carriages break down and have everybody die," Joseph said. "Of course, you've always got to figure in some loss. That's the course of things out here. I figure if we only lose one in ten, we'll be doin' a fine job. But that just goes for the greenhorns and Europeans. Sure, I lost a few scouts gettin' this far, but that was a freak accident that shouldn't have happened in the first place. Every one of them should have known better. It's dangerous when you begin to take things for granted. That's when you lose your way and unknowingly risk your life."

"Two hundred wagons must mean over five or six hundred people, if not more." Will whistled a long note. "Do you really think that so many Easterners will be crazy enough to cross such land when they aren't fit for the job?"

"I figure White folks will do anything for something free and a good promise," Joseph smiled. "I have no doubt that fools will line up for miles to be the first to arrive. Of course, free land only lasts for so long, but that should give enough folks time to get a foothold that it takes, and towns will start to pop up on the West

Coast, just like Oregon City. You just wait and see. That's why I'm bettin' my money on the Oregon Trail."

"Oregon Trail?" Forrester asked. "I've never heard it by name."

"Nor has anyone else." Joseph chuckled. "That's the beauty of the whole thing. We get in at the ground floor as it's built up. I tell ya, this is the future, youngins."

"How old are ya, Joseph?" Virgil asked. "If ya don't mind my askin'."

"I'm forty years young." Joseph smiled. "I reckon you and me be just about the same age."

"Yessir, we're the same age, all right," Virgil replied. "These young folks still don't know how lucky they are. Just wait until we get to be Angus McFarlin's age. I wonder how old he is."

"I asked him once, and he told me he didn't know and wasn't interested in knowin'," Levi said. "I asked Rusty Steel too, and he knows, but he ain't sayin'." He laughed.

"I figure when you're forty, you're still not old enough for age to be a worry," Virgil said. "Mind ya now, I've seen city folk that were forty, and they were on their last legs. It all depends on how you live your life. If you're in it for the long run, you must limit your whiskey and ponder on when and how you risk your life. Most city bums be drunks."

"There sure were enough men drunk back at the Rendezvous," Dahteste said. "I've never seen so many crazed men on whiskey. Now I understand why Crow Chief Hachta doesn't want his warriors to go to the Rendezvous. He said Indian blood and whiskey don't mix well."

"I doubt that anybody's blood mixes well with too

much whiskey," Virgil said. "I'd say the secret is in the doses. I only sip at my whiskey so I can enjoy it for hours without getting giddy or sick."

The next day, they all felt it as soon as they set out. They had breakfast of cast-iron frying pan biscuits and bacon with lots of hot coffee. Everything seemed to be fine then. But as soon as they stepped onto the trail, they felt eyes on them.

It wasn't just a feeling either. They were all sure: somebody was out there who wasn't there before. And if they were hiding, they were probably up to no good.

THE SOUTH PASS

DESPITE THE FEELING THAT THEY WERE BEING WATCHED, the party continued riding north. But now, they had their rifles cradled in their arms, and the women held a pistol in each hand—one for the Indians and one to use on themselves if they were captured. Joseph rode out front with Captain Forrester, Levi took up drag, and Dahteste watched their flanks with Virgil and cared for Betty.

Even though Miss Crockett didn't appear afraid, they assumed she was putting on a brave façade despite the nervous tension running through the small party. Nobody could be that cool under such pressure. Then again, maybe she'd never experienced what they had, or she would know better and be as scared as them. As they rode through the morning, the feeling got stronger, like they were walking into a trap.

Joseph held up his hand and they pulled their horses to a stop. The animals were nervous—they felt it too. They listened for out-of-place sounds, but they heard nothing strange. Levi and Dahteste sniffed the air and shook their heads. Still, the feeling lingered.

Midday came and went, and nothing happened, so Levi decided to swing around in a big circle and see if he saw anybody following them. If they were there, he would find them. His tracking skills had always been good from his life as a child in Indiana forests on the Ohio River. After a season in the Rockies, he tracked with the best, including the Indians.

Levi dropped off his new tan gelding, Trigger, and let it follow Dahteste's Appaloosa. It clopped after her horse like a cub follows its mama bear. When Beaver's feet hit the ground, he was off at a dead run. He raced for a gully that ran down the center of two hills. As he made his mad dash for cover, his heart redlined. He knew if anybody saw him now, they could circle him and cut him off, and that would be it.

He crouched as soon as he was undercover and listened. He gobbled air as he huffed and puffed, making it impossible to hear anything but his pounding heart and laboring lungs. He forced his breathing to slow down, and his heartbeat dropped enough that he could hear the constant breeze rustling the long buffalo grass. It made a perfect place for someone to hide and wait on their prey. If he were an Indian, he would find a place at night and wait until the enemy came to him. He kept that in mind as he entered the grass that came up to his waist.

Levi raced from one hiding place to another, making a large half-circle until he was a mile behind his friends. Now it was imperative that he be as quiet as a leopard, or he would be discovered, and his ploy would be for nothing. He checked the wind one last time, and confirmed he was still downwind. Indians could smell a White man from quite a distance. That was why Levi never used soap—because it left a distinct smell that the Indians sensed immediately.

He moved from blind to blind, always making sure he stopped with good cover in case he was discovered and had to fight his way out. Now, he was only a half mile behind his friends and still he saw no one and nothing. He suddenly began to doubt his first instinct. He shook his head. He trusted his instinct over his logic now. His instinct was fine-tuned from so many Indian and bear attacks he had lost count. He moved toward the threat even though he didn't know what it was.

The tracks were the first thing he saw that gave him a positive identification. After that, Levi had no doubt as to his course of action. They suddenly appeared a half mile behind his horse, which was still following the mountain men. His instinct had been right, after all. Now that he knew what he was up against, he had to tread carefully and make sure he made no mistakes, or it could cost him his life or, worse yet, the lives of his wife and friends.

Johnson counted five sets of tracks in all. He wondered if there were more circling him that very instant. A chill ran up his spine as he shot a look over his shoulder, but nothing was there. Levi suddenly felt vulnerable, but he shook it off. He reached deep inside himself for a fist full of courage and moved forward. His wife was ahead of him and in imminent danger, so it was all up to him. He had to eliminate the threat before it got to his friends and family.

Beaver slowly moved toward the danger. He began to run again as he measured his pace, so he didn't get winded before the clash. As soon as he got them in his sight, he ran with a renewed energy to close the gap before they realized he was behind them. Then it would be too late. His heart hammered between his ears as he sprinted the last twenty yards then stopped to take the first shot. They still hadn't noticed that they were now the prey and not the hunters.

Levi raised his rifle and took the shot, immediately dropping the weapon. As quick as lightning, he pulled two pistols and dispatched two more threats. The smell of gunpowder lingered as his ears rang. As soon as the other wolves smelled the blood of their dead or dying brothers, they turned and fled. Levi took one last shot for good measure as the aggressors disappeared into the brush and out of sight. Hooves pounded the earth. Joseph and the captain came racing to the back of the party with their pistols drawn. Three massive animals lay dead with bullet holes in their heads. One twitched its leg.

"I've never seen such big wolves," Joseph said. "How'd ya know they were following us? They were after you, Levi. You were ridin' drag."

"I doubt they would have stopped with one," the captain said. "Where there are five wolves, there could be more if they smell blood."

"I felt it all morning, just like you," Levi replied. "I thought it was Indians, though. It never crossed my mind wolves would be bold enough to take on a party of six. They must have been starvin' to risk such a thing."

"Let's keep moving," Joseph said. "Now, they can eat their friends if they want. More scavengers will come with the smell of fresh blood. Maybe mountain lions too, since it's a fresh kill. We better be on our way and let nature take its course here. You saved the day, Levi Johnson. That was quite a trick."

Now, the feeling of eyes following them vanished. They all relaxed and got as far away from the dead wolves as possible. Soon, coyotes sent out the alarm, and they began to yap from all sides. Some of the varmints neared the dead wolves with caution. They were one of the most dangerous animals in the wilderness, especially in a pack and at such an enormous size. Vultures nosedived for the target only to have an invasion of hungry scavengers racing for the bloody carcasses. As soon as the party of humans was out of sight, it was a free-for-all. It looked like all the animals on the plains were hungry.

The smell of death was heavy in the air. Swarms of crows suddenly appeared. By then, the party was just disappearing over the rise in the land, and the wild animals were left to fend for themselves. Levi looked back; flocks of buzzards still circled overhead, and he could still hear the coyotes.

They resumed the same riding formation, but now they felt alone, so they walked their horses quietly north. The leader looked into the distance. He knew it couldn't be far now. They should see the place where he'd left his missionaries any time if he hadn't mistaken the trail. They were arriving at the South Pass.

Walker could see the twenty-mile-wide, sagebrush-covered, saddle-topped mountain pass with a gradual incline of endless prairie, so he knew he had to be there, but it was vast and endless. He still didn't see his friend or the people in his charge. This was where they would cross the Continental Divide.

They continued for a few hours more until Joseph

Walker saw the rock formation. He sighed relief as he wiped his sweaty brow with his sleeve, stopping to pull out his spyglass and have a look. He couldn't see anybody, but buzzards flew overhead there too. He wondered if they had succumbed to the sun, thirst, or maybe even the same wolves that were after them. Or maybe there were Indians. They hadn't seen any signs, but that didn't mean they weren't there.

"Hold on," Joseph whispered. "Something's out there. We better be expectin' trouble. I don't see anybody up on the camp, so they could be hiding, but from what? Maybe wolves ain't the only thing out there. I sure as heck hope they're still alive."

Walker nodded to Forrester as they spread out. Dahteste stayed with Betty as the four men fanned out to see if they could scare up any Blackfeet waiting to prey on the missionaries. In minutes, two Indians popped up and ran for the other side of the hill. Just before they reached the summit, another Blackfoot jumped to his feet. He had been hiding in an uneaten tuft of buffalo grass. As soon as they saw armed reinforcements had arrived, they took flight. Three Indians couldn't take on six armed White men. When there was only one frontiersman and all the eastern greenhorns, they'd felt their chances were good. Now, they made their escape before they were the ones who became the prey.

Sheriff Walker pulled his pistol and shot off a round. The crack echoed in the distance. It was the signal that they were coming, and that Rory's wait was over. He looked at his glass again. Distant images were suddenly so close he felt he could reach out and touch them.

Quail took flight from the sound of the gun. The

men were jumpy, so they swung their barrels toward the birds, but there were no more Blackfeet Indians to worry about. There had only been three hoping to wait Rory and his missionaries out. Maybe till they died of thirst.

THE MISSIONARIES

RORY BREAKER KNEW THEY COULDN'T HOLD ON MUCH longer. He was beginning to wonder if Joseph Walker had fallen victim to an Indian raid or even highwaymen. Sure, he knew not to expect things to happen in a timely manner in the wilderness, but it was now that he needed him to show up and not tomorrow or the next day. Things were getting dodgier daily, and he didn't know how long they could hold out, especially with the people in his charge being so entirely out of their environment. They were like children playing with dynamite.

They'd come straight from the city and volunteered to work as missionaries in the Oregon City Mission. They had expected to travel through rich, lush green valleys and mountains but instead were struggling across endless plains with nonstop wind. That is, when they weren't in the middle of the most terrifying prairie storms they could ever imagine. Lightning-racked trees stood broken, dotting the distance. When the storms hit the prairie, there was nowhere to hide.

Now, thoughts of imminent doom began to creep into their brains, and they questioned the logic of following Rory's orders. Reverend Smith had secretly spoken to Reverend Brown about striking out on their own if it came to that. What choice would they have once they ran out of water? It was apparent the men they'd hired to take them to Oregon weren't up to scratch. It seemed like a simple enough proposition, but there hadn't been anything simple about the journey from the start back in Montana.

Blackfeet Indians had had them circled in for the last three days. Nobody dared come in or go out of the camp. The only thing that had saved them was the fact that Joseph and Rory had located an excellent campsite with unbeatable cover before he left to find help. They were on a hill that had been eaten to the nub by a herd of fifty thousand buffalo, so they had plenty of chips for firewood and a clear field of fire.

The crop of rocks at the top allowed them good cover and a place to tend to their personals and not lose their scalps. Lucky for Rory's thinking ahead, they had stocked up on chips the first days before the Blackfeet Indians arrived. Since they showed up, Rory's fear kicked up a notch every day until it got his full attention, and now, he was chewing at the inside of his mouth.

Since he was the only one there with any knowledge of fighting Indians, he didn't dare venture out to see if he could calculate their force. Nor was he prepared to risk the marksmanship skills of the greenhorns from some big city back east to give him cover. Sure, they were on a mission from God, but they might have thought about being a little more prepared for the environment they were to travel. At least they claimed to be decent shots. Hopefully, they wouldn't get that far and have their grit tested. Rory doubted they would do well.

They all huddled under the cover of rock, and with high ground, so the Indians couldn't successfully attack. Sure, there was always the option of a night attack, but it appeared that maybe they didn't have a large enough force to execute it successfully. Then again, Rory knew that nobody knew what went on inside an Indian warrior's brain. They could be numerous and just playing games before the slaughter. He had seen similar things happen before.

"Mr. Smith," Rory whispered. "How are your folks holding up?"

"I sure am glad that you and your boss thought to fill a barrel with water. The sun is relentless, and my mouth is so dry my lips stick to my front teeth," Smith said.

"Yeah, I've been chewing dirt for a spell myself," Rory replied. "You'll get used to it in the end."

"What are we going to do, my son?" Reverend Smith asked. His voice was gentle, but his eyes were angry.

"We ain't gonna to do anything but wait and hope Joseph's found some good scouts and Indian fighters. Until then, we have to hunker down and hope they don't decide to come at us at night. My guess is that there're only a few that stumbled on us, so they figure rather than risk one or more of 'em gettin' shot, they think they can starve us out. Lucky for us, we've got the water."

"Yes, but it's not going to last forever," Reverend Smith said. "I only took enough to wash my feet this morning. I haven't had a proper bath for days."

"You've been washin' up with our drinkin' water?" Rory asked incredulously. "What kind of fool are you? Iffin Joseph doesn't come back, that's all the water we've got. The next person I catch washin' up with water is gonna get shot."

"What do you mean, if Joseph doesn't come back?" Smith asked. "Did you hear that, Brother Brown?"

"Now, don't you start on me too, Reverend Brown. I've got enough on my plate."

Of the ten couples, eight of the men were ministers. It made Rory nervous he'd let a swear word slip and offend the pastors. He had kept his communication with them to a minimum, claiming he couldn't talk and guard at the same time. The truth was, he didn't know what he would do if Sheriff Walker didn't come back. Joseph had always returned when he left him guarding something before. The only reason he could think of that would keep him from his word would be if he were dead.

Just as quickly as the thought entered Rory's mind, he pushed it back into a dark recess of his brain. He was a superstitious man and believed if you thought about bad enough, it would come to be. He didn't even want to ponder Joe not coming back. If he was on his own, he might be able to sneak out at night, but there was no way he could vanish into the darkness with this bunch of white collars.

He dug his hand deep into his pocket and fingered his lucky four-leaf clover. It was tied to a rabbit's foot on a pigging string, and he stroked that too. He crossed his fingers and hoped Joseph would arrive soon.

"Don't you folks worry," Rory said. "Joseph will

show up sooner or later. He ain't let me down yet, so I see no reason he'll let us down now."

Rory took the occasional pot shot at the grass where he'd hide if he were an Indian just to let them know they had guns and were still alive. No Indians jumped up or ran, but still he knew they were there.

Another day of boiling sun passed as the evening neared and still no sign of Sheriff Walker. If he didn't make it in the next day or two, they probably would get hit by the Indians. Rory reminded himself to check the water again and move it to where he hid so he could control how it was used. No more water was to be wasted by washing feet. He had never heard of someone doing something so stupid in a land so arid. It just went to show him that they had no idea of what they had gotten themselves into.

At this point, Rory Breaker didn't think he could save the twenty missionaries and their five servants. If Joseph didn't show up soon, they would perish. Of course, he could abandon them and try to sneak away at night on his own. Then his chances of escape would be acceptable to fair. But could he abandon his charges when Sheriff Walker told him to keep them safe? He suddenly realized he would have to sacrifice either his life or his word, and he hadn't broken his word, ever. He didn't plan on starting now.

Despite the dismal-appearing future, Rory again pushed the negative thoughts aside and into the dark recesses of his brain, gritted his teeth and continued to keep watch. He hadn't slept for days.

That night, he sat and stared at the moon until his neck ached. His trained ears were ever listening for any out-of-place sounds. The moon cast a silver sheen on everything before him. He strained his eyes to look for any strange movement in the grass. During the day, it never stopped moving, like a breathing sea, but at night, anything that moved would be an enemy and not the wind.

RORY BREAKER

RORY STRUGGLED TO MAKE IT THROUGH THE NIGHT AND not fall asleep. Yet, he knew that would probably be when the Blackfeet attacked if they attacked at all. At this point, he assumed they were just waiting for them to run out of water and die. Of course, the Indians had no idea that they had stocked a good supply of water in barrels. Joseph was smart enough to foresee he might be delayed, so he made sure the animals could be kept safe and there was water for them and the people.

Now, the water supply had dropped so low Rory knew he had to stop watering the horses. Next would be the mules. He blocked the poor use of water by putting the barrel by his position and sleeping beside it at night. Still, as religious as they were, they all tried to steal the revered liquid. Some took a little, and others, like their leader, Reverend Smith, stole a lot, just because he couldn't live with dirty feet. Breaker marveled at how water became so important that a man of faith bent to petty theft. He had heard that in the Arab countries, water was thought to be more valuable than gold.

Would a man of wealth trade his riches for a glass of water when he was dying of thirst? Breaker believed he just might.

Smith and Rory bickered every day over this waste, but since the preacher believed he headed the wagon train and not Rory, there wasn't much he could do. He didn't want a full-blown mutiny on his hands. Then they would probably strike out on their own and slowly die along the way as the Indians stole everything they had, little by little, including the horses and mules. The only way Breaker had avoided total mayhem was by looking the other way when the head of the group stole to wash his precious feet.

Who knew, maybe it was some religious ceremony that he practiced daily. Since Rory came from out west and had never been east of the Missouri River, he didn't know the ways of folks in the big cities. Oh, sure, as a boy he went to church when there weren't too many chores to do on the ranch. But that was a long time ago, and since he now worked for Joseph Walker, he rarely had the time to catch a sermon. He usually watched over the sheriff's office when the boss went and did his Sunday duties as a lawman and town leader.

If that don't take the cake, Rory Breaker thought. *Washin' your feet every danged day. Sometimes, I don't get a chance to wash up for a month then hopefully, it's in some cool river.* He daydreamed of fresh ripples washing over his body as he began to nod off.

Rory had been awake for four days and the heat had him beaten into the ground. He had cut *his* rations to half that of the missionaries. He figured he could handle the dry stretch that would soon come better than the people in his charge. He knew that

when the animals began to drop dead from lack of
water, the Easterners would panic, and it wouldn't
take but a day or two at most for them to die of thirst.
A man can go for a long time without food but
without water in such an environment, death came
quickly.

A wet stain showed on the crown of his hat. Sweat
ran down his face and dripped off his nose and chin. His
eyes became heavier and heavier as he began to nod. He
could hear the missionaries rustling in their bedrolls as
they waited in the shade. Rory smelled smoke. One of
the missionaries must be making lunch. The aroma of
coffee teased his sense of smell.

Somewhere deep in Breaker's conscious or subcon-
scious, a gunshot rang out. At first, he thought he was
hearing things—maybe he had fallen asleep, and he
was dreaming. He was exhausted and half asleep and so
hot he was dizzy. He shook his head and blinked his
eyes. Sweat shook off his hair like a wet dog. Then he
dared pop his head up and have a look above the rock
cover.

That was when he saw six riders, and the one in the
lead was Sheriff Joseph Walker. He had come through
in the end. Rory heaved a long sigh of relief. The nightmare was over. He had never been in charge of such
highfalutin Easterners, and he didn't want to repeat the
experience ever again. Now, he could let his boss take
care of the greenhorns.

As he watched, the first two Blackfoot Indians
jumped up and ran for their lives. They were farther
away than he expected. Finally, a last warrior jumped to
his feet not fifty yards from Rory's camp and ran for the
other side of the hill. One had been much closer than

he thought, but he also saw he was right about their numbers and why they hadn't attacked.

In the end, there were only three warriors. Had he known that before, he would have ventured out into the night on his own and taken their scalps, but how was he to have known? He had only known that Indians were out there waiting to kill them and steal whatever cargo they wanted. If he had gone out alone, the scalp taken might have been his.

Rory stood to his feet, grabbed his hat, waved it in the air, and yelled, "Joseph! Come on in, pard. We've got ya covered."

As the trappers, trackers, and Indian fighters rode into the greenhorns' camp, the White missionaries seemed distrustful of the Indian woman. The others they looked at with mild disgust because they were all covered in dust down to the wrinkles in their clothes and faces. One of the men was so big he resembled a grizzly bear. The Indian woman was small, but still, she looked dangerous. The missionaries had never heard of peaceful Indians other than the ones who stayed in the mission and had adopted their Christian ways.

"I'm Levi Johnson, and this is my wife, Dahteste," Levi said to the puzzled faces. "We be married right and proper." All the white collars left Johnson a bit unsettled, too, and he didn't quite know what to say.

Joseph saw his new friend was struggling with the travelers, so he butted in. "This is Virgil, Captain Forrester, Levi, who just introduced himself, his Crow wife Dahteste, and we have another traveler who just joined our group to Oregon City. This here's Betty Crockett."

Joseph expected somebody to recognize the name,

but these people obviously weren't interested in tales of mountain men and Indian fighters. To the rest, Davy Crockett was an American hero known from Washington, DC, to the Wild West. They didn't understand how anyone in the country wouldn't know who he was. To them, he was one of the original pioneers and one of the heroes who gave their lives at the Alamo against General Antonio López de Santa Anna.

Joseph shrugged and asked, "How did my man Rory treat y'all? Everybody looks as fit as a fiddle. I don't see any graves." He chuckled.

"To be honest, we had lost hope in your man Rory Breaker," Smith said. "And in you too, Joseph. Not only did he not provide us with sufficient information about your whereabouts, but he also yelled at us for washing our feet. What kind of man expects gentlemen to go unbathed? We aren't heathens, sir; we are gentlemen and men of God."

"You say you used the drinking water to wash your feet?" Joseph asked as his chin dropped to his chest. "If he called ya a fool for doin' so, I reckon he had all the right in the world. How dumb can a man be to use valuable drinking water where there is no more available? And for washin' his feet? I'm sorry, Reverend Smith, but I find that kind of stupid myself. Are there any more complaints about the man who saw that you weren't scalped while I was gone? You did see them Blackfoot Indians, right? Maybe some of ya ought to take a good look at yourselves and rethink that opinion you've arrived at insofar as my best scout. That man could run rings around you lot in an Indian attack. It was due to him those three Blackfoot braves didn't have your scalps and all."

"I hardly think three Indians could deal with our fancy rifles," Smith replied arrogantly. He obviously looked down his nose at Joseph now too. "Like I told you, we all know how to shoot. I don't like to repeat myself, sir."

"Oh, I have no doubt you know how to shoot at paper targets. But how is your shootin' when the other party is shootin' back or is a movin' target and not standing still? Have any of you men killed another human being in an act of violence?"

"Why, of course not," Brown retorted, obviously shocked. "We're Christians. We don't go around shooting people. We pay ruffians like you to do such things for us."

"Y'all don't like to get your hands dirty, now do ya?" Rory Breaker grumbled. "You look down your nose at us when it's *you* we should be lookin' down our noses at. You're nothin' but a bunch of old ungrateful fools."

Both Reverends Smith and Brown stood too close to Breaker. The small but dangerous man didn't like people towering over him. He wondered for a moment if they were going to have a go at him after all the talk of peace and forgiveness. His hands bunched into fists.

"Two to one ain't exactly fair," Levi said.

"Which way do ya mean?" Rory asked. "It ain't fair for the two of them, or it ain't fair for me?"

"That's enough, Rory," Joseph said. "They paid us to do a job, and that's exactly what we'll do. If they don't like us, well, that's just their loss. We'll see how they feel after the next nine hundred miles ahead of us. That'll tell who's prepared and who's not."

The new arrivals were surprised by the tone of voice of the missionaries. They had expected them to be kind and generous, but they were initially snobbish and arrogant. Of course, they were all educated and could probably read and write so well they wrote books. But reading and writing didn't win you any prizes out in the wilderness unless you were taking notes on all the mistakes you'd made along the trail. Then it might be worth something to someone in the future.

"That was a hard hundred miles." Virgil yawned as he dismounted and stretched his back. He immediately began to tend to his horse.

The missionary's animals were grazing between the rocks. The buffalo hadn't fed all the way to the top of the hill, so there was still some pasture. As they moved forward mowing the prairie like a big scythe, they left patches of uneaten vegetation. It was thick and healthy, and the tired animals ate their fill as the men removed their saddles and bridles and brushed them down.

Once all the horses and mules were taken care of, they made a new campfire for themselves and sat around the burning buffalo chips. The combustible was odorless and made little smoke but provided bright orange coals. The Easterners didn't like to touch the sunbaked dung, another dirty job they left for Rory.

They rested the remainder of the day after the hard trek from the Rendezvous. Virgil got busy and made black beans and strips of fried bacon. Betty made frying pan biscuits and a pot of thick coffee. The sun crossed the sky once again and vanished over the end of the world. There wasn't a single sound on the prairie. Not even the coyotes sang that night.

Reverend Smith walked over to the wagon master's fire and said, "Would you like to eat with us, Miss

Crockett? I believe you'll find us quite educated, and we won't leave you feeling distressed."

"Why, I'm just fine where I am," Betty replied as she tilted her head back and looked down her nose. "These people saved my life and that of seven friends of mine. I couldn't think of a better group of friends to share my time with." She smiled wickedly. "Maybe you should look at yourself before judging others by their strange appearance. I am afraid the ones who're dressed oddly here are you people and me. I long for the day one of these fine men makes me a suit of buckskin shirt and britches."

Smith was shocked, as was Brown, who stood just behind him. They turned and hurried back to their flock, leaving a wake of dust in their trails.

"You sure did send them packing." Captain Forrester laughed. He had another look at the attractive woman with yellow hair. He couldn't help but stare.

"How old did you say you were, Captain?" Betty asked as soon as she caught the West Point officer staring. She was a bold woman, and his face blushed like a rose.

"Why, I'm twenty-eight, ma'am." The captain smiled. He felt something funny in his stomach like a little ball of energy, and he felt a little dizzy.

"You don't have to call me ma'am. You don't mind if I call you Will, do you? You can call me Betty." She smiled, and her eyes twinkled like the stretch of stars overhead.

The captain sucked in a bolstering breath and gobbled air. It was all he could do not to bust out laughing. He suddenly felt happy, and he wasn't quite sure why.

Levi lay back on his saddle, and Dahteste leaned her head on his chest. They were all tired, but it wasn't that big of a deal for people used to living in such harsh conditions. They had food, combustibles, water, and good company. What more could a mountain man ask for?

Dahteste blinked her big brown eyes at Miss Crockett and smiled. She snuggled closer to her man, her eyes became heavy, and she fell asleep after a hundred grueling miles to the South Pass and what was just about to become the Oregon Trail.

"*Whew.* Just when I thought I was getting used to dodging bullets," Forrester said. The captain got up, sighed, looked over his shoulder, and walked out of the camp without a word. It was anybody's guess where he was going and what he was up to. Probably to sneak around the campsite and look for trouble, and he probably wouldn't have to go too far to find it.

A Look at Book Seven:
Unforgiven: A Western Double

Some debts are paid in lead. Others never get paid at all.

Unforgiven

Rusty Steel and Angus McFarlin ride out from the Rendezvous with two thousand dollars in gold coins—and a trail full of outlaws waiting to take it. Trappers are being ambushed and killed for their hard-earned coin. The road home may be their last.

Meanwhile, Levi Johnson, his wife, Dahteste, Captain Will Forrester, and Virgil Lovejoy join Sheriff Joseph Walker to scout a group of missionaries bound for Oregon. Shoshone warriors guard the land, and the brutal terrain doesn't take kindly to strangers. Betty Crockett, niece of a legend, has her sights on the captain—but his demons may run deeper than she knows.

Hell on High Water

When two more mountain men are attacked, Levi and Will hunt the men responsible—only to find a ghost from the past. White Ghost, long thought dead, returns to spread terror across the Rockies.

As the blood trail winds through the high country, Dahteste and Betty grow closer, and a bold plan is hatched to win the captain's heart. But on this frontier, nothing comes easy—and not everyone survives the storm.

AVAILABLE DECEMBER 2025

ABOUT THE AUTHOR

 Born in 1886 in Southern Ohio, Ash Lingam grew crops, raised cattle, and doted on the young boy. Ash's family was among the early settlers in pre-Revolutionary America. He has traced his lineage back to around 1746 when his ancestors immigrated from Europe to the aspiring American Colonies.

A retired marketing executive, Ash devotes his spare time to training police dogs and writing novels. He has found his niche in the Western, historical fiction, and adventure genres. With his vast vault of experience, he never runs out of sources for new stories. He has lived in eleven different countries and worked in a total of forty-six to date, Ash has written approximately 130 novels, short stories, and poems. More than one hundred of his eclectic titles help the American frontier come alive for his readers.

https://www.ashlingam.com/